Home to
Chicory Lane

Center Point
Large Print

Also by Deborah Raney and available from
Center Point Large Print:

The Face of the Earth
After All

**This Large Print Book carries the
Seal of Approval of N.A.V.H.**

Home to Chicory Lane

— A Chicory Inn Novel —

DEBORAH RANEY

CENTER POINT LARGE PRINT
THORNDIKE, MAINE

This Center Point Large Print edition is published
in the year 2015 by arrangement with Abingdon Press.

The text of this Large Print edition is unabridged.
In other aspects, this book may vary
from the original edition.
Printed in the United States of America
on permanent paper.
Set in 16-point Times New Roman type.

ISBN: 978-1-62899-433-9

Library of Congress Cataloging-in-Publication Data

Raney, Deborah.
Home to Chicory Lane : a Chicory Inn novel / Deborah Raney. —
 Center Point Large Print edition.
pages ; cm
Summary: "Now that their kids are grown, Audrey and Grant Whitman
have converted their home into a cozy bed-and-breakfast. But then their
youngest daughter shows up during opening weekend with a loaded
U-Haul—and no husband. Now they'll have to figure out how to help the
young couple in addition to running a new inn"—Provided by publisher.
 ISBN 978-1-62899-433-9 (library binding : alk. paper)
 1. Bed and breakfast accommodations—Fiction. 2. Large type books.
 3. Domestic fiction. I. Title.
PS3568.A562H66 2015
813'.54—dc23
                                                    2014041782

For my wise and wonderful parents,
Max and Winnie Teeter,
who've given all of their children
such a wonderful heritage of faith.

Acknowledgments

As I begin another new series, I'm all the more aware that no book ever comes into being by one person's efforts. It would take an entire volume to thank all those who ultimately made this new story possible, but let me name just a few to whom I'm especially beholden for this novel:

Ken Raney, my favorite person in the whole wide world, with whom I've enjoyed the last four decades of life—each year more than the one before. I love you, babe! Let's see if we can do like your grandparents and spend eighty-two years together! We're almost halfway there!

Courtney Walsh, creative and amazing friend, whose casual comment, "You have so many neat family stories. You should write a book about a big extended family!" got these characters swirling in my imagination. It never would have happened without our fun conversation that night, Courtney!

Tamera Alexander, critique partner of more than a decade now (we're gettin' old, friend!) but so much more than a business friend. Thank you for your constant encouragement and for walking this mostly fun but often frustrating path beside me.

Steve Laube, agent extraordinaire, thank you for a dozen years now of wisdom, guidance, psychological insight (aka talking me down from the ledge when necessary), and always that great wit that makes hard times easier and good times "gooder."

Ramona Richards, Jamie Chavez, Susan Cornell, and the rest of the crew at Abingdon Fiction, thank you for your expertise and insight in seeing the diamond in the rough this book was before you got your talented hands on it.

To my parents and kids, grandkids, in-laws, outlaws, dear friends, and kind acquaintances: you each enrich my days more than you will ever know. Thank you for everything you pour into me and squeeze out of me. I am rich in so many ways because you are in my life.

I

"So, *Mrs.* Whitman, is everything ready?" Grant stood under the archway dividing the formal dining room from the parlor, smiling that cat-that-swallowed-the-canary grin Audrey adored. And had for nearly thirty-five years.

She went to lean on the column opposite him. She loved this view of the house—no, the *inn*. She must remember to refer to it as such. This wonderful house where they'd raised their five kids and where she'd played as a little girl had finally become *The Chicory Inn*. The stately home just a mile outside of Langhorne, Missouri, had been built by her maternal grandparents on a wooded fifty acres with a clearwater creek running through it. Now it was her fifty-five hundred square-foot dream fulfilled. Or at least that was the plan.

Audrey gave her husband a tight smile. "I'm as ready as I'll ever be. I just know I'm forgetting something."

"Come here." He opened his arms to her.

She stepped into his embrace, desperately needing the strength of him.

"Everything looks wonderful, and anything you forgot can't be too important. Just look at the weather God supplied—sunshine, cool October breeze, and the trees are at their autumn peak. Even the chicory is still in bloom in the ditches. Made to order, I'd say."

She nodded, feeling as if she might burst into tears any minute.

Grant pulled her closer. "Can't you just enjoy this weekend? It's no fun if you're in knots the whole time."

"Were we crazy to invite the kids home for this?"

He kissed the top of her head. "We were crazy to *have* kids, never mind five of them. But hey, look how that turned out."

"I wish your mom could've been here."

He cleared his throat. "Trust me, it's better this way. Besides, you know she'll find a way to get in her two cents, even from the wilds of Oregon. What do you want to bet she'll call, just as guests are arriving, to make sure you didn't forget anything?"

She loved Grant's mother dearly, but the woman did have a way of trying to run the show—even when it wasn't her show to run. Grant was probably right. Cecelia—or CeeCee, as the kids called their grandmother—had timed her trip to visit Grant's brother perfectly.

Audrey's cell phone chimed, signaling a text message.

"See?" Grant gave her an I-told-you-so grin. "There she is."

She checked her phone. "Your mother barely knows how to make a call on a cell phone, let alone send a text. Oh, it's Link. He's running late." She texted a quick reply to their son.

"Link late? Well, there's a huge surprise."

She laughed, grateful for the distraction. Their son was notoriously tardy. But after she put her phone back in her pocket, Audrey turned serious. "Oh, Grant . . . What if this whole thing is a big fat flop?"

"And why, sweet woman, would it be a flop, when you've poured your heart and soul and passion into it for the last eight months?"

"And most of your retirement funds, don't forget." The thought made her positively queasy. It wasn't as if he could just return to his contractor job tomorrow and get back his 401K. "Not to mention a lot of sweat equity."

"And don't forget the blood and tears." He winked.

"And your blood *pressure,*" she said with a look of warning. "How can you joke about this, Grant? What if we—"

"Shh." He tipped her chin and silenced her with a kiss.

She knew Grant had been relieved to get out of the rat race his job had become. In fact, his doctor had prescribed retirement along with the blood pressure meds he'd put Grant on last fall. The past year of renovations had been anything but relaxing, but things would settle down now that the remodel was finished. Maybe this was all a sort of blessing in disguise. She let that thought soothe her. For the moment anyway.

The doorbell rang.

"That'll be Corinne." She pushed away from him. "She promised to help me with the hors d'oeuvres."

"I don't see why we couldn't just have chips and salsa or pretzels or—"

"And don't forget your tie." Audrey scooped the despised *noose,* as Grant had dubbed it, off the end of the hall tree and tossed it at him.

He caught it and dangled it by two fingers as if it were a poisonous snake. "You're not really serious about that?"

"Serious as a heart attack."

Grant's grumbling faded behind her as she hurried to answer the door.

Their eldest daughter stood on the wraparound veranda with almost-two-year-old Simone propped on one hip.

"Corinne?" Audrey sagged. "I thought Jesse was going to watch the kids?"

"He is, but I think Simone's cutting teeth, and I didn't want Jesse to have to deal with that, too. You know how he gets when—" Corinne stopped mid-sentence and eyed her mother. "It'll be fine, Mom. Dad can watch Simone if we need him to."

"No, your dad has a whole list of things *he's* in charge of. I need him." She pushed down the resentment that threatened. "Never mind. You're right . . . it'll be fine." She reached for her youngest granddaughter and ushered Corinne into the foyer.

Corinne walked through to the parlor, her eyes widening. "Wow! It looks gorgeous, Mom. You've been busy."

"I just want everything to be perfect. Just this one time." She didn't have to look at her daughter to know Corinne was rolling her eyes.

"Just this once, huh?"

She ignored the sarcasm and tweaked little Simone's cheek. "Are those new toofers giving you trouble, sweetie?"

The baby gave her a snaggletoothed grin and wiped her turned-up nose on the shoulder of Audrey's apple green linen jacket.

"Simone!" Corinne's shrug didn't match the grimace she gave Audrey. "Well, at least it matches."

Audrey did not find that amusing.

Corinne swooped in with a tissue, which made Simone screech like a banshee. Which made Huckleberry come running, barking as if he'd just cornered a squirrel.

Great. Just great. "Can somebody please take this dog outside? How did he even get in here?" Audrey hated raising her voice to her family, but she knew too well that the playful Lab could undo in two minutes everything they'd spent a week preparing. "I want him outside until the last guest leaves."

"Come here, Huck," Corinne coaxed, stroking the sleek chocolate-colored coat. "You bad boy."

"It's okay. I'll take him out." Audrey handed the baby off to Corinne, put Huck outside, and came back to the sink. Grabbing a damp dishcloth from the basin, she scrubbed at her jacket, exchanging the toddler's snot stain for a dark wet spot. She prayed it would dry before the first guests started arriving.

The clock in the foyer struck eleven, and a frisson of panic went through her. They had less than two hours and so much still to do. She heard Link's voice at the front door. Maybe she could enlist him to watch Simone for a few minutes. Like his brother Tim, Link had always had a way with kids.

"Hey, Mom. Dad said to report in." Tall and rugged-looking like his father, Link appeared beneath the arch of the kitchen doorway. "Smells good in here." He gave Audrey a quick hug before snatching a bacon-wrapped canapé from a silver tray. He popped it in his mouth before Audrey could protest.

She placed herself between her son and the gleaming marble counter full of food. "There are snacks out in the garage for you kids, but I'm not joking; this stuff is off limits until we see how many people show."

"Got it, Mom. Off limits." In one smooth motion, Link gave her a half-salute and reached behind her for a sausage ball.

"Cut that out! Shoo! Out of my kitchen!"

"Place looks good, Ma."

Grant appeared in the doorway. "Reporting for duty."

Link shot his dad a conspiratorial grin but obediently backed into the entryway. Audrey wondered for the thousandth time why some sweet young girl hadn't snapped up this handsome son of hers. But that was a worry for another day.

"Hey guys," Audrey said, "can you bring in some folding chairs from the garage? Maybe just half a dozen or so. I don't want to set up more than we need."

"You'll need more than six." Grant sounded so sure the day would be a success. "Bring a dozen, Link."

She hoped he was right. But if not . . . Well, there would be no problem getting rid of all the food she'd made. The good ol' Whitman family reunion they'd planned for the rest of the weekend would take care of that. The thought brought a pang of longing with it. It was wonderful to have most of her family together, but it wouldn't be the same without Landyn and Chase.

15

And Tim. Nothing would ever be the same without Timothy.

Landyn Spencer craned her neck to check the Interstate traffic behind her in the rearview mirror, but all she could see was the U-Haul trailer she was pulling. The extended mirrors on the behemoth were smeared with a dozen hours of rain and dust.

New York was thirteen hours behind her, and with the sun finally coming up, she realized she was in familiar territory.

She'd left the city after ten last night, starting out on only four hours of sleep. She'd been watching the lit-up Empire State Building fade into the skyline in her rearview mirror, and not until she'd passed through the Lincoln Tunnel and come out on the New Jersey side had she finally allowed herself tears.

That was a mistake. She'd been crying ever since. But enough. She had to get hold of herself before she got home. She swiped at damp cheeks, took a deep breath, and steadied her gaze on the road in front of her. If her eyes got any more swollen, she'd have to pull the Honda over. And if she did that, chances were good the stupid thing wouldn't start again. Then she'd *really* be up the Hudson without a paddle. Besides, right now, she just wanted to put the past—and Chase Spencer— as far behind her as she could.

She still couldn't believe that her husband of six months had gone so far off the deep end. Without even discussing it with her, he'd let their great, albeit small, apartment on the Upper West Side go—sublet their *home* to a stranger—and rented a fleabag excuse for a studio apartment in Brooklyn. What was he thinking?

He *wasn't*. That was the problem. He'd let his art rep convince him that living in Bedford-Stuyvesant near some stupid gallery that was supposedly the next hot thing would jumpstart his career. The agent had told Chase the studio would pay for itself in a matter of months—and probably herald in world peace too.

Well, fine. Chase had made his choice. But they were newlyweds. *She* should have been his choice. Oh, he claimed he wasn't forcing her hand. But if she did what he wanted and followed him to Brooklyn, it meant an almost two-hour commute for her every day. They saw each other little enough as it was! Had he thought any of this through? No, he had not. And despite what Chase said, leaving Fineman and Justus, and a marketing position she loved, didn't leave her with many options. Especially not now . . .

The tears started again and she shook her head. She couldn't even let herself think about that right now.

She attempted to distract her maudlin thoughts with the stunning colors October had painted on

17

either side of the Interstate. She thought she'd crossed over into Kentucky, though she didn't remember seeing a sign. If Chase were here, he'd no doubt be sketching the trees or shooting photos in a vain attempt to capture the vivid colors. Then he'd complain that the pictures didn't even come close, and she'd have to—

A horn blared behind her. She checked the mirror and then the speedometer. She was barely going fifty in the left-hand lane. Stupid cruise control had quit working again. Heart pounding, she accelerated and tried to whip back into the right lane only to have the trailer tug her over the line into the passing lane. She finally managed to maneuver to the proper lane, and she glared hard at the driver as he passed her.

It was a stupid, childish thing to do. She was the one in the wrong. But the guy had almost scared her into having a wreck. It would serve Chase right if she had an accident. She quickly checked the thought. He wasn't the only one she had to think about. Mom and Dad had already lost one child. Her throat tightened at the thought of her brother. If they had to go through that again, she wasn't sure they'd ever recover. Besides, Mom and Dad didn't know she was on her way home. If she had a wreck, no one would know why she was on a road all alone, miles from New York.

It did make her smile to think about what her parents' reaction would be when she pulled into the driveway. She hadn't seen Mom and Dad since her wedding in April, and it would be fun to surprise them. Suddenly she missed them the way she had that first summer she'd gone away to church camp and learned the meaning of "homesick."

But how could she tell them she was leaving Chase? After only six months of marriage. She could hear her dad now. "Landyn Rebekah Whitman," he'd say (somehow forgetting she was now a Spencer), "you get in that car and you drive yourself right back to New York." He'd be mad at Chase, too, but she'd be the one who'd get the talking-to.

Well, they didn't know the details. And they wouldn't. Chase had fought hard to win her parents over, and she wasn't going to make him out to be the bad guy now—even though he was. One hundred percent, he was. It still made her furious.

No . . . worse than that. It broke her heart.

She was beginning to understand why her parents had been skeptical about Chase in the first place. He was letting this . . . *delusion* of getting rich and famous selling his art sidetrack him. Not that he wasn't good. He was. He had a ton of talent, but that didn't mean he could make a living at it. And their finances didn't exactly allow for risky investments right now.

Chase had landed a job in New York right out of college, working in the art department for a small local magazine. It was a job that used his art skills, and one with room to grow.

But then this nut job art rep had seen Chase's work and gotten him all wired with delusions of grandeur. In a way, she understood. Chase hadn't received much encouragement growing up. His dad left when he was five, and he'd been raised by a single mom who seemed to have a new boyfriend every other week. The minute Chase graduated high school, Mona Spencer had followed some guy out to California. She'd come back for their wedding on the arm of yet another flavor of the week, but Landyn didn't expect to see her again unless she and Chase took the initiative to make a trip out West someday.

Still, despite his rough childhood, and a couple of wild years in high school, Chase had defied the odds and turned into a good guy. A really good guy. Their youth pastor from Langhorne Community Fellowship took Chase under his wing, and by the time Landyn was old enough to date, he was toeing a pretty straight line. Well, except for that tattoo. Dad had come completely unglued when he heard Chase had gotten inked. She'd finally calmed him down by explaining that Chase's Celtic cross—on his collarbone, so it was hidden under most of his shirts—was a symbol of his faith and of the permanence of God's love for him. Landyn had always loved her husband's tat—one he'd designed himself. She'd even toyed with the idea of getting one to match. But so far the fear of her father's reaction and the lack of cash had prevented her—not to mention the disturbing image of herself as a grandma with a shriveled tat on her chest.

After Chase proposed, Mom and Dad insisted they go to counseling before getting married— more intensive than the required premarital counseling—with Pastor Simmons. And though she'd balked big-time at the suggestion, Chase had been willing. And when their sessions were over, she was certain Chase Spencer was ready to be the husband of her dreams—even if her parents weren't convinced.

Maybe she should have listened to them.

Because now he'd quit his job and all but forced her to quit hers. Forced her to run home to Missouri. Except she didn't have a home in Missouri anymore either. Her parents had turned their house into a bed-and-breakfast, and her room was now a guest room at the Chicory Inn. *Real original, Mom.* From what her sisters said—and from the photos Mom had e-mailed her of the finished renovation—Landyn wouldn't even recognize the place.

Sometime this week was the big open house for the inn, too. She'd told her parents she and Chase couldn't get away—which was true at the time. But now she had no choice. She'd stayed with a friend from work for three days, but if she'd stayed there one more day, she'd have had one less friend. So she'd loaded up what little furniture Chase didn't take with him, and she was headed back to Langhorne.

At least in Missouri she wouldn't be shelling out two thousand dollars a month in rent for some roach-infested studio. And she'd be a world away from New York. And him.

2

The first guests arrived at one o'clock sharp. Audrey should have known Lawna and Fred Farley, from half a mile up the road, would be first to ring the doorbell. She had no right to resent them coming. She'd invited all their neighbors and friends, and she wanted them to come, despite the fact they'd likely never book a night in the inn. But, as Grant had suggested, they might be persuaded to reserve a night for visiting family members at the county's newest and most quaint bed-and-breakfast.

Still, Audrey knew Lawna well enough to know the woman's main mission today was to critique the decor, the food, Audrey's standard of cleanliness, and the Whitman children and grandchildren—and then report back to anyone in Langhorne who would listen. Lawna's Tease, Tan 'n' Tone, the beauty/tanning/fitness salon the Farleys had opened in Langhorne a year ago (Grant called it Tease, Tan 'n' *Talk*) would provide the perfect venue for her purposes too.

Audrey pasted on her best smile and opened the door. "Welcome!" Behind them, two more cars pulled up the long driveway and parked on either side of the Farleys. She didn't recognize the people getting out of those vehicles. Maybe this day wasn't going to be a bust after all. "Here, let me take your jacket, Fred."

"I've got it, Mom." Bree stepped in and took the corduroy jacket Fred shrugged out of.

"Bless you, sweet girl." Audrey didn't know what she would have done without their precious daughter-in-law this morning. Not only had she cheered Simone up—and cleaned her up—but she'd somehow managed to whip the rest of the family into shape too. It was no wonder Tim's wife was so good at her job as an event planner. "I owe you one," she whispered to Bree after Fred and Lawna had wandered into the parlor to inspect the renovation.

"Look out there," Bree said, pointing to the knot of people gathered on the front veranda. "And the weather is perfect. If we get too big of a crowd we can just send people outside."

"It is perfect, isn't it? And bless you, too, for thinking we'll have a crowd."

"Of course you will." Bree hung Fred's coat in the closet.

"Tell the girls we're ready for the tours." Audrey went out to herd the guests inside where Corinne and her sister, Danae, were preparing to host guided tours of the inn. The girls' husbands, Jesse and Dallas, had taken the three grandkids for a ride in the wagon with instructions to keep the little girls occupied as long as possible.

Hurrying down the stairs toward the small flock of guests, Audrey noticed there were now six cars in the makeshift parking lot and another coming up the drive. Pulling a U-Haul trailer. Hmm . . . She hoped no one expected to get a room tonight. They already had a dozen bookings on the calendar just from word of mouth and what little advertising they'd done. But they purposely hadn't reserved anything this opening weekend since they'd asked the kids all to stay the weekend to celebrate the grand opening—a christening of sorts, and probably the last time they'd have so many of their family all under the same roof for a while.

The white car towing the U-Haul moved slowly up the drive, but instead of following the signs to the designated parking Grant had roped off, the vehicle pulled around beside the detached garage where the kids always parked when they came to visit. The car looked a little like Landyn's Honda, and for a minute Audrey dared to hope her baby girl had—

Wait! Squinting, Audrey shaded her eyes against

the sun's glare. The girl getting out of the car . . . It *was* Landyn.

It was all Audrey could do to take the time to direct her guests inside, but she managed to tactfully do that before flying down the steps and across the front lawn.

Landyn's hair was a mass of pale ringlets around her face, and even with huge sunglasses covering her eyes, she looked exhausted. But she was beaming from ear to ear. "Hey, Mom!"

"You stinker, you. Couldn't get away, huh?" Audrey caught her youngest up in a bear hug, then looked past her to the passenger side of the car. "Where's Chase?"

"I came by myself."

"You drove? Honey! That's a long trip to make by yourself. Did you drive all night? Oh, never mind! I'm just so glad you're here! Wait till Dad sees you. He's going to absolutely flip out."

Landyn laughed and opened the back door of the Honda to retrieve a small suitcase. "What's with all the cars?"

Audrey furrowed her brow. "What do you mean? It's for the open house. People came. I thought that's why *you* came."

"Oh—of course."

"You forgot?"

"No, I mean . . . I knew it was this weekend. I just forgot it was today. I—I figured you'd have it on a Sunday or something."

Something seemed . . . *off*. But Audrey didn't have time to press her right now. "Here—" She reached for her daughter's bag. "What else needs to come in? And what on earth is in the U-Haul?"

"Oh—" Landyn eyed the trailer as if she'd also forgotten she'd towed it halfway across the country. "Some furniture and stuff. To put in storage. We can unload it later. It looks like you have a good turnout."

"Better than I thought we'd have. And we're just getting started. It goes until six. Are you hungry? We've already eaten, but I can fix you a plate."

Landyn hitched her purse up on one shoulder and locked the car. "Thanks . . . not hungry. And I'm a mess. Can I sneak in the back and freshen up before I have to see anyone?"

Audrey scrambled to think where she could put Landyn. The other kids had already filled all the guest rooms—and the covered porch. "You can clean up in the master bath for now. I'll take it off the tour until you're out."

"Tour?"

"Your sisters are giving tours of the inn."

Landyn raised a blond eyebrow over the rim of her sunglasses. "Whoa . . . So it's the *inn* now? Fancy schmancy."

Audrey felt the sting from her daughter's snarky tone but tried not to let it show. "Come on. I'll sneak you in. You can surprise everybody after you get cleaned up." She hefted the suitcase in

26

one hand, put an arm around Landyn, and squeezed her close. "I'm sorry Chase couldn't make it, but I'm so glad you're home."

And she was. She was thrilled her baby girl had decided to surprise them, but Landyn's timing could not have been worse. The master suite on the third floor was Grant's and her retreat. It would never be booked, but she'd wanted to let people see the impressive space this one time at the open house, and she'd said as much in all the advertisements.

She toyed briefly with sending Landyn into town to clean up at Grant's mother's empty house, but that was no way to welcome a newlywed daughter home. Their guests would just have to understand.

Grant left a foursome of his golf buddies bragging in the front yard and went to greet a new carload of guests who'd just come up the driveway. Audrey would be delighted with the turnout for her open house. He hadn't seen her for at least an hour, but through the open windows he could hear the pleasant murmur of conversation inside. And above it, Corinne and Danae's well-rehearsed tour guide lingo floated down from the open windows. His two eldest daughters' voices sounded so much alike he couldn't tell where one left off and the other began.

Their kids had done them proud today. He

tugged at his tie, which now hung in a loose loop around his neck. He'd be glad when the last guest pulled out of the drive and he could don shorts and flip-flops and just hang out with his family. He had steaks marinating in the fridge in the garage, and Audrey assured him there'd be plenty of leftovers from the open house to round out the meal. She'd no doubt be exhausted after this day, but he'd talked her into skipping church so they could sleep in tomorrow. "God will understand," Grant assured her when she protested.

And the girls, including Bree, had all agreed to stay long enough to clean the floors and get the house back in shape after half of Clemens County and beyond had traipsed through it.

"Hello, folks. Welcome." He stretched out a hand to two middle-aged couples who'd emerged from a Lincoln Town Car. He glanced at the license plate. "Tennessee? You've come a ways."

The driver of the car laughed. "We're visiting my brother here. He and Doris live just up the road in Cape Girardeau."

"Ah, I see. Well, you Tennesseans definitely win the prize for coming the farthest. So far."

He directed them through the front door and spied the tail end of Corinne's tour group of six heading out to the backyard. "I'm not sure where my other tour guide is, but why don't you help yourself to some refreshments and I'll see if I can track one of the girls down."

"Oh, thank you, but we just ate." The driver's wife patted her ample belly. "Don't worry about us. We can just do a self-guided tour."

The quartet seemed harmless, but Audrey had warned them all about letting people roam the house unattended. "I'll give you the grand tour myself," he said. "We can start on the third floor and work our way down."

As they climbed two flights of stairs to the master suite, Grant noted points of interest—not necessarily the things Audrey would have chosen to highlight were she guiding the tour, but the gentlemen seemed interested while their wives oohed and aahed among themselves over the decor.

"This is our private living quarters, but my wife wanted to show it off today." Grant pushed the door open and motioned for the group to precede him into the room. "Audrey's invested a lot into this proj—"

The women gave a little gasp, and Grant followed their gaze to the bed. Someone— someone wearing Audrey's lavender polka-dot bathrobe—was curled in a fetal ball in the middle of the down comforter Audrey had paid a small fortune for. But it wasn't Audrey.

The body stirred and sat up looking dazed.

What on earth? "Landyn? What are you doing here?" He turned to his guests. "I'm sorry, but would you excuse us for a moment, please?"

Murmuring unwarranted apologies, the two couples pivoted and nudged each other out of the room, obviously feeling awkward—and probably wondering why there was a pretty young woman sleeping on his bed.

"Daddy!" Landyn squealed and rolled off the bed and into his arms.

"I thought you couldn't come! Does your mom know you're here?"

She giggled. "She snuck me in the back way. I—wanted to surprise everyone."

"Well, you certainly did that." He glanced back at the door, relieved to see the guests heading downstairs.

He held her at arms' length. Her eyes still looked sleepy. "Where's Chase?"

"He couldn't come. I . . . came by myself." Landyn looked around the room. "It doesn't even feel like the same place."

"Did Corinne and Danae take you on the tour?"

She shook her head. "I haven't seen anyone but Mom."

"You're kidding."

She grinned. "I used your shower. I was just going to rest my eyes for a few minutes and—I guess I fell asleep. Sorry if I scared off those people." She motioned toward the door.

At that minute, the door opened and Audrey came through it. "Oh! I missed the reunion." She

30

beamed up at Grant. "I wanted to see your face when you saw her."

"You would have liked to see the faces of your out-of-state guests when I brought them up for the tour and there was a strange woman in our bed."

"Dad!"

Audrey gasped. "Are you serious? Oh, dear . . . I'd better go down and explain. Which guests?"

"The ones from Tennessee."

"Someone came all the way from Tennessee?"

"Visiting relatives in Cape. Sorry to disappoint."

"Okay. I'll go do damage control. Meanwhile, we need to get this room back in shape."

"Or close it to the public," he said, aiming a worried glance at Landyn. "You look tired, baby girl."

"She drove all the way from New York by herself," Audrey said on her way out the door.

"You drove straight through? Is Chase working?"

"Yes—He couldn't get off." A split-second hesitation that planted a seed of worry in Grant's gut. "But I didn't want to miss the family reunion."

He studied his daughter. Now wasn't the time for questions, but he sensed there was something she wasn't saying. "Well, get dressed," he said finally. "I'll take you on the tour myself." He gave her another quick hug, surprised at the lump that swelled in his throat.

He hadn't seen Landyn since her wedding . . . was it six months ago already? It was hard to picture his baby girl as a married woman.

And he hoped there wasn't already trouble in paradise.

3

Landyn rummaged through the small suitcase she'd brought in, looking for something halfway presentable. She settled on skinny jeans and a crinkle-look blouse that was a few wrinkles beyond crinkled. Still, it was better than the ratty T-shirt she'd arrived in. She pulled her hair into a thick ponytail and went out to the hall to find Dad.

He walked her through the second-floor bedrooms, and when they got to her old room, her sisters and Bree were there talking with two elderly women Landyn didn't know.

Corinne spotted her first. "Landyn! What are you doing here, baby sister?"

The squeal-fest that followed lightened her heart considerably.

"I can't believe it's really you." Danae reached out to finger the hem of Landyn's blouse. "Look at you, all metro and New York-y."

Landyn laughed. "You goose, I bought this in Cape two years ago."

"Well, you wear it *tres* New York."

They giggled like middle school girls at a slumber party.

Bree turned to the abandoned guests. "Why don't I finish the tour? These girls haven't seen each other in a while."

"Sisters," Dad explained.

The women cooed as if they'd just seen a basket of kittens.

Landyn hugged Tim's wife—she refused to think of Bree as Tim's *widow*. "Thanks, Bree. We'll catch up later, okay?"

"So what do you think?" Corinne asked after the guests were out of earshot. "Do you like the house?"

"The *inn,* you mean?"

Her dad grinned. "Mom's got you trained already?"

Landyn frowned. "It will always be a house to me." But she had to admit, the place looked amazing. Of course, Mom had e-mailed photos throughout the remodeling process, but everything looked even better in person. She'd never considered that she might have inherited her artistic talents from her mother, but it struck her now that it was true. So many of the decorating elements on this floor were exactly what she would have chosen—refurbished hardwood floors and cream-painted woodwork and wainscoting that gave a cozy, traditional feel to the century-old house, but paired with bold, contemporary rugs and textiles. And her mother's unique yet subtle decorative touches made each room truly extraordinary. "Mom really outdid herself on this project."

"Did you ever have any doubt?" Dad looked pleased.

"I guess I never thought about it."

"Well, be sure and tell her. She's poured her life into this place this past year. It'd mean a lot to her to hear that you approve."

Landyn looked around her old room and affected a pout. "I'm still not very happy she took down my Twilight posters and sold off my lava lamps."

Dad laughed, and she remembered how much she liked making him do that.

"By the way, where's my dog? You didn't sell off Huck, too, did you?"

"Unfortunately, no. He's still here, wreaking the usual havoc and eating us out of house and home. Mom just didn't want him in the house until after everyone leaves. He's been relegated to the backyard."

"Poor Huck."

"Have you *seen* the backyard?" Danae pulled a curtain aside. "It's a dog's paradise out there."

Landyn went to peer out the window. "Oh, wow! That's gorgeous. Dad, did you do that your—Hey, there's Huck." She waved and tapped on the window. "Huckleberry! Hey, boy!"

The dog lay in the shade on a patch of lush grass, wagging his tail, oblivious.

"I'm going down to see him."

"So what else haven't you seen yet?" Danae asked trailing her out into the hall.

"I haven't seen any of the downstairs except what I saw when Mom snuck me up the back stairs through the sunroom."

"Oh, wait till you see the family room. You'll love it." Danae led the way down the curved staircase.

They were on the landing when a thud, followed by a high-pitched wail, made them all lean over the rail looking for the source of the commotion.

"Did somebody fall?" Corinne hurried past them.

Danae followed, but Landyn hung back, peering over the rail into the foyer below where half a dozen people stood in a circle looking as if they might break into a chorus of "Kumbaya" any minute.

"Please stand back," Dad said, taking charge. "Corinne, go find your mother. Where's the dog? Did Fred trip on Huckleberry, Lawna?"

Landyn looked again and realized the group was gathered around a man lying on the floor.

"Heavens, no." The voice belonged to Lawna Farley, their long-time neighbor. "I haven't even seen the dog. Fred just fainted. He does this at least once a week. His blood sugar, you know."

Landyn let out a relieved breath. Hopefully Fred hadn't broken anything. It would be the pits if Mom and Dad got sued before the inn even officially opened. She blamed six months in New York for the cruel thought and reminded herself that here in the heartland people didn't sue each other over every little thing.

Mom came in from the veranda, breathless—and looking beautiful. Landyn had noticed it earlier when her mother greeted her at the car. She didn't remember her mother ever being so pretty. And she looked nowhere near fifty-eight, or however old she was now. Landyn had lost track. It was strange how, now that she was a married woman herself, she saw her mother through different eyes. And wondered why she hadn't seen the *person* her mother was beneath the bossy mom persona.

"Fred? Can you hear me?" Mom knelt and helped Mr. Farley sit up. She offered him a glass of water and fanned him with one of the new brochures for the inn. "Lawna, why don't you bring your car around? Grant will help Fred out. You probably ought to have a doctor check him over."

Landyn suddenly felt remorseful for the way she'd treated her mother in recent years. Not that she'd ever been out-and-out mean, but she'd let stupid things that shouldn't have mattered annoy her. And she'd pushed Mom away when she was just doing what came naturally for mothers—trying to protect their babies.

Landyn had been the last one, the one that emptied her parents' nest. Maybe it wasn't so surprising that Mom had poured herself into the bed-and-breakfast the way she had. Heather Crupp's mother had a nervous breakdown when Heather left for college. So even though Landyn hated the way her parents had changed the house she grew up in, maybe she should be grateful Mom had chosen a healthier way to handle the empty nest.

Even if it did ultimately leave Landyn homeless.

Audrey surveyed the kitchen, not sure she could keep her eyes open long enough to join her family for supper. But it was a good kind of weary. Make that *exhausted*. Almost two hundred people had signed the guest book today and they'd gotten almost twenty new reservations on the books, too.

Grant dinged his fork against a glass and waited for everyone to quiet down. "Let's pray, and then we can chow down."

Hands clasped around the table and when they were all connected, Grant squeezed her hand and began the familiar mealtime prayer. "Lord, thank you for the loved ones gathered around this table, thank you for bringing Landyn safely home. We are grateful for this food and the hands that prepared it, and we ask that you would bless it for the use of our bodies that we may better serve you."

A chorus of amens went up and the conversations that had been going at full throttle before Grant called for silence revved back up. But he raised a hand and waited until they quieted again. "Thanks for all your help today, guys. Mom and I couldn't have done it without you." He leaned across the corner of the table and pulled her close to kiss her forehead. "Other than Fred fainting in the foyer, I'd say the day was a success, my dear."

"Fred Farley fainted in the foyer." Link grinned. "Sounds like a nursery rhyme."

Landyn picked up her brother's chorus. "Our friend Fred Farley fainted and fell in the foyer."

"On Friday!" chimed five-year-old Sari, catching the spirit of the game, even if she had the day of the week wrong.

"Good one, squirt." Jesse gave his daughter a pat on the back.

"And Saturday," yelled Sadie, not to be outdone by her big sister but not quite getting the gist of the joke either. Still, they rewarded her with more laughter.

"And finally . . ." Landyn clutched a serving spoon like a microphone. "This just in: on Friday, family friend Fred Farley fainted and fell face-down in the foyer . . ." She bit her lip, obviously scrambling for more f's.

Giggling, Corinne grabbed the spoon from her

sister. "Not far from Fred's fine family farm." She thrust a victory fist in the air and brought it down with a triumphant "Yes!"

"Funny," Danae deadpanned.

Link had just taken a swig of Diet Coke, which he promptly spewed through his nose. And of course that started a whole new round of hilarity.

Audrey went for a dishrag and started blotting up the soda that beaded on the tablecloth. But she couldn't curb her own laughter long enough to do a decent job. Suddenly she didn't feel so exhausted anymore.

"Do the Farleys still own that spa place?" Landyn asked.

"You mean Tease, Tan 'n' Tone?" Jesse said with a glint in his eye.

"Are you serious? It's called Tease, Tan 'n' Tone?" Landyn made a comical face. "Terrific!"

Link clutched his chest. "You guys are killing me."

His laughter was contagious—so much like his brother's had been. When he and Tim were teenagers, Audrey used to love to get them started just to hear their infectious cackling.

"The Tease, Tan 'n' Tone—in town?" Grant winked at Audrey.

She rolled her eyes at his lame attempt, but oh, her heart was full. Despite everything, she and Grant had been blessed beyond words with this family. She was sorry Chase couldn't have come with Landyn, but since he hadn't even been at his job for six months, it was unlikely he'd accrued any vacation time. She was surprised Landyn had been able to get away. She'd barely had a minute to talk to her youngest with all the guests, and now with the rest of the family here. She didn't even know how long Landyn was staying.

Somebody's phone rang—one of those crazy ringtones that was a few bars of a song. Not a melody Audrey recognized, but it didn't sound like a very happy tune. Landyn slipped her phone from the pocket of her jeans.

"It's Chase." She scooted her chair away from the table and went down the hall.

Audrey didn't hear Landyn answer, but something was going on with those two. A mother didn't miss when her daughter *cringed* at the sound of her husband's ringtone.

4

Landyn considered pretending to have a civil conversation with Chase, but she hated the lies she'd already told. Instead, she slipped into the powder room near the foyer and waited for the call to go to voice mail.

Chase hadn't tried calling her even once until now. Fine. She wasn't in any big hurry to talk to him either. A wave of nausea rolled over her. Now she was lying to herself. She missed him like crazy.

When his voice mail message signaled, she clicked on the icon and listened.

"Landyn, what the—"

Real nice, Chase. Your first words to me in three days are curse words? She rolled her eyes and finished listening to his message.

"I went to our apartment and it's empty! Where *are* you? I *was* just mad, but now you've got me worried. Call me."

He was mad? Oh, that was rich. She wondered if he'd gone to the apartment looking for her or just to pick up the rest of his stuff. It didn't matter. She hadn't heard anything close to an apology in his message.

But what was she going to say when she went back to the table? *Chase says to tell everyone "hi" and he's sorry he couldn't come.* No. She wasn't going to keep lying. She didn't owe any explanation. But they'd expect one and—

Her stomach revolted, and she was grateful she was already in the bathroom. She dropped to her knees in front of the toilet. A knock at the door made her break out in a sweat.

"Landyn? Honey, are you okay?"

She wiped her mouth on her sleeve and forced her voice not to tremble. "I'm fine, Mom." Another lie. "I'll be out in a minute."

She flushed the toilet and washed her hands

and face, praying her mother wouldn't be waiting outside when she opened the door.

"Honey? You're white as a sheet." So much for answered prayers. Her mom grasped her shoulders. "What's wrong? Did you get bad news?"

"I'm fine, Mom." She brushed past her down the hall, but felt her mother dogging her, and then a hand on her shoulder.

"Landyn . . . What is going on?"

"Oh, Mom . . ." She turned and crumpled into her mother's waiting arms. "Chase and I . . . We're—separated."

"What? Chase left you? What happened?" Mom held her at arms' length and looked her in the eye. "What is going on?"

Landyn could barely speak. "Can I just . . . go to bed? I don't feel well."

"Honey, you need to tell me what's going on."

"Mom, I don't want to talk about it right now." She hated the agony she saw on her mother's face, but she really didn't have the strength to get into it right now. "Where can I sleep?"

"Oh . . . You take the Butterfly room. I'll have Danae and Dallas sleep on the hideaway sofa in the basement."

"No, it's okay. I can sleep down there. Is my stuff still in your and Dad's room?"

"You go on down. I'll bring your stuff." Mom

started for the stairs. "And don't worry. I'll make excuses for you."

Her voice caught on a sob. "Thanks, Mom." Her phone rang again. Chase.

"Do you want me to tell him you can't talk?"

"No. I—I'll take it."

Mom disappeared and Landyn made a split-second decision. "Hello?"

"Landyn. Thank the Lord. I've been trying to find you. What is going on?"

"Tried to find me, huh? You called exactly one time, Chase. Did you forget it shows up on my phone when you call—or don't call?"

"Where are you? What'd you do with all our stuff?"

"I'm at home."

A beat of silence. "Home where?"

"Where do you think? The only home I have now. At Mom and Dad's."

"You *have* a home with me, Landyn. I told you that."

"You can't just make decisions like that for me, Chase. I'm your wife, not your little girl."

"Whatever happened to 'whither thou goest, I will go'?"

It stung to have her wedding vows thrown back in her face. "I think that promise implied some measure of mutual agreement." Her stomach roiled again and tears threatened, but she would not let him see her vulnerability.

"Please come home, Landyn. I can't do this without you."

"Maybe you should have thought of that before you let someone else have our apartment—our *home!*"

"I told you, babe . . . I had a chance at this place, and I couldn't let it get away. I feel like this is what we're supposed to do. Especially since we found someone to sublet that same day!"

She let the "we" slide for the moment. "Supposed to do, as in God told you?" That's what he'd said before.

"I know you don't buy it, but yes."

"And we, as in you and me? Then why didn't God tell me?" Her voice rose, and she started down the basement stairs so the rest of the family wouldn't hear her.

"I—I don't know. Maybe you weren't listening."

Her jaw clenched involuntarily, and heat made her skin prickle. "I'm sorry, Chase, but this conversation is over. We . . . we can't agree on this, so I don't know what else there is to talk about."

"Wait! Landyn, don't hang—"

"I've got to go, Chase. I'm sorry." She clicked End and slumped onto the lumpy couch. She tried to work up tears. Wished for the cleansing they usually offered. But right now she was all wrung out. She felt nothing.

She'd prayed. She really had. Maybe not with

the right attitude, but she had to get over this feeling of betrayal before she could utter a genuine prayer. There was no way it could be right for a husband to make a decision of this magnitude without even consulting his wife. No way! Besides, this was not part of the deal. They had a plan and Chase was wrecking it to pieces.

He claimed he didn't have a choice. That it was an opportunity he was handed and he had to make a split-second decision. He said he'd only done what he felt God was leading him to do. But that wasn't an excuse for completely rearranging *her* life, was it? Even if he did think God told him to. It sounded to her like an excuse to do what Chase wanted to do. And she would not let him set a precedent like that in their marriage.

Audrey sank into the overstuffed chair in the master bedroom and gave in to the tears that had threatened all day. "I'm sorry, Grant. I . . . I don't know what I was thinking."

Soft strains of Mozart from Grant's iPad only made her melancholy deeper. She punched a feather pillow and hugged it to her chest, feeling like an angst-ridden teenager.

He peered at her over the e-book he was reading. "Why are you apologizing?"

"Because!" She punched the pillow again. "We spent our life's savings fixing up this place. You sacrificed everything, Grant, and it looks like this might have all been a horrible mistake and—"

"Mistake?"

She stared at him. "Everything that could go wrong did go wrong. Just look how it turned out!"

"How it turned out? What are you talking about?" Grant looked incredulous. He closed the cover on his iPad and tucked it into a shelf on his nightstand.

Audrey fingered the hem of her pillowcase. "Seriously? With Landyn showing up in the middle of it all, Huck running amok, the whole Fred fiasco . . . We'll probably get sued, and—"

"Audrey." He slipped off his reading glasses, put them on the nightstand too, then drew her into his arms.

"I thought the cake was a little dry, too, didn't you? I don't think I'd use that recipe again unless I add—"

"Babe, *babe* . . ." He laughed. "Everything turned out fine. And I have never been happier in my life."

"What?" She shifted in the bed to look up at him. "Are you crazy?"

"Probably." He chuckled. "Okay, certifiably. But . . . I don't know . . . something about today just felt so right. All our hard work really paid off. I—I guess I never thought about this part when I was scraping popcorn off of ceilings and hanging from the roof attaching twinkle lights."

She giggled, the image of him hanging off the

eaves all too real. They'd had a huge fight that day. "But—"

"Did you see people's faces when they saw the transformation? And how many nights did you book today?"

"Seventeen . . . Maybe eighteen." She was still in awe that people had committed dates to their calendar on a whim like that. "Of course, half of them will probably cancel, and the rest are getting such a huge discount that we won't make a penny on—"

"Shh . . ." He placed a finger gently over her lips. "Can't you just enjoy our success? Just for tonight."

Raucous laughter floated up through the furnace vent from the room below . . . Link was no doubt regaling his siblings with stories of their childhood escapades. Audrey smiled. "It is kind of nice having all the kids under our roof again."

He affected a look of horror. "Just for the weekend, remember."

"I know, I know." Well, except for Landyn. But now wasn't the time to tell Grant about that. "But you've got to admit it's nice."

"You did see the grocery bill, didn't you?"

She furrowed her brow. "Now *that* was scary."

"I'll say."

At breakfast the next morning, Audrey looked around her "empty nest." How was it that she'd

47

shooed five kids off to college and now there were six adults in pajamas at her breakfast table —seven whenever Landyn finally got up—and three unattended toddlers crunching cornflakes into the brand new Berber?

She laughed and flipped another griddle full of pancakes. Bree had come back to have breakfast with them and help with the clean-up. Audrey couldn't have loved that girl more. Her sons-in-law, too. They'd been so lucky—no, so *blessed*—with the people their kids had chosen as mates. Of course, they'd prayed for the ones their children would marry since each of them were born.

She watched Link playing with the kids—a big kid himself—and her heart filled. Even at twenty-eight Link exhibited the symptoms of "middle child syndrome," often seeming to feel over-shadowed by the other kids' accomplishments. Tim's heroic death on a windblown hill in Afghanistan had only made that worse. How she prayed Link would find a wonderful girl who could help him appreciate his amazing qualities.

For a while she'd dared to hope something might develop between Link and Bree. A few months ago, she'd even suggested he invite Bree out to dinner.

But when he figured out she meant on a *date,* he'd been furious. And disgusted. "She's Tim's wife, Mom. She's . . . practically my sister. What are you thinking?"

48

"She's not his wife. She's his widow."

Grant had taken Link's side, though, chiding Audrey for interfering. So she'd stayed out of it since. But sometimes when she thought about Bree finding someone else, grief consumed her as if it had only been yesterday that the uniformed officers had brought the devastating news to their door.

Landyn was now the same age Tim was when he'd died. The thought sent a pang through her. Audrey wasn't superstitious, but she'd be glad when Landyn celebrated her next birthday. Too many reminders.

As if reading her mind, Grant looked up from his newspaper. "Are you going to let your youngest daughter sleep her life away?"

"She wasn't feeling very well last night. It won't hurt anything to let her sleep in."

"How long is she here for, do you know?"

Audrey shook her head. "I barely got to talk to her yesterday." Though it was true, it felt like a lie.

"Well, I hope she's not planning to unload that U-Haul in my shop."

Audrey winced. "I think that's exactly what she's planning. At least she used the word *storage*."

A frown creased her husband's forehead. "Did she also use the word *temporary*? What do they own that's big enough to need a U-Haul anyway?"

Audrey shrugged, eager to change the subject.

She heard Huckleberry at the back door and went to let him in.

"Huck! There you are!" Landyn, still in the long T-shirt she'd slept in, came down the back stairway and made a beeline for the dog. He went into happy spasms, alternately licking her face and barking at her and Grant, as if to announce "my girl's home!"

"Do you want pancakes, honey? Did you sleep well?"

"I slept okay. And no pancakes. But thanks. I think—" A funny expression came to her face, and she scrambled to her feet and headed down the hall with one hand over her mouth.

Grant gave Audrey a what's-up-with-her look. She only shrugged. But she was starting to have her suspicions. She wondered if Landyn had told Chase yet.

5

The trees in Central Park were nearing their peak of autumn color, and Chase Spencer chose an empty bench and plopped there, still breathing heavily from his morning run. He'd overslept and had only done two miles today, but it wasn't like anyone was going to give him a hard time for wimping out.

No, that was Landyn's job. And from the sound

of things, she'd given up on him. He slumped on the bench and tilted his head to look at the massive oak branches overhead, composing a painting in his mind. If only he could capture the true colors and textures on canvas. But his work always fell short of what he saw in his mind's eye. Sometimes he wished he could shut off the images that were always there. Colors and patterns, light and shadow, ink stippling and watercolor swirls. His profs had called it a gift. And there was a time he'd viewed it that way, too.

But recently, it felt like more of a curse. One he couldn't seem to escape, but one that dogged him no differently than what he imagined an addiction to alcohol or weed would.

God what am I supposed to do with this?

It was a question he'd asked himself. And God. And Landyn. He and God were usually on the same page. Why couldn't Landyn just go along? Why was that so hard for her? It wasn't like he'd asked her to follow him to Africa to be a missionary—though sometimes he thought she might have sooner done that than let him have his dream.

He was an artist. It wasn't an occupation. It wasn't a hobby, as Landyn too often referred to it—revealing more than she knew. No, it was *who* he was. He could no more help that God made him that way than Landyn could help being a woman. It wasn't his fault that society made it almost impossible to make a living as an artist.

And now he had his chance—his one chance—to make a go of it, and she wanted to throw it away. For security. For money.

He hadn't seen that coming. Not when they'd been in youth group together growing up, not when they'd worked together in the computer labs on campus for work-study when he was a junior and she a doe-eyed freshman, and she'd brought him empty journals to fill with his ink drawings. Not when he'd taken her on dates to art galleries and dreamed confidently about the day it would be his work hanging there. Certainly not when they were engaged and she went out of her way to sing his praises—*Chase Spencer, my art genius fiancé*—to anyone who would listen.

But as soon as it meant giving up a nice apartment and moving into a studio, as soon as it meant giving up the security of the paltry savings account they shared, she'd freaked out on him and accused him of sabotaging their marriage and "abandoning" her.

Why couldn't she understand that this was the opportunity of a lifetime? God couldn't want him to hide his talent and bury his gifts. He was being obedient to the God they both claimed to believe in, and Landyn was punishing him for it. Even weirder when she'd always been the more spiritual one in their relationship. *Oh, ye of little faith, Landyn.*

Well, he'd show her. He would prove to her that

he'd been right all along. He still loved her. And when she was ready to admit she'd been wrong, that she'd thwarted God's will in his life—a pretty serious offense as he saw it—then he'd forgive her. And take her back.

Because he missed her like crazy.

His cell phone chirped and he checked the screen. It was the gallery. His heart ramped up a notch, but he forced a nonchalant tone. "This is Chase."

"Hey, Chase. This is Patrick Everhardt. Miles Roberts probably told you I'd be calling?"

"Yes, he did." *But on Sunday?* It still bothered him that the Sabbath was just another day in this city. Oh well, when in Rome . . . "Good to talk to you, Mr. Everhardt."

"Listen, we're impressed with what Miles showed us. We'd like to set up a meeting, see if we can get something in the works for you."

"Hey, that's cool. I'd be glad to come in and talk to you." He sounded smooth even to his own ears. It was a good thing they couldn't hear his heart trying to escape his chest.

"Miles explained how our commissions work?"

Chase frowned. "He said you might be able to get me a little upfront money." It had shocked him to learn that galleries took a fifty percent commission. "Is that a possibility? Just something to live on while I do some of the pieces he thought we needed to fill out the show."

"I wish we could, man. But we just set up two other debuts, and we can't really do anything else right now. But I guarantee you'll see it on the backside. And we can help you with some of the framing. Maybe you have someone—family or a friend—that could float you a loan to get you through?"

"Yeah . . . Sure, I'll work something out." Everhardt was a big dog. Chase wasn't about to let this chance slip out of his hands. And if Everhardt would cover framing some of his work, that was a huge expense off his back. He was struggling to come up with enough matted stuff for a small show Miles had scheduled for next week.

Maybe it wasn't all bad that Landyn had run home to mama. He didn't exactly have time for a wife right now. He checked the thought, recognizing it for what it was. Him, on the defensive because he knew he wasn't worthy of her. Had always known it. And if he ever forgot, Landyn's dad could be counted on to slip in some subtle reminder.

It still steamed him a little what her parents had *required* him to do before saying "I do" to their daughter. Counseling. Like he was some kind of nutjob. Landyn had been quick to point out that most couples went through some kind of counseling before they walked down the aisle— a lot of pastors required it before marrying a couple. Or so she'd said.

He'd loved Landyn since he was eighteen. She'd been sixteen the first time he saw her, so he'd loved her from afar until Grant finally came around and let them hang out together. But even after they started dating, Chase had spent most of those years figuring Landyn would eventually realize she could do better than him.

But after they got married . . . Well, he'd just thought it would take a little longer for it to catch up with him.

But he wasn't giving up yet. Maybe this time apart would give him time to prove to her that he could make it as an artist. Even if he had to get a second job and work around the clock. He'd do whatever it took.

The trees along the creek whispered in the morning breeze, their leaves trembling in rich shades of red and purple and gold that made Landyn think of Chase. He would have been pulling samples off every tree and rushing back to the house to mix paints in an effort to match the incredible beauty on paper. And she would have chided him for the irony of missing a moment while trying to capture it.

She missed him so much. Not the Chase she left in New York. No, she missed the Chase she'd first fallen in love with three years ago on a summer day at Lake Wappapello. But he'd changed. Or maybe she was the one who'd changed.

Her stomach turned somersaults and she folded her arms around herself and slumped down with her back against the rough trunk of the massive Osage Orange tree. If there was anything on the acreage that represented the Whitman kids' childhood, it was this gnarly, spreading hedge tree—"the climbing tree" they'd dubbed it, for obvious reasons.

Huck trotted up from the creek bank and plopped down beside her. Patting his warm coat, she pulled his head onto her lap, not minding that his muzzle was still wet from his visit to the watering hole. "Did you miss me, Huckleberry? Huh, boy?"

He looked up at her, panting, then laid his soggy head back on her thigh.

"I sure missed you." She pushed his muddy paws away from her jeans and scratched behind his ears.

It had felt strange to be back home, especially inside where nothing looked the way it had when she'd lived here. But down here by the creek, everything was like it should be, untouched by Mom's wand of change.

It wasn't that she wasn't proud of her mother. And impressed with what she'd accomplished. Dad, too, though she knew he'd mostly just executed what Mom had drawn up. What they'd done with the house was truly remarkable. Landyn recognized that. Besides, it wasn't as if she had any claim on the place—and even if she did, Mom and Dad had only increased the value of the old house.

But it wasn't home anymore. Not even close. She remembered Corinne, the first time she came home from college for the summer, saying wistfully, "you can never really go back home." Her sister had graduated college long before the renovation, so maybe Landyn would have felt just as adrift if the house was exactly the way she remembered it. Still, seeing the drastic changes they'd made, realizing that the home she'd loved was gone, left a hollow feeling inside her.

A swell of nausea made her wrap her arms tighter around her midsection and close her eyes. She leaned her head against the tree trunk and let the breeze fan her. She hadn't told anyone about the baby. She'd hardly admitted it to God, much less talked to him about it. But she couldn't pretend much longer. "Oh, Lord. What am I going to do?"

The only answer was the trickle of the creek in the distance.

Grant studied the U-Haul parked across the yard, then looked at Landyn beside him on the bench in Audrey's fast-fading rose garden. "So what have you got in there?"

Landyn followed his line of sight. "Just some furniture and stuff. It's not full."

"What, you don't need furniture in New York?" She didn't giggle like he expected.

"Dad—I'm not going back." She looked at her hands in her lap, picking at a hangnail.

"What do you mean?"

"Chase and I . . . We had a disagreement. He let our apartment go and rented a hole in the wall in Brooklyn. So I had to—come home. He's determined to make it big with his art. Some guy promised him a showing in a gallery in Bedford-Stuyvesant and he fell for it."

"So you just left him? Just giving up on him, like that?" Dad snapped his fingers in that way that annoyed the snot out of her.

"I didn't leave *him,* Dad. He pretty much made his choice when he chose to sublet our apartment without even telling me. He didn't even give me a chance to discuss it. He just signed the contract on the spot. It would have cost me a fortune to commute back to my job from Brooklyn. I would have had to find a job in Brooklyn and start from square one."

"Wait . . . You quit your job, too?"

"I didn't have a choice, Dad. I can't afford to live in Manhattan on my salary alone."

"And you don't call *this* starting from square one?" He motioned between them on the bench.

His youngest daughter's news hit him like a fully-loaded river barge and he gripped the lip of the bench, feeling the splintered wood beneath his fingers. He'd known something wasn't quite right with Landyn, but he sure as blazes hadn't seen *this* coming. He'd been shocked at the salaries Landyn and Chase were drawing fresh out of college—until he heard how much their apartment rented for. But in this economy it was flat foolish to quit a decent paying job.

He looked toward the house and prayed for Audrey to appear on the back porch. She was always the one with the level head when it came to crises with their kids. But even she would have plenty to say about this. He took a breath and forced a calm he didn't feel into his voice. "Let me be sure I understand. Chase moved to a different apartment without telling you?"

"Oh, he told me, but not until after he'd already signed the new lease and sublet our old apartment. You should see this place, Dad. It's one room—and that's being generous. And Chase has his art studio set up in half of it. At least half. Everything else—including our bed—was supposed to go in the other half. You know how late he stays up sometimes to finish a painting. How was I supposed to get up at six every morning if I'm trying to sleep in his art studio with floodlights and his music blaring? It would have been outrageous for me to try to commute."

"Well, he must have had a reason for doing that." What was the kid *thinking?* "He did expect that you'd move with him, right?"

She shrugged, looking near tears. "He said he did. But it sure doesn't seem like it. He didn't even *ask* me, Dad." She pounded the arm of the bench. "He just did it. Without even thinking how it would affect me. How it would affect *us*."

"But . . . He must have *some* reason for making that decision." He wanted to give his son-in-law the benefit of the doubt, but he was running out of excuses for Chase Spencer.

"He just said he felt like it was what we were supposed to do—as in what *God* wanted us to do."

Grant winced before he could hide his emotions. Chase had gotten a rough start. But he'd turned into a good man. Or at least Grant had thought so. They'd seen a dramatic change in the kid over the past five or six years, watching him grow up in their church. And later, when they'd finally allowed Landyn to start dating Chase. It was a change Grant liked to take a little credit for, given how much time Chase had spent at the Whitman house. But enduring the childhood Chase did, and only coming to faith as a teen, their son-in-law had always been a little . . . *radical* in how he applied his faith. "So what does Chase think about you coming back here?"

"He doesn't like it." She looked down at her tennis shoes the way she had when she was a kid telling him she didn't know who ate the last cookie. "But Dad, there's nothing for me there anymore."

"You do realize you're calling your husband 'nothing' when you say that?"

"You know what I mean. I can't live that way. Even if I could commute, we can't make it on my salary alone there."

"What do you mean? Chase still has *his* job. Right?"

She hung her head. "Not exactly a paying one."

"Wait a minute. Chase quit his job too?" It was all Grant could do to keep his voice level. What were these stupid kids thinking? "So, what are you living on?"

Landyn looked at her lap, her face coloring. "He's picking up some tutoring at the college, but he hasn't gotten a real paycheck in over a month. He's sold some art here and there, but we've mostly been living on my salary and the last of our wedding gift money."

"Landyn! How long has this been going on?" His blood reached a rolling boil. "Why didn't you tell us?"

"Because I knew you'd have a cow, just like you're doing. It's not like Chase isn't working at all, Dad. He works harder than anybody I know. He's determined to make it as an artist."

"Fine, but his first priority should be providing for his family. Somebody needs to set him—"

The screen door slammed and Audrey came across the lawn toward them, waving. This news was going to break her heart. But as bad as he felt about that, he was relieved to see her, to have her input.

"You two look pretty serious," Audrey said, when she got within earshot. "Am I interrupting something?"

"I was just telling Dad about Chase."

"Oh." Audrey gave him a hangdog look.

She may as well have slapped him. "You knew? Why didn't you tell me?" This wasn't how they operated. As long as he'd known his wife, they'd never kept secrets from each other.

She lifted one shoulder. "I knew a little, but she wasn't ready to talk about it last night."

Landyn hung her head. "I don't think the whole world needs to know all the gory details. And I didn't want to ruin your open house."

He shot his wife a look meant to say "we'll talk about this later."

"Listen, Grant . . ." She answered his look as if he'd spoken the words. "It's not like you and I have had all the time in the world to talk."

He conceded her point with a sigh.

Audrey took a seat on the other side of Landyn and put an arm around her. "You want to fill me in?"

While Landyn spilled, Audrey shook her head and interjected "oh honey" and "I'm so sorry" where he had laid blame and chided Chase. Grant was sorry he'd immediately passed judgment on the kid, but even hearing the story a second time didn't change his opinion. A man's first responsibility was to take care of his wife. If he couldn't do that, he had no business being married. Still, they were already married. Unless they'd gotten divorced and had failed to inform him of that, too. The thought was only halfway sarcastic.

Audrey reached for their daughter's hand and clutched it between both of hers. "Is there anything else you want to tell us?"

Landyn looked up at her mother through hooded eyes. "What do you mean?"

"Honey . . .?" Audrey pressed.

Grant had no idea what she was getting at.

Apparently their daughter did. Her face crumpled and she threw herself into her mother's arms. "Oh, Mom . . . What am I going to do?"

"What is going on?" He looked at Audrey over their daughter's limp form and mouthed, "What?" He knew it was irrational, but he felt somehow betrayed by Landyn and Audrey both.

"Silly man." Audrey reached to stroke his cheek before going back to stroking Landyn's hair. "You're going to be a grandpa again," she whispered.

"Oh, dear Lord." It was a prayer. A fervent one. Oh, he firmly believed children were a blessing from the Lord. But right now it looked for all the world that this particular blessing just might grow up under *his* roof—a frightening percent of which was still owned by the First Bank of Langhorne.

6

Downtown Cape Girardeau hadn't changed a bit in the two years since Landyn had last been here. Corinne and Danae had invited her to meet them for a late lunch at Bella Italia. "But not too late," Corinne had said. "We want to beat the Tuesday Happy Hour crowd."

Landyn had spent yesterday helping Dad unload the U-Haul and return it to Cape Girardeau, then she'd helped Mom get the house—the inn—ready for guests tonight. It would feel weird to have strangers staying in the house. She was glad for an excuse to get away, and besides, she hadn't gotten a chance to talk to her sisters since Saturday. She looked forward to catching up with them, but she was nervous too. She had a feeling they knew about her and Chase —and maybe about the baby too—but she needed to make it official. And she wasn't sure how her sisters would feel about either piece of news.

Her two older sisters had always been closer to each other than to her, which was understandable since she'd come along later—after Link and Tim—the *caboose* of the family as her brothers called her. Even though she loved Corinne and Danae—and knew they loved her—she some- times felt like a third wheel when the three of them were together. A *much loved* third wheel. But still . . . and her moving to New York had only widened the gap.

Through the window of the restaurant, she saw them at a table just inside. She waved, and taking a deep breath, pushed open the door and motioned to the hostess before weaving through the lunch crowd to the table. She slid into the chair across from Danae, with her back to the street. "Hey, sisters."

"You look a little more rested than last time I saw you." Corinne gave her a one-armed hug.

"We already ordered." Danae pushed a menu across the table to her. "Mom said you drove straight through from New York. That's just crazy, Landyn."

"I stopped a couple times and slept in the car. Mountain Dew and Starbucks were my copilots."

Corinne made a face. "You should be careful, honey. All that caffeine's not good for the baby."

She hesitated. "Mom told you?"

Corinne glanced at Danae. "Actually, Dad told us."

"Wow. News travels fast. Well, aren't you going to say congratulations? Or something besides 'don't drink so much coffee'?"

"I wasn't sure if . . . Dad made it sound like you weren't too happy about the baby. But of course. Congratulations." Corinne patted her back, making Landyn feel like she was twelve again.

"Congratulations, Landyn." Danae's smile didn't reach her eyes. "I'm really happy for you guys."

"It's just"—Landyn shrugged—"really bad timing. For me and Chase both. Did they tell you about that situation, too?"

"Sort of," Corinne admitted.

"Just so you guys know, Chase doesn't know I'm pregnant."

"What?" Corinne's jaw dropped. "When were you planning to tell him? How could you keep something like this from him?"

She rubbed her stomach and tugged at her shirt. "I feel like I'm already showing. What's up with that? When did you have to start wearing maternity clothes, Corinne?"

Her sisters exchanged a quick look, and Landyn braced herself for an onslaught, but Danae only rolled her eyes. "You are not showing, Landyn."

"Depends on which kid you're talking about." It seemed Corinne was giving her an out, but Landyn knew her sister well enough to know she wasn't finished with her questions about Chase. "With Sari I was so eager, I had my skinny bones in maternity tops at two weeks. By the time Simone came along, I waited till I absolutely couldn't squeeze into my regular clothes any-more. But then styles are a little different now, too." She tugged on the sleeve of Landyn's shirt.

"You can probably wear that top all but the last couple months. I've got some stuff—shirts and shorts—you can borrow if you want. If I can remember where I put them."

"Just don't wear them out," Danae said. "I had dibs, remember." She shot Corinne a look and reached for Landyn's menu, studying it as if she hadn't already ordered.

Landyn hadn't thought how her news might affect her sister. Danae and Dallas had been trying to get pregnant for several years with no success. The last she'd heard from Mom, they were trying to save up for some kind of fertility treatments.

"Don't worry, I'll save everything for you," Corinne said, patting Danae's hand, her voice falsely bright. "You'll probably be wearing them right behind Landyn."

Danae took a sip of her coffee. "How are you feeling?"

"I'm sicker than a dog half the time and I feel fabulous the other half."

Corinne laughed. "Sounds about right."

Landyn touched Danae's arm. "I'm sorry. I truly wish it was you and Dallas this had happened to."

Her sister shrugged. "It's not like you did it to spite me. And I'm happy for you. I really am. I just . . . I wish it was me." Danae looked past her and tapped the menu. "Here comes our server.

Do you know what you want? The meatball sandwich is to die for."

Landyn shook her head. The mere sound of the word *meatball* turned her stomach.

The server set a glass of water in front of her. "Have you decided?"

"I think I'll just have the minestrone. And maybe a small salad."

"So, what *is* the scoop on Chase?" Danae asked as soon as the server was out of earshot. She seemed eager to change the subject.

Landyn gave them the short version.

"He'll come to his senses." Ever the big sister, Corinne patted her hand. "He loves you too much."

"I know he loves me, but I think he loves his career more. He's determined this is what *we* are supposed to do. Me, not so much. End of story."

"Landyn . . . You can't just give up on your marriage." Corinne looked shell-shocked. "You haven't even been married a year! And with the baby—"

"I haven't given up on anything. I just don't see that I have a choice right now. Can we talk about something else? Where are your munchkins?"

"Jesse's mom has them."

"That's sure handy having them in Cape. How are they doing?"

"They're good."

Landyn scrambled for something to talk about and landed on the weather. "We should have sat out front. This might be our last chance before the weather goes south." She hooked her thumb over her shoulder toward the patio seating at the front of the restaurant. The afternoon sun canted beneath the awning and splashed inviting patches of light across the red-and-white checkered tablecloths.

She and Chase had sat out there on a hot August night on their first serious date. She pushed the thought away and prayed for their food to come.

Danae craned her neck to look past Landyn out the plate glass window. "Hey, that looks like— Isn't that Chase right there?"

Even though she knew it couldn't be him, Landyn's stomach turned another somersault. She swiveled in her chair to follow her sisters' lines of sight. "Where?"

"He went by already. I could swear it was him. Did you see him, Corinne?"

Landyn shook her head. "My husband, Chase?"

"What other Chase do we know? See, sis, I told you," Corinne said, smiling. "He loves you enough to come after you." She studied the street outside the window.

"Chase is in New York. You need to have your eyes checked, Danae."

"Well, if it wasn't him, he has a twin brother."

"It better not be him. He can barely pay the rent on the stupid studio, let alone buy a plane ticket back to Missouri. Besides, he's not going to just show up without letting me know he's coming back."

Or was he? Suddenly showing up out of the blue sounded like exactly the kind of thing Chase Spencer might do. Especially if *God* told him to. She had to work to not roll her eyes at the thought.

The server appeared with their food, and her sisters dived in like they hadn't eaten for weeks. But Landyn picked at her salad and couldn't keep from surreptitiously checking the store-front window over her shoulder. She knew how unlikely it was that it *was* Chase Danae had seen, but the idea that he might show up in town filled her with an emotion she couldn't quite identify.

Was it *hope?* All she knew was, she wished Danae had never seen Chase's supposed look-alike because now, she missed her husband more than ever. And she was starting to think maybe she needed to high-tail it back to New York and try to talk some sense into the man's head. Because as much as she wanted a baby some day, she could not do this alone.

But neither was she going to use this baby to manipulate her husband. They had to resolve things before she told him the news. Chase had to decide to work things out because he loved her and wanted to be with her, not because he felt obligated since she was carrying his baby.

7

It was still too hot to relish pulling warm linens from the dryer, but Audrey was not complaining about the six loads of laundry she'd done this morning. Those fresh-smelling sheets and fluffy towels were evidence of guests—*paying* guests—at the inn. A couple more weekends like this and they might have enough to pay this month's mortgage without dipping into what was left of their meager savings.

She blew out a breath at the absurdity of the thought. With the exception of a couple of years when she and Grant had three kids in college at the same time, they'd never struggled to pay their bills. Grant had always made good money as a contractor, and he'd invested well with their savings and later with the money she'd inherited when her father died. It was that inheritance that had given her the leverage to convince Grant the Chicory Inn was a viable investment.

But it seemed the more they'd torn out of the original house, the more problems they'd unearthed. In the end, though they'd ended up with almost a brand new home, they'd also sunk most of their savings into the project. She'd lost many a good night's sleep worrying about how they'd recoup that loss before they needed money to retire on.

She pulled a queen-size fitted sheet from the dryer and wrestled it into submission. She frowned, remembering how she'd argued that running a B&B would be like being retired. "Just like being retired and hanging out with company every day," she'd chirped—like an ostrich with its head in the sand. She did enjoy having guests, but it was anything but leisurely.

"Here, you need a hand with that?"

She jumped, but Grant stilled her, kissing the back of her neck.

"You scared me! But your timing couldn't be better." She shook out the sheet and Grant caught the opposite corners. He met her in the middle and they did the sheet-folding dance that had become sweetly familiar over the past month. Her husband had never folded a sheet in his life before they opened the inn. But since then, he'd been all in with her when it came to housekeeping. Audrey loved the feeling of partnership running the inn had given them. She just hoped that partnership feeling extended to paying the bills.

With the sheet folded in quarters, she met him again with her half, and wrapped him in a hug, the still warm sheet sandwiched between them. "Didn't you say you wanted to get between the sheets with me?"

He gave a wry laugh and kissed her forehead. "That wasn't exactly what I had in mind."

She shushed him and put a stack of folded

linens in his arms, then motioned for him to follow her upstairs.

"This looks promising . . ."

"Don't get your hopes up, buddy. We have guests checking in at four."

"Rats!" Grant snapped his fingers. "Well, a man can hope, can't he?"

"Oh, there's always hope. And extra brownie points if you'll help me get this room put together."

They worked together making the bed, Audrey snapping the sheets smooth over the mattress and folding crisp hospital corners while Grant stuffed half a dozen pillows into cases and placed them just so on the bed the way Audrey had shown him.

"I feel kind of bad making Landyn sleep in the basement. Especially—in her condition. That hideaway is miserably uncomfortable. But it doesn't make sense to move her into one of the guest rooms when we'd just have to kick her out whenever the inn fills up."

"We could just 'book' the room, you know."

She shook her head. "That's one hundred dollars we'd lose every night if we gave her the cheapest room."

"But we don't fill it up every night, Audrey. And it's not like she's going to be here long-term."

She stopped in her tracks and stared at him. It

took him a few seconds to feel her eyes on him, but she waited until he met her gaze. "You don't call nine months long-term?"

"First, she's already . . . what, three months pregnant?"

"Closer to four, I think. She hasn't even been to a doctor yet."

"Is that wise? Shouldn't she have seen a doctor by now?" He waved his own questions away. "Never mind. Okay, so it'd be more like five months—assuming she stayed until the baby came. But there's no way those two won't work things out."

"You think?" Sometimes Grant's optimism drove her crazy. "Do you know something I don't?"

He shrugged. "They'll work things out."

"I don't know . . . Landyn can be so stinking stubborn when she wants to be."

"Hmm . . ." He scratched his chin. "I wonder where she gets that."

She snapped him with an empty pillow case. "She might get some of it from me, but I happen to know her father contributed his share of stubborn genes too."

"Proud of it." He puffed his chest out and preened until he got a laugh out of her.

That was always his goal. Get her to laugh. And it was one of the things that had drawn her to Grant thirty years ago. But some things were no laughing matter—no matter how you looked at them.

"Audrey—"

His tone got her attention and she looked at him, waiting.

"I think we should put Landyn in one of the guest rooms. It was hard on the kids to lose the house they grew up in. But her most of all. The guests in this house will never be more important than our kids."

"Oh, just stick the knife in and turn it, why don't you?"

"Well? Am I right?"

"Of course." He had her dander up now. "You're always right. And what if they all want to move in?"

"Now you're just being ridiculous."

She flopped the last decorative pillow on the bed, harder than necessary. "I don't know if you've noticed or not, but we have a boatload of bills to pay. And booking paying guests is the only way those bills are going to get paid."

He came around the bed and put his hands on her shoulders, but she shrugged him off. "The bills will get paid. And besides, Landyn is not going to be here in nine months, or even five months. She'll come to her senses and they'll work things out."

"What about Chase coming to his senses?"

"What do you mean?"

"Well, it sounds to me like he's the one calling the shots here. Do you think Landyn should have just followed him blindly to that dump?"

"Listen, I don't like it any more than you do, but is what Chase did worth a divorce? I do not want to see her throw her marriage away over a disagreement. And after six months? That's just stupid."

"But he didn't even ask her, Grant. He made a life-changing decision *for* her. When he had to know she wouldn't agree. And all because he's chasing that foolish dream of being an artist."

"I know . . . I don't like it either. His first priority should be to take care of his family. Especially when his 'family' is my daughter. But I've been thinking about it, and I wonder . . . would you rather he didn't have dreams? Dreams are important, Audrey. Sometimes important enough that you just have to suck it up and do whatever it takes to let your partner live their dream."

Grant had never once tried to make her feel guilty about the bed-and-breakfast—her dream— but she was pretty sure he wasn't talking about Landyn and Chase anymore. And it did make her feel a little guilty. "Grant, I—"

"Because if you don't honor the dreams of the ones you love most, you face the rest of your life knowing you kept that person from being every-thing they could have been."

"Is that why you . . . humored *me?* With the inn?"

He shook his head. "I never said this was about the inn. Or about you."

"But—"

He took her shoulders and kissed her, quickly, before she could slough him off again.

Before she could find her voice, he changed the subject.

"She does need to get her stuff out of my shop. I did not build that to serve as free storage for our kids."

"Can you make room for her things in the shed?"

A gleam came to his eyes. "Tell you what. If you can make room for Landyn in here— upstairs—I guess I can make room for her stuff in the shed. Deal?"

She sighed, knowing when she'd been had. "Deal."

Gallery visitors milled in front of the brick wall where Chase's paintings were on display. Not a bad showing for a Friday afternoon. Clusters of patrons took in the show's offerings, reading the descriptions in the program and quietly discussing the merit of the artists' work.

Chase stood a distance behind the browsers, straining to hear their murmured comments. There was a fine line between being close enough to decipher their words, and so close that he drew irritated glances. His photo on the program was a self-portrait that was abstract enough to preserve his anonymity, but he still felt self-conscious.

He'd worried that his agent had thrown the show together too quickly, used too many older works. But so far the reviews—both published, and overheard in the gallery—had been mostly positive. The *Times* had even blurbed the Everhardt show, which wasn't until next month. He wondered if Landyn would pick up a copy and see the blurb in the Arts section. Was there even any place to buy a copy of the *New York Times* in Missouri? She'd never been much of a computer nut, so he doubted she'd think to look for the reviews online. If she even cared.

He walked to the end of the large room and slowly back again, pretending to peruse the program, which he practically had memorized by now.

He heard the door behind him open and turned to see his art rep, Miles Roberts, enter the gallery. He waved and went to greet him.

"Hey, Chase. How's the show?"

"Well, I don't think I've sold anything yet, but the buzz is good—so far."

"Oh, you've sold something all right." Miles looked amused.

"What do you mean?"

"Two of your pen-and-inks went for a grand each."

Chase's jaw dropped. "Are you serious, man?" Wait till he told Landyn! If this wasn't confirmation that he'd been right to grab this opportunity, he didn't know what was.

"I wouldn't joke about something like that," Miles said. "Don't go out and spend my commission though."

Miles was kidding. And Chase didn't tell him that he'd forgotten to figure the rep's commission that would come out of every check before he ever saw a dime. He for sure didn't tell Miles he'd already spent a good chunk of his windfall on the trip back to Missouri last week. Charged it to a credit card, which he'd promised Landyn he would use only in emergencies. Well, it had felt like an emergency at the time.

In retrospect, it had been a stupid thing to do— a waste of time and money. Especially when he'd had no intention of talking to Landyn or even letting her know he was there. The only silver lining was that the airline was oversold on the first leg of his flight, and he'd let them bump him in exchange for two-hundred dollars toward a future flight. He'd tucked that voucher into his Bible and whispered a prayer that he could use that ticket to bring Landyn home. Home to New York.

In the meantime, he'd needed desperately to see her. To make sure she was okay.

Ha. She was okay all right. He'd seen her Honda parked downtown in Cape in front of Bella Italia.

For a minute he'd dared to hope she was inside, crying, remembering their first date and having a change of heart about leaving New York.

He should have known better. No, she was happy-go-lucky at lunch with her sisters. He gave a dry laugh.

"What's funny?" Miles's voice jarred him back to the moment.

"Oh . . . nothing. Just thinking about what my wife will say when I tell her about selling those pieces."

"That's funny?"

"Never mind." He waved him off. "Private joke."

"Please don't tell me those were your wife's favorite pieces you sold . . . I've got more wives mad at me because I sold the work that made them fall in love with their husband."

"Don't worry." Landyn had never even seen those pen-and-inks. He'd finished them after moving to the Brooklyn studio. "At this point, I think Landyn would sell *me* if somebody offered her a grand."

"Well, she ought to be thrilled. This won't put you in a new tax bracket or anything, but a sale's a sale. We'll take what we can get. And there's still a few days left in the show."

"Hey, I'm just happy to be in a tax bracket period."

The art rep seemed to think that was hilariously funny.

"Do I need to put in an appearance here every day while the show's running?"

"No sir. What you need to do is hightail it home and get back to work. And I suggest you hold off on the watercolor for now. Do some more pen-and-inks instead. Get a few framed like the ones that sold. We'll reimburse you for the frames, but those we know we can ask a grand for. We want to hit the market while it's hot."

"I'm on it." Chase gave a little salute.

"Congrats, man." Miles put out his hand. "You're off to a great start."

Well, at least he could pay off the credit card. That was a relief.

So he'd sold some of his work. For a good price. He should be dancing in the streets. But if he did, he'd be dancing alone.

8

"You're really not going to tell him?" Corinne had cornered Landyn on the back porch while Corinne and Jesse's three kids romped with Huckleberry in the backyard at the inn.

"What good would it do?" A mockingbird screaked a reply from the climbing tree down by the creek, but Landyn ignored it. "Chase is being so stubborn about this. He's just sitting in that lousy studio waiting for me to admit I was wrong and he was right. I'm not saying I've been perfect in this whole mess, Corinne, but he hasn't either."

"That may be, Landyn, but that's not my point. You can't just not tell Chase he's going to be a father. Besides, I have a feeling once he knows that, he'll change his mind. I know Jesse manned up big-time when I got pregnant with Sari. Chase is a good guy. He'll do the right thing."

Landyn regarded her sister. She had no doubt that her sisters—and probably Bree too—had talked about her behind her back. And she knew Corinne was mostly concerned for her, didn't want her to be unhappy. But weren't sisters supposed to side with you on something like this?

Instead, it seemed like her whole family had a big campaign underway to get her to go back to Chase. They'd all made her feel like a first-class jerk for leaving him. Even though she was pretty sure not one of them would have put up with the stunt Chase pulled.

She slipped off her shoes and propped her feet on the sun-warm porch rail. "Are you telling me that if Jesse came home one day and said, 'Oh, by the way, I sold our house and we're moving into a one-bedroom dump in Sikeston,' that you'd be fine with it?"

Corinne giggled. "Sikeston? What hat did you pull that out of?"

She gave a droll smile. "Work with me, sister. That's the best analogy I can come up with. But you get what I'm saying. And I happen to know you would *not* put up with that from Jesse! No matter how much you love him."

Corinne sighed. "I already said that's not the point." She put a hand on Landyn's arm. "Honey, you don't want to raise a baby by yourself. I don't care what Chase did, you don't want to go through a divorce. You haven't even been married a year. You guys have managed to get along with each other since you were just kids. Don't let that go lightly."

Landyn glared at her. "I never said I wanted a divorce. I just want—"

"Where do you think this is going to end up if you hold out on Chase?" An edge came to Corinne's voice. "He should know he has a child coming into this world. Jesse would never forgive me if I didn't tell him about *our* baby. This is Chase's child, too, you know."

Landyn feigned shock. "No. Really? I had no idea that's how it worked."

"Stop. You're just being a brat now."

"And you're treating me like I'm still twelve years old and you're the almighty big sister."

"Well, you're acting like you're twelve, and— I *am*."

"Almighty?"

That made Corinne laugh again and eased the tension a little.

The children's shrill voices in the backyard

drew their attention. "Sadie? What's wrong?" Corinne went to the corner of the porch and leaned out over the rail.

"Sari won't let me be the mom." Sadie trotted to the porch with Huck tagging after her.

"Well, can't you both be moms?"

The four-year-old put hands on hips. "But there's only one Simone."

"Well, you'll just have to take turns with her being your baby."

Simone's head shot up and she toddled away from them, wagging her head at her sisters. "Huh-uh. No baby!"

Corinne and Landyn cracked up. Landyn wondered if Corinne knew how much she admired her. Could she ever be as patient and calm as Corinne always was with her kids? A tremor of sheer terror ran through her at the idea of having a baby who depended on her every waking moment.

The little girls' argument escalated and Corinne jogged off the porch to mediate.

When she came back she gave Landyn's back a pat. "All I'm saying is that you've got to talk to him, Landyn. You can't just hide out and ignore him. You need to work this out."

"What if we can't work it out? What if he won't budge?"

"You'll work it out. I know you will. Even if it means being separated from him for a while until you both cool your jets a little, at least you're working on it. He needs to know you're committed to him, no matter what. Even if you can't ever reach an agreement on this."

"I don't see how we can stay married if we don't ever reach an agreement on this!"

"Then you might have to agree to disagree, Landyn. Couldn't you do that—if that's what it took to save your marriage?"

Landyn took a deep breath. "I don't want my marriage to end. Oh, Corinne, this isn't how I thought being married would be at all! Not at all. We haven't even had our first anniversary and—" Her voice broke and tears came, surprising her. She'd been too angry to cry before.

Corinne wrapped her in a hug. "Just talk to him. And listen to him. We're all praying for you guys. You'll work things out. I know you will—with God's help. But you've got to take the first step."

She pulled away, anger seeping in again. "Why? That's what Mom said, too. But why can't *he* take the first step. Chase is the one who started this. I was just minding my own business, working my tail off . . . It's what we agreed to, by the way. The deal was he would do this for three years while we got established, then he could make a go of his art thing. Instead I've spent most of our marriage trying not to panic while he chases every pipe dream and takes dead-end jobs for the sake of his precious art. I'm sorry, but I don't feel like I did anything wrong!"

"I'm not saying you did. But Landyn, sometimes marriage is about forgiving and taking responsibility even when it's not your fault. I'm not saying it's easy, but I am saying it's right. Sometimes."

"Easy for you to say. Jesse would never do something like this."

"Oh, sure he would. Maybe not that exact thing, but trust me, Landyn, at some point, every person who's ever been in a marriage gets selfish. Your honeymoon might have ended a little sooner than most, but you would have gotten there eventually."

"Wow, thanks big sister. You're really cheering me up."

Corinne's grin warmed her. "Being married is the best thing that ever happened to me, Landyn. But that doesn't mean it's easy. You're going to make selfish choices and self-centered mistakes, and you're going to hurt each other sometimes. Even when you're both Christians, you're also both human."

"Yeah, and that's what ticks me off the most. He played the God card on me."

"You mean because he said he thought he was doing what God wanted him to do?"

She nodded.

"What if he is? I'm not saying I agree with him," Corinne added quickly. "Yes, he should have consulted you on something that affected your life so drastically. But have you considered that maybe he really did think God was directing him to do what he did? You said he had to make a decision right away to get that place."

Landyn shook her head. "I'm sorry, but I don't think God works that way."

"No . . . Hear me out. I'm not even saying God actually did direct him. But if Chase *thought* it was God, then you kind of have to admire him for obeying."

"If that's the case, then you have to admire the 9-11 terrorists and all the other religious fanatics who claim they were just doing God's work."

Her sister shot her a quit-being-difficult look. "Is Chase a religious fanatic, Landyn? Is he trying to blow up buildings?"

"Well, no . . . But—"

"Then can you give him the benefit of the doubt? What if you called him, and just assume for the duration of the conversation that Chase really did think he was following God's leading?"

"And what will that accomplish?"

"Well, for one thing it will help you talk to him without this . . . this *fury* I've seen in you every time you mention his name."

"I *am* furious. Who wouldn't be?"

"You have to put that aside if you're going to have a civil conversation with him."

She closed her eyes and blew out a breath. "I don't know if I'm up for this."

"Pray about it, Landyn. Please. That's all I'm ask—"

"Mo-ommy!" Sadie came running up the porch steps just as Mom opened the back door. "She's doing it again!"

"There you girls are," her mom said. "I wondered what happened to you."

Sadie grabbed her grandma's hand. "Gram, Sari won't let me have Simone to be my baby."

"Two moms, only one baby," Corinne explained.

"Isn't there a story like that in the Bible?" Landyn teased. "A sword was involved, as I recall."

Corinne and Mom gave her the stink eye in unison.

"Don't you even bring that up," her sister said. "Solomon I'm not."

"Well, I'm not Solomon either, but I have an easy solution for the two-moms-one-baby problem," said her mother.

"What? Make Huckleberry be one of the babies?"

"Better than that."

"What's a solution, Gram?" Sadie's eyes sparkled.

"Come with me. You too, Sari. I'll show you." Her mother winked over the little girls' heads and Landyn knew she was heading up to the attic —or what had been an attic before the remodel— for the ragtag collection of dolls the Whitman girls had loved before they'd all outgrown them.

"I'm surprised Mom hasn't just given you those dolls—for the girls."

Corinne shook her head. "If the dolls were at our house they wouldn't hold half the magic they do when they're at Gram's house. Besides, that wouldn't be fair to you and Danae. You might have girls too someday."

Where did this storehouse of knowledge come from? Landyn sighed. Would she just automatically know these things after her baby was born? Somehow she doubted it. Mom and Corinne were both oldest sisters. Maybe that was where they got their knack with children. But Danae had it too. She just hadn't had a chance to use it yet.

Landyn had never even babysat as a teenager. She'd played with dolls when she was little, but usually her dolls were passengers in the plane she was flying or they were customers at the restaurant where she was chef. Sure, she wanted kids. Chase did too. It was something she dreamed about sometimes, but they'd both agreed it was way down the list for them. Like five years down the list.

Now it was more like five months down the list. Panic swelled, constricting her breath.

"Are you okay, Landyn?"

She swallowed the lump in her throat and slipped her shoes back on. "I'm fine. I'd better go in now. I need to—"

She drew a blank. Who was she fooling anyway? She didn't have one thing to do, one responsibility. She'd run some errands for Mom and spent one morning at Corinne's watching the girls while her sister baked for a funeral dinner. She'd loved every minute with her sweet nieces, but it wasn't like her family couldn't get along without her.

The reality was, she'd become a charity case to them. And she couldn't live another day in this limbo, not knowing what her life would look like a month from now. Or five months from now.

Something had to change.

9

Audrey ripped sheets off the beds as if her vendetta was against the linens rather than the people who'd slept on them. She ought to be grateful for a long weekend when they'd filled up every available room. And she would be if this group hadn't been such a royal pain in the derriere.

A dozen teenage girls—scholarship pageant contestants—had descended on the inn, sleeping three and four to a room—and with only one set of adult sponsors who apparently went off duty six hours before the girls finally quieted down.

The perfume-saturated entourage had all but

trashed the place, tracking November's mud in from the backyard, and leaving dirty dishes—the ones they didn't break—in virtually every room of the inn. She wouldn't be surprised if something valuable turned up missing when she finally got the place put back together enough to take inventory. As it was they were going to have to replace half a dozen towels that had been stained with enough makeup to paint Mount Rushmore.

The pageant had done a photo shoot on the kids' climbing tree down by the creek and it had been all Audrey could do not to traipse down there and supervise herself. If they'd damaged the ancient tree, she would have seen that heads rolled.

At least the chaperones had paid the bill in full—but not before talking Grant into giving them a hefty discount since half of the girls skipped breakfast. Never mind that Audrey had cooked for all of them, and she'd seen at least three of them grab muffins for the road on their way out the door.

Good riddance. She'd be drafting a new policy about ratio of chaperones to teenage guests. But at least the group had paid, which was more than she could say for their last guests, whose check had bounced both times she tried to deposit it. She hated to change the inn's policy of taking personal checks, but neither could she afford to be scammed.

Especially not while their youngest daughter was depriving them of the income of one guest room. Audrey wished she didn't have to be so miserly, but they did have bills to pay. And she didn't think Landyn had a clue how much it was costing them to lose that room's income.

She chided herself the minute the thought left her thick head. She and Grant had talked about this before they'd ever signed on the dotted line. They never wanted their kids to feel like they played second-fiddle to the inn. Of course, when they'd signed on the dotted line, they hadn't known the bottom line would be so thin. Or that one of the kids would move back home.

Blowing her bangs out of her eyes, she gathered enough towels for an army from the bathrooms and lugged the laundry to the hallway. She slid open pocket doors, revealing the washer and dryer hidden there. The mountain of linens was daunting, but she was grateful not to be hauling them up and down two flights of stairs.

"Hey, Mom." Landyn poked her tousled head out of the room that had been hers as a teen. She looked up and down the hallway, then spoke in a stage whisper. "Are they gone?"

"Yes. But they left plenty for us to remember them by." She poured liquid detergent into the receptacle and started the washing machine. "Did you get any sleep?"

Landyn made a face. "Are you serious? It

sounded like we were hosting the World Series up here. I swear that one girl had a laugh that could grate cheese."

Audrey laughed. "Listen, I'll do the downstairs rooms, but would you mind making up the beds on this floor?"

"Oh." She made a face that said, *I suppose, if I must.* But she nodded. "Okay . . . sure. What time is it?"

"Almost noon."

"Okay. I'm going back to bed for a while. Could you tell Dad to keep the noise down?"

Audrey bit her lip and measured her words. "We have guests checking in before dinner, and Dad has to get the lawn mowed before they show up."

Landyn huffed and rolled her eyes.

"How did you ever sleep in New York?" It came out sounding testier than she'd intended.

"It's *supposed* to be noisy in New York."

"Well, guess what, sweetie? It's supposed to be noisy at a bed-and-breakfast, too. Especially when it's lunchtime."

"Whatever." Landyn disappeared behind her door.

"Don't forget about the laundr—"

The slam of the door clipped short her reminder.

Speechless, Audrey wanted to march in after her, grab her "baby" by the shoulders and shake some sense into her pretty, curly head. Landyn had always been a bit of a drama queen, and, truth be told, she and Grant had indulged her.

They had to shoulder some of the blame. But it was time for Landyn to grow up.

Audrey reminded herself that there were hormones at play here, too. And exhaustion—both physical and emotional. She'd give her daughter the benefit of the doubt. This one time. But she was not going to put up with this indefinitely.

Two hours later when Audrey finally had the downstairs rooms ready for guests, she went up to check on the upstairs. She heard the roar of the riding mower in the side yard and loud music coming from Landyn's room. *And she thought those teenagers were noisy?*

Audrey peeked into the room across from Landyn's. The beds were exactly as she'd left them, stripped clean. She went to check the dryer. Empty.

Fuming, she opened the lid to the washing machine and stuffed the wet linens into the dryer, then slammed the lid to the washer.

She went down the hall and knocked on her daughter's door. "Landyn? I've got people arriving in two hours and the bedding didn't even get put in the dryer." She pushed open the door.

Landyn growled and pulled the blanket over her head. "You never said they needed to go in the dryer."

"Well, they weren't going to jump in there by themselves."

"Mother. I thought you'd already put them in. I

didn't know that was part of the job." She spoke in that long-suffering, patronizing tone that had always made Audrey want to spit nails when Landyn was a teenager. It hadn't improved now that her daughter was a married woman.

She looked at her watch. "Well, if they *had* already been in the dryer, they would be wrinkled beyond repair by now."

"Sorry." Landyn's voice was dull and held no remorse. She threw off the covers and eased her slender legs over the side of the bed. The long T-shirt she'd slept in clung to her thin frame, but her tummy definitely had a new roundness to it. And it struck Audrey that if she hadn't figured out before that Landyn was pregnant, she would have begun to suspect now.

Her baby, pregnant. And she was afraid it was not under the best of circumstances. *Please, Lord, help them work things out.*

"The bedding is in the dryer," said Audrey.

"I'm getting in the shower."

"Well, please don't be long."

"The clothes have to dry don't they?"

That was the straw that broke the camel's back. Audrey snapped, willing her voice not to quiver the way it usually did when she was angry. "Landyn, for three weeks now, Dad and I have not asked you for much of anything. We've given you three meals a day, and a room that we could otherwise be renting out." She knew, even as she ranted, that she was probably going to regret her words later, but right now it felt like they needed to be said. "We've put gas in your car, and we've handed over cash when you needed it. I don't think it's too much to ask to—"

"You're going to bring up that loan now? I *said* I'd pay you back. Good grief, Mom, it was fifty dollars. I never would have asked to borrow such a huge sum of money if I'd known you were going to hold it over my head the rest of my life."

Audrey took a deep breath. "All I'm asking for is a little help. I need these rooms ready no later than four o'clock and I need to know you're not going to forget again."

"I didn't forget the first time. And no offense, but it is driving me stark raving nuts to be treated like a child."

"Then maybe you should quit acting like one." She turned on her heel and left.

Landyn turned the water as hot as she could stand it and stood under the spray, fuming. Hot tears mingled with the flow from the shower head, then swirled down the drain.

It had been a mistake to come home. Not that she'd had any other options, but it was obvious Mom had changed. It seemed she had more important priorities in her life than her children now. And Dad would only back Mom up—the way he always had. Right or wrong.

She needed to get out of here. She needed to talk to Chase. But despite what her sisters believed, she could not tell him she was pregnant. If he agreed to reconcile only out of a sense of duty—or worse, because he felt trapped—their marriage would fall apart anyway. No, if he was willing to work things out, it had to be because he truly wanted to be with her. And because he was genuinely sorry for wrecking their lives.

The thought made her bow her head under the pulsing spray. She felt like a hypocrite hiding her condition from her husband after raking him over the coals for making such a life-changing decision without consulting her. But it wasn't like she'd gotten pregnant on purpose. She ran her hand over the small bump in her abdomen. She was carrying a part of Chase inside her. Something they had made together. Something precious.

She turned off the shower and squeezed the water from her hair. Grabbing blindly for the towel, she suddenly knew what she had to do. She would leave tomorrow. She dressed and dried her hair, then stuffed a few clothes in her suitcase so she wouldn't chicken out and change her mind. The thought of making that drive again was almost more than she could stomach, but then, the thought of staying here—where she was nothing but a burden—was worse.

She'd have to use their credit card. And for the baby's sake, she would not drive straight through this time. However, she had to see Chase and find out if they had anything worth saving.

She wouldn't tell Mom and Dad until morning. They'd only try to change her mind. And her mind was made up.

10

The first chill of winter gusted down Brooklyn's alleyways. Chase pulled his jacket up around his neck. The apartment would be freezing, but turning up the thermostat never seemed to raise the temperature as much as it did the utility bill.

Despite a few good shows where he'd sold some of his larger works, he didn't have money to burn on heating bills. The small balance in their savings account was growing. Not as fast as he would have liked, but at least he wasn't going backwards any longer.

And he'd made strides in paying down their credit card. But he hadn't paid it off like he'd hoped. Their finances were precarious.

Their. Such a loaded word. He tried to think in terms of Landyn coming back. As if they had a future together. He didn't know if it was true, and every day he didn't hear from her, every day she ignored his phone calls and texts, the yeast of doubt fermented. But he was determined to stay the course.

He had a feeling all it would take was three words to turn his wife's heart back to him. *I. Was. Wrong.* But for him to speak those words, let alone set them to paper, would be a lie. And he refused to win Landyn back with a lie. Because if he did, eventually he'd have to get back to the truth.

Truth. He wasn't sure what that was anymore. But he did know the only thing that would make Landyn happy right now was a lie.

He stopped off at the corner grocery and paid twice what he would have at the A&P for a salami and some cheese. And a two-liter of Coke. You'd think he would have lost a few pounds without Landyn's cooking to tempt him. But he was eating junk and though Landyn had taken the bathroom scales, he was pretty sure he was up at least five or six pounds.

He exhaled a breath that froze on the air in front of him. He wasn't going to lose sleep over five pounds. A man could choose worse vices than salami and cheese. And M&Ms. The luxuries helped him endure the long, lonely nights.

He wasn't a perfect man. Not by a long shot. But he'd heard God on this. Of that he was certain. Not an audible voice, but in that strange, holy vocabulary that spoke as clearly to his heart as the English language spoke to his mind.

It seemed a strange thing for God to talk to a man about. *Take this apartment and let the other one go. Do it today.*

But he *had* heard the "order." He couldn't deny it, much as Landyn had made him question what he'd heard. Now, he only hoped he didn't lose his wife while trying to obey his God.

"The beds are all made up, Mom."

Audrey peered past Landyn into the room their guests had vacated this morning. After their spat over the laundry yesterday, this was a refreshing change. "Thank you."

Landyn shrugged. "I'm not sure the pillows are the way you like them. I think they look okay, but I know you're picky about that."

"I'm sure they're fine. Thanks, honey."

Landyn disappeared into her room but emerged again, pulling a large suitcase behind her. Her backpack was slung over her shoulder.

Audrey stopped short. "Where are you going?"

"I've got to see Chase, Mom. I have to talk to him."

"You're not driving to New York?"

"Well, I'm not walking." Her daughter's giggle sounded more like a sob.

"Honey . . . Wait. Let's talk about this. Does he know you're coming?"

"No. I'll call him when I get close. I don't want to give him a chance to tell me not to come."

"Landyn, please . . . Why don't you book a flight? I doubt it would cost any more than the gas and hotels you'll pay for. Just . . . At least wait until Dad gets home."

"Where is he? I wanted to tell him good-bye, but he wasn't in his office, or out in the shop."

"Were you going to tell me good-bye?" She tried to keep her tone light, but she was afraid the wrong answer would bring tears.

"Of course I was. I just—" She set the suitcase by the door in the foyer. "I didn't want to give you a chance to talk me out of going."

"Exactly like I'm doing, huh?"

"Exactly." For some reason, the smile her daughter gave her broke her heart. Maybe because it made her look fourteen again.

"Sweetheart, you have a baby to think about. You don't want to be on the road alone. What if your car breaks down? Or you get sick?"

"Dad worked on my car a little. It'll be fine. And I promise I'll call if anything goes wrong."

"That's not the point, Landyn. Dad and I can't just drop everything and come and get you if you get in trouble."

"I'm not planning on getting in trouble."

"You didn't plan on getting pregnant either." Audrey regretted the barb the minute it was out, but Landyn didn't react. "Honey, at least let us check into bus tickets, or maybe you can book an Amtrak trip."

"That would take three times as long, Mom. And I can barely afford the gas. I sure can't afford to book tickets. Not to mention I want to leave now. I made it here just fine driving, and I was just as pregnant then as I am now."

"Yes, but I didn't *know* you were pregnant then."

Landyn laughed—not the sarcastic mocking Audrey had grown used to from her, but genuine laughter. It warmed her to realize she still had the power to elicit that from this child of hers.

"Couldn't Chase come here? I'm sure he would if he knew about the baby and—"

"No, Mom. I'm not telling him. And nobody else better tell him either." She dropped her head. "I don't want him making any decisions for the wrong reason."

"Landyn, a baby . . . finding out he's going to be a father . . . what better reason could there be to work things out between you? Think about it."

"You don't think I haven't?" She let her backpack slide to the floor. "Mom, that's *all* I've thought about since I started to suspect I was pregnant."

Audrey sighed. Why had she and her daughter butted heads so sharply almost since the minute Landyn had pulled into the driveway three weeks ago? They'd had their moments when Landyn was a teenager, for sure, but nothing like this. Was it just the volatile cocktail of pregnancy hormones tangling with menopausal hormones?

She wished she could talk to Corinne and Danae about it, but she'd decided long ago that unless it was truly a matter of life and death she would never gossip about one of her children to the others. She'd seen too many families damaged beyond repair that way. But that didn't change the fact she was worried about Landyn. She never would have pegged her youngest as one who would let something so relatively trivial threaten her marriage.

"Landyn, will you please at least wait until Dad gets back? He will be so hurt if you leave without saying good-bye. And what about the other kids? Do Corinne and Danae know you're leaving? And Link?"

Landyn shook her head. "No one else knows. I just decided myself. I didn't want anyone trying to talk me out of it. I need to do this."

A bolt of inspiration struck Audrey. "Honey, is it possible that's how things happened with Chase?"

"What do you mean?"

"Could he have felt so strongly about taking that studio apartment that he did it quickly—so no one would try to talk him out of it?"

Landyn bit her bottom lip. "That doesn't make it right."

"But it makes it fine for you to take off without telling any of us good-bye?"

"You don't know the details, Mom."

"Maybe not. I just want you to be safe. And I

want you to be happy. That's all any of us want for you, honey."

Seeming unmoved, Landyn picked up her backpack and hoisted it over her shoulder. "Please tell everyone good-bye for me. I—I'll call you along the way."

"Do you need money?" Not that they had any to give.

"No. I'm fine. See you, Mom. Don't worry about me."

Audrey stood glued to the beautiful new hardwood floors in the foyer, knowing there was nothing she could do to change her stubborn daughter's mind. Grant would probably be upset she didn't call him, but she'd seen that fire in Landyn's eyes before. There would be no stopping her. All they could do now was pray.

II

"Why didn't you call me?" Grant had been angry with Audrey plenty of times over the past year and a half, especially in the course of remodeling the house. But he couldn't remember ever wanting to wring her neck the way he did now. "What were you thinking, letting your pregnant daughter drive out of here on a whim? It's a thousand miles to New York, Audrey. One thousand miles!"

Audrey rinsed a handful of silverware and

distributed it into the dishwasher basket. "You think I don't know that? She's twenty-three, Grant. Besides, she made that drive two weeks ago and she got here just fine."

"I don't care. She's carrying our grandchild. She never should have driven *one* of those miles, let alone a thousand." He picked up the frying pan from the stove and set it hard—too hard—on the counter beside Audrey.

To her credit she took it from him without comment and rinsed it under the hot running water. Warm steam rose between them. "She was carrying our grandchild two weeks ago, too, Grant. We just didn't know it."

Audrey was using that tender voice she used when she was trying to diffuse his anger. Well, he wasn't ready to be diffused. Not by a long shot. "Have you heard from her yet?"

"No. I tried to call about ten minutes ago and got her voice mail. But you know her, Grant. She's going to make us worry a little first."

"Yes, and may all her children be just like her."

"Grant—"

"Well . . . It'd serve her right," he muttered. "What time did you say she left?"

"It was about nine, I think."

He looked at his watch. She'd been on the road four hours. Four down, twelve to go. And knowing Landyn, she'd try to drive it straight through again. "Do you have Chase's number in your phone? We need to let him know she's on her way."

Tight-lipped, she dried her hands and retrieved her cell phone from the charging station on the bar counter. She swiped the screen, scrolling through her contacts, then handed him the phone.

He would need to apologize to Audrey later. He'd spoken too harshly and blamed her for things that were not her fault. But he was too mad and too worried right now. He punched Call and waited.

"This is Chase. You know what to do."

Blasted voice mail. What good were cell phones if people just let every call go to voice mail? He tapped his foot on the wood floor, waiting for the beep. "Yeah, Chase, this is Grant. Listen, give me a call the minute you get this. I need to talk to you. It's . . . about Landyn."

"Grant! You're going to scare him to death." Audrey snatched her phone back from him.

"Well, maybe it would do the boy some good to be scared."

"He's not a boy. Besides, put yourself in his shoes, Grant. For just one minute."

Her words were instantly convicting. He hated how she could do that to him. He exhaled. "I know, I know . . . I'd probably *be* Chase in this situation."

She put a hand on his cheek and he covered it

with his own, his anger seeping away. "Yes, you would."

"You're right. Is that what you want to hear?"

"I'm right. As always." She grinned up at him.

He tried unsuccessfully to make his voice stern. "Not so fast, woman. I'm not conceding everything."

"Not yet anyway."

He pulled her close and held her, feeling stronger in her embrace. He knew she was feeling the same with him. That cord of three strands worked its miracle again, and he rested his chin atop his wife's head and whispered a silent prayer of thanks.

After sitting on the tarmac at LaGuardia for almost two hours, the plane finally took off. Chase put in his earbuds, leaned his seat back, and closed his eyes. He would never admit to anyone— except Landyn—that he had used the two-hundred dollar voucher from his last flight to fly to Missouri. Even with the voucher, it had cost him over a hundred dollars out of pocket. And he wasn't in Missouri yet. This rift between them was going to be their financial undoing.

But he didn't care. He would go get his wife, and he would win her over if it was the last thing he did. And if it took them the next twenty years to pay off the stupid credit card, it'd be worth it.

His agent had freaked out a little when he told

him he was leaving New York again. Especially when Chase admitted he'd bought a one-way ticket and didn't know when he'd be back. He'd promised Miles that he could work—paint—from Missouri. But he'd only been able to fit a few basic art supplies in his carry-on. He was pretty sure Landyn's parents would let him set up a work space at their place, but it would cost a small fortune to buy the supplies he needed. And even more to ship any finished art back to Miles.

But he'd do it, if that's what it took.

It was three short flights back to Cape, but between Philadelphia and St. Louis, he slept. And dreamed of Landyn. The girl he'd loved since the first day he'd laid eyes on her. He woke groggy and disoriented to the flight attendant tapping his shoulder.

"Sir, I need to ask you to put your seat in the upright position in preparation for landing."

He went through the motions, but the dream was still so vivid, and it filled him with a longing he hadn't felt in a while. Landyn. *Please God, somehow turn her heart back to me.*

He couldn't imagine his life without her. All his dreams, all his desires were wrapped up in his beautiful wife. The day she'd walked down the aisle with a smile only for him, he'd thought it too good to be true. Too good to last. And now it seemed as if maybe those misgivings had been warranted.

But he wanted to share a life with her. Build a family with her.

The thought instantly produced a stab of fear. Children. Someday, maybe. If he didn't spend every dime he made flying to Missouri on a win-her-over mission. But Landyn wanted a family. Someday. Certainly not now. They could barely put food on their own table, let alone think about other mouths to feed. Little . . . *people* to be responsible for. But God had a lot of work to do on him before he was ready for that.

As he trudged up the jetway into the St. Louis airport, his cell phone vibrated in his pocket. He waited until he got into the terminal, then found a seat at an empty gate in front of a flight board, searching for his departure. Good. He had a few minutes to catch the short hop into Cape Girardeau.

He had a voice mail message from Landyn's mother. He clicked Play and listened, surprised when it was Grant Whitman's voice on the recording. Landyn's father sounded odd, and his message was cryptic. Too cryptic. But he said it was about Landyn. Chase's gut knotted. Something was wrong.

He almost couldn't make himself call Audrey's phone, but he did, and was relieved when it was she who answered instead of Landyn's father. "Audrey? It's me."

"Hi, Chase. Thanks so much for calling back."

Her friendly tone sent relief surging through his veins. "Is everything okay?"

"I think so. You—haven't talked to Landyn have you?"

"No. Why?" The knots in his gut tightened again.

"She's on her way back. She wants to talk to you."

"Back? To New York?"

"Yes. She left here about nine."

"Nine this morning?" He looked at his watch. It was five fifteen. Surely Audrey didn't mean what he thought she meant. "When was her flight? Was she flying in to LaGuardia?"

"Oh, no . . . I mean she drove. Took her Honda."

"Are you kidding me?"

"We tried to stop her, Chase."

"Well, I hope she's not sitting on the side of the road somewhere. That Honda is not dependable."

"Grant did work on it some. I'm not sure if he got it fixed but it seemed to be running okay—"

He heard Grant in the background asking what was going on, and Audrey trying to explain. In a minute she came back on. "Are you there, Chase?"

"I'm here."

"Landyn didn't want to talk to you over the phone. She wanted to talk face to face."

He didn't know if that was good or bad.

"I just hope she'll stop somewhere for the night," Audrey said. "But in case she drives

110

straight through, we wanted to let you know she was coming."

"Audrey, I'm not in New York."

"What?"

"I'm sitting in St. Louis. At the airport. I've got a flight into Cape tonight. We board in twenty minutes."

"You're in Missouri?" Audrey's voice rose on a squeak.

"Yes. I came—to talk to Landyn. Unbelievable," he muttered.

"This is crazy." Audrey's squeak turned into nervous laughter.

"Listen, I'm going to hang up and try to catch her before she gets any farther. When did you say you last heard from her?"

"We haven't. Not since she left here around nine."

That didn't concern him too much. Landyn was notorious for not answering her phone. But he had to catch her before she got too far. Still, if she'd already been on the road for almost eight hours, she was halfway there. "I'll try to get hold of her. Have you tried texting her?"

"Yes. Texting, calling, sending smoke signals . . . You know how she can be."

He blew out a breath. "Okay. I'll see if she'll answer me. Surely she'll stop for the night if she hasn't already. We can catch her before she heads out again in the morning."

Audrey sighed on the other end. "I just hope she does stop for the night. She drove straight through on the way here."

"Are you kidding me?" Anger boiled in his belly. "What was she thinking?"

"Chase, I think—"

For a minute he thought they'd gotten cut off. "Audrey?"

"I'm here. I'm sure we'll get hold of her. Grant just sent her a text. Let's all keep trying. We'll get her turned back around toward home as soon as we can."

"If you reach her before I do, tell her to stop someplace for the night. She can put it on our credit card. Tell her I said so."

"Okay. I guess—I'll let you go so you can try to reach her. You'll stay with us, of course. I haven't made Landyn's room up yet. Do you need someone to pick you up at the airport?"

"No, don't worry about it. I can rent a car."

"Nonsense. We'll pick you up. Our guests are all checked in for the night. We can get away. What time does your flight get in?"

He searched his pocket for his boarding pass and relayed the airline information. "This is crazy! Why didn't she call me before she left? I don't think she even has a key to the apartment."

"Oh, no." Landyn's mom suddenly sounded on the verge of hysteria. "Well, does she have a friend she can call, someone she could stay with?"

"Don't worry. We'll catch her before she gets much farther."

Chase didn't think his words convinced Audrey any more than they convinced him.

12

"Have you heard from her yet?" Audrey felt bad greeting Chase at the baggage claim with those words, but she was desperate to know Landyn was okay.

He shook his head and her hopes dimmed. Imagining her daughter alone on the road some-where—maybe trying to drive into New York after dark—put a heavy stone in the pit of her stomach.

To her surprise, Chase put down his bag and embraced her. "It'll be okay. Landyn knows how to get around in New York. She has friends there that she can call."

She took a deep breath and blew it out with a prayer. "You were lucky to get a flight on such short notice. Here . . . Grant's parked right over there." She pointed to their Highlander parked across the drive from the baggage claim at the tiny airport. "When did you last try to call her?"

He hiked his duffel back onto his shoulder and fished his phone from his pocket. "About twenty minutes ago—the minute we landed. But I'll try again as soon as we get in the car. I want to say hi to Grant first."

She leveled a look at him. "I'd try her one more time . . . first, if I were you. Grant's pretty worried."

He gave her a wry smile and punched a button on his phone. He put it on speaker phone and Audrey heard the burr, then an immediate switch to voice mail—Landyn's voice.

Chase brightened. "That's the first time I've gotten her voice mail. Always before it was the system—like she had her phone turned off."

"Thank the Lord. Maybe she—"

Chase's phone beeped and he held up a hand and spoke into the phone. "Landyn, hey. I'm at the airport in Cape with your parents. We've all been trying to get hold of you and we're starting to get worried. Call me. Or call your mom . . . But call *somebody*. I'm serious." He hung up and shrugged.

Audrey wasn't sure she liked how casually he was taking this, but he probably knew Landyn better than they did these days. She led the way across the drive and watched while Grant greeted Chase—rather curtly, she thought—and helped him put his luggage into the back of the car.

She motioned for Chase to sit up front with Grant, and climbed into the backseat.

"So . . . any news?" Grant kept his hands at two and four on the wheel, his eyes straight ahead as he pulled away from the curb.

Chase brought him up to speed.

But Grant didn't respond until they were on the highway. "It's ironic that in this age of communication overload, you two can't even get your schedules straight."

It may have sounded like he was teasing, but Audrey hoped Chase didn't laugh because she knew Grant saw nothing funny about this whole fiasco. She didn't either, but she had to admit Chase's calm demeanor had eased her mind considerably. And he said Landyn had friends she could call. That was something. If she hadn't lost her phone—or forgotten her charger. Why wasn't she answering her phone?

The rain came down in sheets, smudging the headlights of early morning traffic and leaving Landyn dizzy and disoriented. She'd slept—if you could call it that—for two hours in a Walmart parking lot outside of Pittsburgh, but other than that, she'd had no sleep in almost twenty-four hours.

This trip had seemed even longer than the same route west, despite the fact she wasn't pulling a U-Haul this time. Her dad had helped her unload the trailer and return it—which pretty much ate up the last of her cash. She was scared to check their credit card balance, especially if Chase was using it too. But she couldn't think about that now.

But she was here. New York, New York. It wasn't even a month yet since she'd left, but it

115

felt like she'd been away for a year. And this wasn't the New York she knew—the Upper West Side—and everything felt as foreign to her as the first day she and Chase had arrived in the city.

She'd just seen a sign that said Welcome to Brooklyn, but her phone was dying and the GPS kept trying to send her back the way she'd come. She knew her parents were probably freaking out that they hadn't heard from her, but she wanted to find Chase's apartment before she called them. Besides, they were in a different time zone and probably wouldn't be up for another hour or so.

If all the text messages and voice mails she'd ignored yesterday were any indication, her parents had told Chase she was coming. Which was exactly why she'd resisted the temptation to even listen to the messages. Her parents—and Chase— would have only tried to change her mind, and she was determined not to lose her courage. She was going to talk things out with Chase if it killed her. And it just might.

She stopped at a light and told her GPS to recalculate. She knew why they called New York "the city that never sleeps." It wasn't even five a.m. and already traffic was crazy. Or at least they would have called it crazy back in Cape Girardeau.

A knock on her car window sent her pulse into high gear.

An unshaven man with wild eyes bent to her window under a battered umbrella, rain funneling over the side. He motioned for her to roll down her window. She reached, without looking, to be sure her doors were locked.

"You lost, missy?" the man hollered through the glass, still making a cranking gesture. "Ya got a couple dollars to spare for a hungry stranger?"

She shook her head and inched forward, praying the light would change before the guy got aggressive. The car in front of her revved its engine and she drove forward a few more inches. Her car sputtered and died.

Frantic, she turned the key in the ignition. The car made a familiar grinding noise, started briefly, then died again. She turned the key. Nothing.

The man had his hand on her door handle now. Landyn laid on the horn and shot up a desperate prayer. She pumped the gas and turned the key once more.

The car sputtered to life and adrenaline flooded her veins. Hunched over the steering wheel, trying to ignore the man outside her window, she looked both ways. When she finally had a clear path, she pulled forward fast enough that the tires left a spray of muddy water in their wake.

The man let go of her door handle and spat a choice expletive at her. She lost sight of him in the rearview mirror, but when the light finally changed, she gunned it for all she was worth.

Her breath came in short gasps and she couldn't seem to loosen her grip on the steering wheel.

After their first few weeks learning the ropes and rhythms of the city, she and Chase had never felt unsafe in New York. But then she'd almost always been with him when they went out. Especially at night.

When her heart finally stopped hammering, she felt a stab of guilt. The guy was probably harmless, just looking for breakfast—or more likely, a drink. But still, it wouldn't have killed her to give him a couple dollars. For all she knew, she might be in his same shoes a month from now.

She thought briefly about going back—driving through for coffee and an Egg McMuffin, finding the man, and giving it to him. She'd seen her dad do that on more than one occasion. Dad would always quote the Bible verse about entertaining angels unaware. She was pretty sure angels didn't use the kind of language this guy had, but he hadn't threatened her. Not really.

But two short blocks later, her guilt subsided, and she drove on in the rain, crossing the Brooklyn Bridge into unfamiliar territory. Manhattan, she knew. But Brooklyn was Chase's turf. And the directions he'd given her to the Bedford-Stuyvesant address when he first moved into the studio were sketchy at best. Still, the GPS should have been able to find it by the address she'd punched in.

Where would she park when she got to Chase's place? She didn't know Bed-Stuy at all and didn't want to have to walk very far. Maybe she should have him pick her up somewhere. And if Brooklyn was anything like Manhattan, parking space was like platinum, but at this time of morning with everyone still in bed, she'd be lucky to even find anything in the residential areas.

Chase had talked about selling his car after he moved to Brooklyn. It'd been crazy enough trying to manage two vehicles when they lived uptown. Chase maintained that in Brooklyn they could get by with public transportation. And Lord knew they could use the money the cars would bring— not to mention the savings in parking fees—but she didn't think he'd sold his old beater yet. He was kind of attached to that beat-up old Toyota Corolla. But she was glad she hadn't let him talk her into selling the Honda. It was nothing fancy, and it threatened not to start about half the time, but it was ten years newer than Chase's old car.

Feeling queasier than usual, she pulled off onto a relatively quiet street and parked under a tree. Rain pelted the windshield as she reentered Chase's address in the GPS. It seemed weird to be thinking in terms of *his* address, *his* apartment, *his* car. They'd been "we" and "us" almost since they met. But then, she wasn't the one who'd forced them apart.

She flipped her phone over in her hand. She'd been determined to surprise Chase. To knock on his door and say, "We need to talk." If she was honest with herself, she'd had visions of him pulling her into a tight hug, begging her to forgive him, promising he would make everything right again.

It was almost six a.m. now. She didn't know what his new schedule looked like, but if she waited much longer he might leave the apartment. And then what would she do? The few friends she knew well enough to call for help would be at work by the time she got uptown, and besides, she did not relish the idea of driving across the bridge in this rain—or even through the tunnel.

No, it was time to call. She checked the street and sidewalks outside the car, made sure the doors were locked, and that there wasn't another panhandler waiting to scare the stuffings out of her. Then she dialed her husband.

13

"Landyn? Finally." Chase sounded more relieved than circumstances warranted. "Where are you?" Or maybe he was just angry.

"I'm here. Why? Is everything okay? You've talked to my parents, haven't you?"

"What do you mean, you're *here?* Where?"

"In New York. Where do you think? I'm here, in Brooklyn—"

"Just great." He sighed.

"What? This stupid GPS doesn't seem to recognize the address you gave me. I *think* I'm in Brooklyn. I came across the bridge anyway . . ." She peered up through the windshield trying to find some landmark that would help him give her directions to his apartment. "I just turned off Atlantic Avenue. There's a Chase Bank and a CVS."

"You just described every other corner in the borough and—" Another sigh. "Landyn—"

"I just turned off on a side street. It's a deluge here. I can hardly see two feet in front of me."

"Okay. Listen to me. You said you came in across the bridge? Which bridge?"

"Brooklyn."

"What? Why'd you go that way? That's *way* out of your way."

"I didn't know," she whined. "It's pouring rain, Chase! I can't see anything—"

"Okay, calm down. Let's see . . ." It sounded like he was studying a map. "You want to get back on Atlantic and head east."

"I can't even tell which way is east. How far am I from you?" She was near tears again. And beyond exhausted. "Could you please just come and get me?"

Dead silence.

"Chase?"

"You haven't listened to your messages yet, have you?"

"You mean Mom's freaking-out call-us-this-minute texts? They didn't want me to come in the first place but—"

"Landyn, shut up and listen for a minute."

Her heart did a free fall. "Why? Is everything okay? Chase?"

"Landyn . . . I'm in Cape."

"Cape?" Her hopes sank. He couldn't be serious. *"Girardeau?"*

"Yes, Girardeau. If you'd ever answer your phone you'd know that. This is ridiculous! Why didn't you return our calls? Your parents have been worried sick. We've all been—"

"Wait . . . My parents are there?"

"I'm at their house. They picked me up at the airport last night. We've been trying to get hold of you ever since. What on earth are you doing in Brooklyn?"

Landyn rested her forehead on the steering wheel, on the verge of tears. "I came to talk to *you*."

He gave a humorless laugh. "You ever hear of a phone?"

"Oh, Chase. What am I supposed to do now? I'm exhausted and I'm sick—" She caught herself. "I'm so hungry, I'm sick." Why hadn't she thought to bring that box of saltines she'd kept by her bed at Mom and Dad's?

"Listen, I'm going to talk you through to the apartment. The super can let you in. I'll call him when you get close. I think there's a carton of eggs in the fridge and some milk that's not too out of date. You can eat something and get some sleep, and we'll figure out how to get you back here whenever you wake up."

"Why didn't you tell me you were coming to Cape, Chase? This is crazy!"

"Yeah, well, I could ask you the same thing. And what are you thinking, driving sixteen hours straight through? That's just insane."

"I didn't drive straight through. I stopped and slept for a little while." *Not to mention stopping forty times to use the bathroom.* But she wouldn't tell him that, of course. "I'm fine. I just want to get to your apartment."

"I know. We'll get you there. Has the rain let up at all?"

The incessant downpour continued to rattle the roof, but she cleared away the fog from the driver's side window with her sleeve and looked out. "Not really, but it's starting to get light outside now. I think I can drive if you'll talk me through it."

He started to rattle off instructions, but she stopped him. "Chase, wait . . ."

"What?"

There was so much she needed to say to him. And to her parents. But now wasn't the time. "Never mind," she said. "Just—get me to your place. Please." The tears came then. If this child she was carrying ever did this to her, she—Well, she'd only be getting what she deserved.

Chase clicked off his phone and turned to face Grant. But Grant didn't miss the huge breath Chase blew out first, and the white-knuckled grip he had on the edge of the marble countertop. The kid's face was gray as an elephant, too. Grant wasn't sure whether it was fear or longing he saw in his son-in-law's expression, but in that moment he was convinced of one thing. Chase Spencer still loved their daughter deeply. And he'd done an admirable job coaching her through what sounded like a very tense situation.

"She made it to the apartment. The super let her in," Chase explained—unnecessarily, since Grant and Audrey had been hanging on every word of his conversation with Landyn.

"Ray's a good guy," Chase said, leaning against the pantry cupboard across from where Grant stood in the inn's kitchen. "He'll make sure she's safe. She was practically falling asleep while I was talking to her."

"Crazy girl," Grant muttered. "I don't envy you having to keep her in line for the rest of your life."

Chase's jaw jutted out and he swallowed hard. "I hope I get that chance, sir."

"You've got to be starving," Audrey said, springing into action the way she did when new guests arrived. "Did you sleep okay? Let me fix you some breakfast. You like sausage?"

"Cold cereal would be fine."

"Nonsense. Let me make you some eggs. I'm cooking for guests in a few minutes anyway. But you don't have to be social," she said quickly. "You can take a plate up to your room."

"You don't—"

Grant gripped his son-in-law's shoulder. "First rule of the Whitman family, son. Don't turn the lady down when she offers you breakfast. Why do you think she hounded me until I built this inn for her? The woman lives to feed people. Let her feed you."

"Thanks. I—appreciate you guys putting me up. And putting up with me." Chase's grin made him look like the kid he was.

"Why don't you go on up and shower, Chase?" Audrey pulled a frying pan from a slot in the custom designed cupboard, already in full hostess mode. "I'll have breakfast ready in fifteen minutes and then you can go back to bed if you want. If you had as restless a night as we did, I know you'll want to."

Chase nodded. "You got that right. And Landyn will probably sleep till noon. Maybe we'll all be thinking a little clearer after a few hours of sleep."

Grant rolled up the sleeves of his chambray work shirt, wondering if this young buck was insinuating that he wasn't thinking clearly. He chose to reject the notion, but said, "Unfortunately, I'm thinking clear enough to know that if I don't get the mowing done this morning, it won't get done at all."

"Don't fall asleep on the mower."

"Audrey, seriously. Have I ever fallen asleep on the mower?"

"Not that you've told me about, but that doesn't mean it doesn't happen."

Chase cleared his throat. "I think I'll head up for that shower now." He turned to Audrey. "Could you tell me where to find a towel?"

"Towels and washcloths are in a basket on the chair by the shower. You can just put stuff in the laundry chute in the hall when you're done. I'll have bedding to do up later today anyway."

Chase thanked her and trudged up the stairs to Landyn's old room that Audrey had assigned him.

It was all Grant could do not to stop Chase and press him with questions—about his job situation, about the rift between him and Landyn. Grant was eager to hear Chase's side of things, and he suspected talking to him might reveal that Landyn's perspective was a bit skewed. There were always two sides. And when a man and a woman were involved, they were often two very different sides.

It struck him that the silver lining in all this might be that they would finally get to know

Landyn's husband better—as an adult—without her around. But their challenge in these next few days would be keeping Landyn's secret from the father of her baby.

He only hoped he and Audrey would still be pulling for the marriage to survive by the time they got the other side of the story.

The studio apartment smelled of paint and turpentine. And pinewood from the frames waiting to have canvas stretched on them. Landyn inhaled deeply. It smelled of Chase, too. She imagined him being with her here on a rainy autumn day in New York. And to her surprise, she realized she missed him. A lot.

She'd forgotten how much she loved the city. Brooklyn had its own sounds, its own flavor, but it was still New York.

After Raymond, the building super, let her into the apartment, she'd showered, then crashed on the futon for four hours. She'd tossed and turned, trying to shut off her mind. But she had her second wind now. She'd seen a little deli a couple of blocks up the street and decided to go get something to eat.

The super had given her a spare key to the fourth-floor studio—on threat of death if she lost it—so after slipping her tennis shoes on, she locked the door behind her and headed down the stairs. The super was in the entryway on a ladder, changing out a fluorescent light bulb.

"Sure didn't sleep long for somebody's been up all night drivin'." His thick accent—a quaint blend of Brooklyn and Italy—made her feel right at home.

"I guess I was hungrier than I was sleepy."

He steadied himself with one hand on the top of the ladder and patted the potbelly hanging over his belt. "I love me some shut-eye as much as the next guy, but I'd be right there with you on the hungry. Ya know where you're goin'?"

"I thought I saw a deli up the street a ways." She pointed.

He raised a bushy salt-and-pepper eyebrow. "That's right, and it's pretty good, but if you know what's good for ya, you'll keep on walkin' two blocks past the deli. There's a little hole-in-the-wall barbecue joint. Best brisket and beans on the continent. You like barbecue?"

Her stomach did a belly flop at the mere thought. "How about breakfast? Is there some-place close that's still serving breakfast? Maybe just a bagel and some eggs?"

"Eggs and bagels what ya looking for?" He shook his head like she'd just made a grave mistake. "Then you were right the first time. It's the deli you want. But you're gonna be sorry you missed out on that barbecue. Don't say I didn't try to steer you right." Raymond looked down at her from his perch on the ladder, shaking his head. But she didn't miss the glint in his eye. He studied her then—for a second too long.

"What?"

He looked away quickly and busied himself putting the cover over the newly installed fluorescent tubes. "Chase never said he was married, that's all. Not till he asked me to let you in to his place."

Her face must have revealed her thoughts because Raymond scrambled off the ladder and came to stand in front of her. He put a hand on her forearm. "No, no, it ain't like that. He never had women up here . . . Nothin' like that. Chase's a good guy. I have a sense about these things. In here—" He tapped his temple. "But he's a talkative guy too. And you're a pretty lady. I woulda thought he'd've mentioned you."

"We're sort of—separated right now."

His eyes went wide. "Separated? No, that's no good. Chase's a good man. You gotta work it out. You both too young to be callin' it quits." He shook his head and tsk-tsked like an old woman. "How long you been married?"

"Six months. Almost seven now, I guess." She wondered if this last month even counted, and hung her head, feeling like more of a failure than she had when she'd told her parents.

Raymond blew a raspberry. "That's crazy. No. You'll make it right. You'll figure it out."

She wanted to ask him how he was so sure.

Especially when Chase had never mentioned he was married.

Raymond took hold of her shoulders and steered her toward the street side door. "You go get your breakfast. Then you can sort it all out better. When's Chase comin' back?"

"I don't know." She gave him an abbreviated version of the crazy story.

"Ah . . ." Raymond shook his head slowly. "It's the O. Henry story."

She frowned.

"You know. The watch. The combs. Chase gives to you the combs but you already cut your hair. You give to him the watch fob. But he already sells the watch."

"Ohh . . . Yes, I remember. To buy her combs. I guess it *is* a little like that."

He smiled. "That story, it works out okay in the end, no?"

She thought for a moment. "Yes, Raymond. It does."

"No, no." He shook his head. "My ma—she's in Italy—*she* calls me Raymond. You call me Ray. Same as Chase."

"Okay . . . Ray."

They laughed together, and Landyn felt like she'd made a friend. And because Ray was Chase's friend, the gap she'd felt between her and her husband closed just a little. She hadn't even talked to Chase since she woke up—not that

130

she needed to. But being at his place, being where he created, she couldn't help feel a little closer to him than she had even twenty-four hours ago.

14

The deli was crowded like a good New York deli should be, and for a change, the heavy aroma of garlic and pickle juice and fresh-baked bread didn't turn her stomach upside down.

She ordered and carried her bagel and decaf to a corner table by the window. She missed her coffee—the real stuff—but Corinne had shamed her into switching to decaf, and she did want to do right by the baby. She took a sip and breathed in the fragrant steam. It wasn't half bad once you got used to it.

The door opened, jangling a string of bells, and letting in a not-unpleasant whiff of diesel fuel from the constant parade of delivery trucks. She spread her rye bagel with herbed cream cheese and crossed her legs, settling in. It was coffee-break time and the streets outside the window swarmed with life. The traffic didn't seem as heavy as it was in Manhattan, but the yellow cabs still made her smile. As did two pigeons splashing in a puddle left from last night's rain.

Even the short time she'd been back in

Langhorne had inoculated her against the cultural vacuum of the small town she'd grown up in. Being in New York again reminded her how very diverse the nation was. And how much she loved that diversity.

She people-watched through two cups of decaf, then found the bathroom before she set out again. Barely in her fourth month, she was already discovering that the have-to-pee-all-the-time aspect of pregnancy was not a myth.

She put some change in the tip jar on her way out the door and took a meandering route back to Chase's place. She probably needed to quit thinking of it that way. It might soon be *their* place. It didn't even hurt to make that concession anymore. Why had it seemed so impossible to give in to Chase's plan? Was pregnancy making her a wimp? *Or maybe it's just making you obedient.*

She looked over her shoulder, half expecting to see someone there, so real the whisper had seemed. But . . . obedient to who? Oh, she'd said those words to Chase in their wedding vows. No one had given her an option. But even making those promises at the altar, she hadn't considered that she'd actually be challenged by them. Love and honor? Sure. Till death do us part? That was her intention—as far as it depended on her. But she wasn't sure she bought into all the submit and obey stuff her mom had always preached about marriage. Still, in recent days, she'd found herself praying that God would help her do the right thing where Chase was concerned. Even if it wasn't exactly the thing she wanted to do. Of course, she didn't seem to know her own heart these days. She certainly didn't know her husband's.

She walked past a Chinese laundry and a pawn shop whose graffitied walls made it look more like an advertisement for the tattoo parlor next door. Across the street was a little food market, and she darted across and went inside to see what she might bring home for dinner.

The manager was a friendly guy, but the heavy smell of onions and some kind of meat roasting made her stomach churn. She made a quick escape as politely as she could. She could come back to the deli later if she didn't find anything to eat in the apartment.

She checked her phone again. Chase had said he'd call, but he probably figured she was still sleeping. She walked on, exploring the neighborhood, and feeling oddly lighthearted and at home here. It seemed curious that she'd lived in Langhorne her whole life and only a few months in New York, yet being back here now—even minus the Upper West Side she'd fallen in love with—she felt as if she'd returned home.

She walked a few blocks, getting to know the feel of the borough. She could see why Chase liked the neighborhood so much, with all the artsy shops and galleries. There were several marketing and PR agencies in the rows of businesses, too. Maybe she could have found work here, though she doubted she'd ever find anything that paid as well as her job in Manhattan had. She'd lucked into that.

She immediately felt ungrateful for the thought. That job had been an answer to prayers—hers, Chase's, her parents', CeeCee's—who knew who else had prayed her straight to her marketing position at Fineman and Justus. She'd tried not to think of what she'd left. And the momentum she'd likely lost having left the company after only six months.

Ray was gone when she got back to the apartment, his ladder put away and the new fluorescent lights brightening up the entry. She climbed the four flights of stairs and, huffing and out of breath, let herself into the studio. Despite the cool autumn temperatures, the apartment was warm. She figured out how to open the windows and moved the futon closer to the breeze.

The apartment was sparse except for Chase's paintings propped against every wall, and more stacked three deep on easels. She knelt to flip through a few of the matted pieces, feeling almost as if she was reading his journal. When Chase painted, he put his whole *soul* on the canvas. He'd always delighted in showing her his in-progress work, and she felt a little guilty that she hadn't ever seen these pieces. At least not that she remembered.

He really was quite talented. And productive. There were half a dozen pen-and-ink drawings matted and acetate-wrapped, as if they were ready to deliver to the gallery. Had he sold work she'd never seen? The thought somehow made her feel sad—and disloyal.

She'd never once considered that Chase's decision to take this apartment might have been made, not on the basis of wishful thinking, but on the fact that he had true talent. And that someone had believed in his gifts. Oh how she wished that someone could have been her. She had believed in him once upon a time—before he'd decided his talent could pay the bills. Now it looked like there was someone who thought it could.

She plopped on her back on the futon and listened to the noises rising from the street below. Pleasant sounds. Friends shouting greetings, cars honking incessantly, passersby in deep conversation, and the occasional blare of a car radio spouting rap or reggae into the autumn air. Not that different from the things she'd loved about Manhattan.

If only she could take back the hurtful things she'd said to her husband. A chance to start over with him. She might not make a different decision about going back to Missouri, but at least she wouldn't have forced Chase to be on the defensive. Not just about his decision, but about his God-given gifts. About the thing she knew defined him. So many regrets.

And who knew, maybe she could have been happy here. Why had she made such a stink about it? Why had she been unwilling even to give it a chance?

But she knew why. She'd never liked being told what to do. According to her parents, she'd been that way almost from the womb. She put a palm over her belly, absently rubbing circles on the fabric of her shirt. Would her baby—Chase's baby—give her as much trouble as she'd given her parents?

She'd deserve it if their baby did. And yet, in that same moment a swell of love rose within her for this little one she carried. It startled—and saddened—her to realize she'd missed more than two months of this intimate knowledge because she'd stupidly not even suspected that the cause of her nausea might be a baby. And even after she realized the likely truth, she'd waited another two weeks before confirming it with a pregnancy test. Because by then the idea of a baby—and the realization of how awful the timing was—terrified her. Paralyzed her. They couldn't afford a baby. Chase didn't want a baby yet. Neither did she.

She rubbed her temples. How could she tell Chase that he'd have to put his dream on hold? Again.

It was possible he already knew. She knew her parents well enough to know that while she'd been ignoring all those phone calls on the road, Mom and Dad may have thought it was important for Chase to know of her condition.

Then again, if her parents had given her secret away—if Chase knew she was pregnant—he surely would have given her a piece of his mind for keeping that kind of news from him.

And also for letting it happen in the first place. He'd made it clear where he stood on kids. At least for now. And she'd agreed. But she was the one responsible for taking precautions. She truly wasn't sure how it had happened. She hadn't missed even a day on her pill cycle.

She closed her eyes. She couldn't even let herself think about how they would make a baby fit into their lives right now. It sure wouldn't be in this tiny studio apartment. And that was assuming Chase was still willing to have her in his life once he found out the secret she'd kept from him.

The clock on the wall in the kitchenette ticked a soothing cadence and the heavy pall of sleep descended. Landyn had just drifted off when her phone rang. Chase's ring. It was almost one-thirty p.m. She reached for the phone, suddenly feeling as nervous as she had the first time he'd called to ask her for a date. "Hello?"

"Hey, baby. I hope I didn't wake you up."

She'd always loved it when he called her 'baby,'

but now, the endearment felt strange. Because the word *baby* had a new meaning for her now. And because their future was up in the air, and they both needed to keep clear heads until they got things figured out. "I slept a little this morning," she said. "But it's starting to hit me now."

"Okay, I won't keep you long. So . . . what do you want to do?"

"I don't know, Chase. When is your flight back?"

"I don't have a flight back."

"What do you mean? Why not?"

"I bought a one-way ticket. It was all I could afford, and . . . I didn't know how long it would take—"

"How long what would take?"

"To get things straightened out—between us."

For a long minute, neither of them spoke.

"Landyn—except for a little in savings, I'm pretty much broke. *We're* pretty much broke. And we can't both be putting things on the credit card without talking to each other."

"I haven't checked our balance in a while. But yeah, I did put the gas on it for the trip home. I'll pay my share off as soon as I can."

"That's not why I brought it up. I want to fly you back to Cape, but I'm going to have to wait until I get paid. Miles has a lead on another sale, so if you can hang out there for a few days until I get my check, I'll book you a flight."

"But . . . You're not coming back here?" She was confused.

His sigh was audible. "I think it might be better if we stay in Missouri for a while. A month or so."

"A month? What would we do there for a month?"

"If you can bring back some of my supplies, I can work from here at the inn for a while. Your parents sounded okay with us staying."

"But what would I do there, Chase? I know you can work anywhere, but I am not going to do laundry and make beds for my mother. Even if they could afford to pay me."

"Who said anything about that?"

"Never mind. It's just—there's nothing for me in Missouri. Why don't you just come back to New York?"

"I know you're not going to want to hear this, but . . . I've been thinking about this a lot. Praying about it and—"

"And here we are again." An exhaustion she couldn't describe came over her.

"What do you mean?"

"You're telling me what to do. Why don't I get a say in this?"

"I'm sorry. But I'm not giving orders. I'm just saying what I want you to do. *Us* to do. What I think would be best. There's a difference. Okay? And I really am praying about it."

"Whatever."

"Landyn, why are you being like this? You used to like it when I prayed."

"I liked it when you prayed *for* me. I'm not so crazy about you using your prayers to manipulate me into doing what you want." She felt her blood pressure soaring and willed herself to calm down. "Can we just talk it out?"

"I don't know. Can we?" Now he sounded angry. Bitter. "Every time I tell you what I think would be best—what I truly feel God is leading our family to do—you go ballistic on me."

"I just want to talk things out together. I want to help with the decisions . . ." She started to say "for our family," then realized it was odd that Chase had used that phrase. Did he know they soon would truly be a family?

"I'm sorry. I'll try to do better. I *am* trying. I'll try to explain everything, but would you be willing to come back to Cape? Just for a while— maybe a month or two—"

"Now it's two?"

"Just until we can decide on something more permanent?"

"We can't make it on one income, babe. And nobody is going to hire me for that short a length of time." *Or* any *length of time once they find out I'm pregnant.*

"No, we couldn't make it on one income in New York, but we could in Langhorne."

"What about your lease?"

140

"I could sublet that place in a heartbeat. That's why I had to jump on it when it came up."

"Seriously, though, Chase. Don't take this wrong, but you were so sure God told you to rent the studio. Why are you changing your mind already?" She really didn't want to start that whole argument again, but he was confusing the life out of her.

"Would you just try, baby? For a month or two?"

"If I agree, then it doesn't make any sense for me to fly back to Missouri. We'll need a vehicle—at least one—so I'd have to drive. Again."

"You're right. I just—didn't want you to have to make that drive again. But you're right. We'll need a car."

"I'm exhausted, Chase. I can't even think about that right now." She couldn't stifle the yawn that came.

"I know. Go to sleep. I'll call you again tonight and we can talk more then. But think about it, okay?"

"I will."

"Did you find something to eat?"

"I went to the deli up the street."

"Oh. Okay. So—is the apartment as awful as you feared?"

"Worse." She yawned again. And met silence on his end. "I'm kidding, babe. It's a long way from our Central Park view but—"

"We never *had* a Central Park view, Landyn."

"Yes, we did."

He laughed. "If we leaned out the window maybe—and held a mirror at just the right angle. On a clear day. During the Equinox."

"Whatever." Even though it was wasted on him, she rolled her eyes. "I'm just saying this is *not* the Upper West Side. And your apartment is tiny. But . . . no, it's not as bad as I pictured it. And Ray's nice."

"Oh, you met him?"

"Yes. Everybody's super friendly here. Not like Manhattan . . ."

"See, I told you."

"I have to admit, I kind of like Brooklyn. Bed-Stuy's pretty cool. It makes me realize how much I miss New York . . . being here."

"I miss *you*." His voice was a whisper.

Don't do that, Chase. "I . . . I miss you, too." And she did.

"So what are we going to do about that?"

"I don't know, babe. I just don't know."

15

"She doing okay?"

Chase clicked off his phone and looked up, seeming surprised to see Grant and Audrey waiting at the kitchen bar counter. "Yeah. She's exhausted. She still hasn't slept more than a few hours, and I think she was about to conk out on me when we hung up. Oh . . . She said to tell you guys hi—and not to worry."

Grant resisted the urge to comment on that one. As if they hadn't been *sick* with worry for the last thirty-some hours. "So she was able to get into your apartment without any problem?"

"Yes." Chase slanted a look his way. "I thought I told you that."

"You did, Chase," Audrey said, patting Grant's arm. "We're just worried about her. We want to make sure she's okay."

"Is that neighborhood safe for her to get around in?" Having his daughter living on the Upper West Side had been scary enough for Grant to get used to, but he'd heard some pretty frightening stories attached to the Bedford-Stuyvesant neighborhood.

"Oh, sure," Chase said. "It's perfectly safe. She's already walked down to get something to eat. She actually said she likes the neighborhood."

Grant thought his son-in-law sounded more like he was trying to convince himself, than he was relaying a fact to them. But Audrey was already kicking him under the bar counter, trying to keep him from pinching this kid's head off for the whole ordeal. So he kept his mouth shut.

"Do you want something to eat, Chase? I could make you a sandwich. Or there's some leftover pizza in the fridge. It's a couple days old, but it's the good stuff—Pagliai's. I think it'll still be okay. I can pop a slice in the oven if you want."

"That'd be great. I am kind of hungry. Are you guys going to eat?"

"We had sandwiches earlier." Audrey slid off the barstool and bustled into the kitchen area.

Grant hadn't gotten that kind of kitchen service —at least not with that kind of a smile—since they'd started the renovation. So, for now anyway, Chase Spencer was a guest in their home, and he'd let it ride.

But these two kids had better figure out what they were going to do with their lives. He'd chided Audrey for being stingy about letting Landyn stay in one of the guest rooms, but he was a little more sympathetic now. Because they were trying to run a bed-and-breakfast, not a shelter for the down-and-out. And if Chase and Landyn didn't come up with a plan for getting out from under his roof pretty quick, he was going to sit them *down* and kick them *out*.

Chase set the warm plate of pizza Audrey had fixed for him on the dresser, ultra aware that a spill would be a disaster in the newly decorated bedroom in the newly decorated inn. He'd always liked Landyn's parents. Her whole family, for that matter. But he'd also struggled with feeling as if he didn't quite measure up.

The Whitmans were all about family. And if

there was one area Chase was lacking in, family was it. And then there'd been that whole thing with the premarital counseling. Her parents had deemed him such a loser that the basic four-session church package wasn't enough. No, thanks to his sorry family history, he and Landyn had to submit to professional counseling before the Whitmans would give their blessing on her marrying the likes of him.

He thought he'd put that all behind him . . . sorted through it, trying to see it from their perspective. But that didn't mean he liked it. Being here at their house now—especially without Landyn, who was usually the buffer between them—brought back all those memories. And though Grant hadn't said so in so many words, Chase was pretty sure the man blamed him for this whole mess.

Someone knocked on his door and he quickly brushed pizza crumbs off the dresser onto his plate. "Come in."

Even though the bedroom had been remodeled since Landyn had lived at home, the knock had set his heart racing and brought back memories of the times Landyn had sneaked him up to her room when they were dating. They'd never done anything—well, nothing too bad anyway—but Landyn's parents had a zero tolerance policy when it came to boys in the bedroom. As that rush of guilt went through his veins now, he realized that policy may have saved them a lot of grief, and he made another mental note for the future day when he and Landyn might have a daughter.

The very thought put a holy fear in him. How could he ever be a father to a daughter?

"You busy?" Grant peeked around the door.

"No. Not at all. Come on in." Chase moved to the edge of the bed and offered the desk chair to Landyn's dad.

Grant straddled the chair and looked around the room. "You have everything you need up here?"

"Sure do. It's very comfortable."

"Well, don't get too comfortable."

"Oh, no sir. I won't. I—"

"I'm just kidding, Chase." Chuckling, Grant put a hand on his shoulder. "I know you're probably even more anxious than we are to have you out of here and back home—Wait . . . that didn't come out right. But you know what I mean."

"Yes, sir." He wasn't at all sure he knew what Grant meant, but he wasn't going to push it right now.

"Listen . . . I wanted to talk to you."

He didn't like the sound of that at all. "Okay . . ."

"I just wondered what plan you have in mind for down the road?"

"Down the road?"

"For you and Landyn. I assume you're committed to the marriage?"

Chase looked him in the eye. "Absolutely." Had

he imagined the *tone* in Grant's voice? An insinuation, perhaps, about Landyn? It almost felt as though his father-in-law knew something he didn't.

"I don't know what you two have talked about since you got your wires crossed, and that's not really any of my business. But as Landyn's dad, I do want to be sure you'll fight for my daughter. She loves you and . . . she's a little mixed up right now, but I think she'll do what's right."

"I—I'm not sure what you mean . . . Mixed up?"

Grant shifted his chair and settled in again. "The story we got is that you let your apartment go and leased the studio without talking it over with Landyn."

"Yes, sir. And I don't know what you'll think about this, sir—"

"Hey,"—Grant held up a hand—"we've been on a first name basis for a long time. Enough of this sir business."

Chase relaxed a little. "I got an opportunity for this apartment at a really good price—a price that would let us put aside some money, even with the commute. I felt at the time like—I *still* feel like—God said take it. The opportunity wasn't going to come around again anytime soon. I know Landyn doesn't agree, but to be honest, I wouldn't do anything different if the opportunity came again." He nudged the edge of the fancy rug with the toe of his tennis shoe. "I think that's what Landyn is having the most trouble with."

Grant looked like he was trying to rein in a smile. "Landyn hasn't wanted other people making decisions for her since she was . . . oh, about two. It wasn't easy being her father, but I've got to say I *really* feel for you as her husband."

He shrugged. "Thank you, sir . . . I mean, Grant."

Grant's expression turned serious. "I admire you wanting to follow God's lead and wanting to be the leader of your family, but if I can make a recommendation . . . ?"

Chase nodded, not sure where this was going.

"I learned a long time ago that my wife has a lot to offer when it comes to wisdom. Sure, there are going to be times when I have to make the decision I believe is right, even if Audrey doesn't agree. But whenever remotely possible, Audrey and I try to arrive at a consensus after we've *both* had a chance to pray—together and separately—about the issue."

Chase opened his mouth to say, "I understand," but he closed it, defensiveness edging up inside him. He wanted a chance to explain his side of things. "Like I told Landyn, this opportunity truly didn't leave time to track her down. She was in an all-day meeting and there was someone else waiting right behind me to take the rental. If I hadn't given my agent a yes right then, we would have lost it."

"Would having your way on this be worth losing your marriage over?"

Adrenaline shot through Chase's veins and he felt his hands balling into fists, almost involuntarily. "First of all, this isn't about having my way. And no offense, but if Landyn divorces me over this—not that she plans to—but if she did, that would be an awfully petty reason."

"And I agree." Grant nodded. "But do you see what I'm trying to say?"

"I think I do. And I hope you see what I'm trying to say. I did what I felt was right at the time. Frankly, nothing has changed my mind. I feel I was following God's leading. And despite Landyn's reaction, I stand by that."

"Have you told her that?"

"I have. I'm not going to lie to her. And I'm not going to apologize for something I don't believe was wrong."

Landyn's dad shifted his chair yet again, moving it a bit closer to the door. Something about his demeanor struck Chase as odd, and it crossed his mind that Grant Whitman might actually be feeling a little intimidated by him. That was an interesting reverse from the man who'd managed to make him all but cower—pretty much since the day Landyn had introduced them.

Feeling emboldened, he rose from the bed. "But I do appreciate what you're trying to say. I'll keep your *counsel* in mind." He hadn't chosen the word lightly and he immediately felt like a jerk for his tone. And for invoking his grudge against Landyn's dad over the counseling.

Grant stood too, rising to his full six-foot-three stature. He took half a step toward Chase, making him feel small again. His father-in-law's intent, no doubt.

"You do that," Grant returned the chair to the desk. "You keep that in mind." He strode to the door and closed it firmly behind him.

16

The sound of sirens in the street below woke Landyn at four a.m. When they had lived in Manhattan, she'd grown accustomed to the constant noise of the city—liked it, even—but she'd dreamed she was back in Langhorne with Chase. She jolted from the futon and went to stand by the window.

She'd slept for several hours after talking with Chase, and now she was wide awake and restless. She ate an apple and some stale crackers and cleaned the apartment, except for the corner where Chase had his easel and art desk set up. It felt strange to see all of Chase's things, with no sign that she'd ever lived here. Except for a photograph of the two of them, which was lying on the side table by the futon. The photo was unframed—a candid shot taken at a friend's wedding two years ago. It was a cheap printed copy of one she'd framed and put on the mantel at their apartment in Manhattan. She didn't know where Chase had gotten his copy, but it lifted her spirits to know he had it in a place he'd see it daily.

Her cell phone rang—Corinne's ringtone—and she rifled through her purse trying to locate it. "Hey, sis."

"Hey, yourself. You doing okay?"

"Mom and Dad told you? Where I am?"

"Yes. You know you're crazy, right? Two road trips to New York in three weeks' time?"

"Guilty as charged. But it wouldn't have been half so crazy if Chase hadn't decided to fly to Cape at the same time."

"It's kind of sweet, really," her sister said. "When you think about it."

"Yeah . . . I guess it kind of is."

"So are you flying back or staying out there?"

"I don't know. Chase's supposed to call today and we're going to try to figure something out."

"You're not going to leave him are you, Landyn?"

"I don't want to."

"Then don't."

"You make it sound so easy. But Corinne, I can't just pretend nothing happened. We had an agreement, a plan, and Chase went back on that. He made a life-changing decision *for* me, and now I don't even know who I'm supposed to be anymore."

"Who you're supposed to be? You've always known who you are, Landyn. It's one of the things

I admire most about you—I'm a little jealous of, if you want to know the truth."

"Well, this has messed with my mind pretty good. Just sayin'."

"Hey, just because Chase made a decision like that doesn't mean he doesn't love you. Or even that he doesn't respect you. It was selfish and thoughtless maybe. But I don't think it was a capital offense."

"Maybe not, but that still doesn't help me. What do I do now?" She looked around the tiny studio. "You should see this place, Corinne. It's the size of a postage stamp. There's not room for a cradle, let alone a crib. He's sleeping on a futon."

"Maybe that's because *you* took the bed. So what did he say about the baby?"

She cleared her throat.

"Landyn? Don't tell me you still haven't told him."

"I told you I don't want him to be willing to work things out only because of the baby."

"But you said he *is* willing. You've got to tell him! Especially now that the family knows. If half the world knew I was pregnant before I ever told Jesse, he would—"

"Half the world had better *not* know. You haven't said anything, have you?"

"No. So maybe I exaggerated a little. But . . . Danae and I, and Mom and Dad—half *your* world knows."

"And you're sure Mom and Dad haven't told him? Mom didn't say anything when I talked to her, but . . ."

"I don't think they'd do that. Not unless you were in danger or something."

Landyn huffed out a breath. "Knowing Dad, he does think I'm in danger because I'm in New York. Bedford-Stuyvesant, no less. Home of Chris Rock and"—she put on her best rapper voice—"The Notorious B.I.G."

Corinne giggled. "I doubt Dad has a clue who that even is." She turned serious then. "You are safe there, right? I mean, it's not a bad part of town or anything?"

"No. I'm fine. And I hate to admit it, but I actually kind of like it here."

"Don't like it too much, little sister. I really don't want my first nephew or niece to grow up a thousand miles away."

"Actually, one thousand fourteen miles away. I can testify to that. But way closer if you fly."

"I don't care. Still way too far. But if that's where God puts you," she added quickly, "and if that's where you have to go to be with Chase, I guess I'll just have to put on my big-girl panties and gut it out."

"Well, I—" Her phone buzzed and Chase's number filled the screen. "Hey, sis, Chase is calling. Can I call you back?"

"Oh, you don't need to. I just wanted to see how

you were doing. Talk to your man. Tell him I said hi. And . . . give him a chance, okay, Landyn?"

"I will."

"I know you will. And *tell* him. Please."

"We'll see. Love you."

"Love you too."

Landyn clicked off and switched mental gears to talk to Chase. "Hi there."

"I didn't wake you up, did I?"

"No. I was talking to Corinne."

"Oh. So you slept okay there?"

"Pretty good." She felt as awkward as she had on their first date. No. That wasn't right. On their first date, everything had clicked and they'd both felt like they'd known each other forever. It had been that way pretty much ever since. Until now.

"So what have you been thinking?" asked Chase.

"About what we should do?"

"That and—just, about us?"

"Chase, I think *us* is a very good idea and—"

"Me too." Relief was thick in his voice. "A very good idea."

"Let me finish though."

"Okay . . ." She thought the wind went out of his sails a little.

"We can't just pretend nothing has changed. It sounds like you're all set. But Chase, I don't know what I'm supposed to do with my life now. I feel like you . . . displaced me. And I don't know where I belong now."

"You belong with me."

"I want to believe that. I *do* believe that. But I still have to figure out what that looks like. Who I am now."

"You are a wonderful woman who I love more than life itself."

"Whatever." She tried to laugh but it came out more like a sob. "I'm just confused, Chase. I don't have a home here. I can't run home to Mom and Dad because I don't have a home there anymore either. I just feel . . . lost."

"We'll find you, baby. I promise. We'll figure it out. Okay?"

"I guess." He wanted it to be so easy. But it wasn't easy. It just wasn't. And he didn't know the half of it.

"Listen. I've been thinking. And—just so you know, I'm asking, not telling."

That, at least, was a good sign. "And?"

"Have you thought about what I said? Would you be willing to come back to Cape?"

"For how long?"

"Just till we figure things out. We can set a time limit if you want to."

How about nine months? "How will we make it though? I don't think we can stay at my parents', and I don't think they can afford to loan us any money. The way it sounds, they've sunk everything into that stupid inn."

"I've got some ideas. Starting with selling my

155

car. Even if you ultimately decided to go back to your job uptown, we wouldn't need two vehicles, especially if I kept working in the Bed-Stuy studio."

"I don't know if I even have the option of going back to Fineman and Justus, Chase."

His pause made her wonder if he hadn't considered that.

"Well . . . any job uptown," he said. "I'm just saying selling a car would give us a little cash to live on while we decide. I—I'm just throwing out some options."

"Are you thinking of selling the car here or driving it back to Langhorne?" She was trying not to shoot down every suggestion he made. And quickly realizing that it was a hard habit to break.

"I don't know. Probably we should . . . I mean, I'd value your opinion. What do you think?"

She laughed. "See, I guess you can teach an old dog new tricks."

"I'm trying. But I gotta tell you, Landyn, it doesn't come easy."

"You don't have to tell me that. Hey, do you think Raymond might know the best way to sell a car here?"

"He sure might. Do you mind asking him? And I'll ask your dad."

"Are you going to ask him about us staying there too?"

"Would it make you mad if I said I have some other ideas up my sleeve?"

"Depends on what you're talking about. And depends on whether you go and commit to one of those without—"

"I know, I know. I'll run it by you first. I promise."

Somehow over the course of the next hour, they managed to recapture—however tentatively—the easy way they'd always had between them. And by the time they hung up, they had a tentative plan, and Landyn felt like they'd called a truce.

Of course, she also hadn't told Chase about the one thing that could put a huge crimp in whatever plans they made.

17

"We'd need the first month's rent and one month's rent deposit. And like I said, the place needs some work."

Chase turned on his heel, taking a three-sixty around the upstairs apartment overlooking Langhorne's Main Street. It was twice the size of the Bed-Stuy studio, and the rent sounded dirt cheap at six hundred dollars a month. But he tried to imagine Landyn going for this—and failed. "Needs some work" was the understatement of the millennium, and the landlord didn't sound too crazy about the short-term deal Chase was trying to negotiate.

Still, the light in this place was incredible. It would be the perfect place to paint. And maybe he'd even drum up some interest in his painting here in town. Local boy makes good and all that.

"Let me talk to my wife and I'll let you know sometime tomorrow. Will that work?"

The man scratched his chin. "I should be able to wait that long."

Chase happened to know—thanks to Landyn's brother—that the studio hadn't been occupied for well over a year, so the owner was probably in a position to deal. He checked his watch. "I need to get this car back to my father-in-law," he told the landlord, "but I'll be in touch."

He headed back to the inn, driver's side window down on the Mariner, his elbow resting on the ledge. He allowed himself a few minutes to covet the vehicle he was driving. He'd never seen himself as an SUV guy, and this was bigger than he and Landyn needed—and manufactured in the twenty-first century, unlike either of their cars. But he sure liked the quiet ride and sitting up higher. Someday he wouldn't mind owning a car like that.

Under the circumstances, Grant had been generous in loaning him wheels. And in letting him and Landyn stay at the inn. But there wasn't any extra space there for Chase to work, so it was important this deal with the loft go through.

After discussing things with Landyn, Chase agreed that if they could sell his car in New York, she would drive hers back to Missouri as soon as the sale was final. And if Chase found a buyer in Missouri first—he'd use the proceeds from the sale to fly back to New York and then they'd caravan back to Missouri in both vehicles. If they couldn't find a buyer at all . . . Well, he didn't have a Plan C. And he'd be glad when he wasn't dependent on the Whitmans for transportation.

But regardless, he thought it would be better if they weren't in New York right now trying to make decisions about what they were going to do with their lives—in the apartment that had caused all the trouble in the first place.

Fortunately, the gallery had sold two more of his pen-and-ink drawings, though small ones, and Miles seemed optimistic that things were going as they should. Chase trusted the man, even when he didn't see the checks coming as quickly as he'd hoped.

He drove back to the Whitmans' wishing he had something more concrete to tell Landyn's father. Grant and Audrey had been helpful, but there was something about Grant's attitude toward him that kept him on edge. He'd heard the old cliché that no father ever thought any man was good enough for his daughter, but this seemed to go beyond that. Something was bugging Landyn's dad, and Chase was pretty sure he was at the center of it. If it was about the rift between him and Landyn, he couldn't even defend himself to her parents without making her look bad. It hadn't been *his* decision to split up.

When he pulled in the drive at the inn, Huckleberry came running. Landyn had missed that crazy dog almost more than she missed her family, and he was starting to understand why. There was something about a dog's unconditional, uninhibited love.

She'd been making noises about getting a dog almost since they'd said "I do." He'd never owned a dog. His mom had been doing good to feed *him,* so a dog was out of the question.

He reached for the automatic opener clipped to the visor and waited for the garage door to go up. Huck followed the car inside, and Chase could see the dog in the rearview mirror panting impatiently, waiting for him to get out.

If he and Landyn ever got settled somewhere, a dog was on his wish list. He had other reasons too. Maybe a puppy would hold off Landyn on wanting kids. He pushed the thought away, but it slithered back. He knew he wouldn't be able to put her off as long as he wanted to. Even though she was excited about her career in marketing, she'd made it clear when they got married that she wanted babies as soon as they could afford it. And whenever she was with Corinne and Jesse's girls, Chase saw that look in Landyn's eyes. That . . . hunger.

The thought made him shudder. Even when they'd gone through those counseling sessions before they got married, he'd never admitted to her—or anyone—how terrifying the prospect of being a father was to him. He didn't have the first clue what it took to be a dad. The only thing he knew about fathers was that they left town the year you started T-ball, when all the other kids' dads were teaching them how to swing a bat and field a ball. And every few years they promised to come visit and take you to the zoo, or the rodeo, or Disneyland. And then you packed your bag and sat on the front stoop from morning till dark, waiting for an invisible hero who never showed up.

He'd been stupid enough to harbor the dream until he was fifteen. Finally his mother had laid it out for him. "He's not coming back, Chase. Not for me, not for you. Not even for a day. And thank God for that. It's time you knew the truth."

He knew now that his mom had done him a favor. But at the time he'd hated her for it. Hated his dad. Hated pretty much the entire world. And then he met Landyn. And found something to love about his life. He always told her she'd saved his life. To which her standard reply was, "No, Jesus did that." Well, right. But he liked to think Landyn was God's way of putting flesh and blood to it.

But she wanted kids someday. And that scared him spitless.

He would never do to any kid of his what his father had done to him. But what if knowing what *not* to do wasn't enough? Even Landyn didn't have a perfect relationship with her parents—and Grant and Audrey had been pretty perfect parents to her as far as he could see. He just couldn't imagine ever having anyone look up to him the way all the Whitman kids did to Grant.

Again, he pushed the thoughts away. He had a few years before he had to worry about that. And right now he had more important family matters to figure out. Like how to be a good husband and provider. How to figure out what God had in mind for him and Landyn.

Leaving the garage door open, he whistled at Huck. "Come on, boy. Let's go."

He jogged out to the front lawn, Huck at his heels. The Whitmans had gotten the dog when Landyn was in junior high and Audrey had told him the other night, when he and Huck were romping in the backyard, "That dog must associate you with Landyn. It's like he thinks he's a pup again whenever you're around." Chase took that as a supreme compliment and liked to claim some credit for Huck's longevity.

He heard the door between the garage and the mudroom open. Huck's ears perked, and Chase looked up to see Grant strolling out onto the driveway. "How'd it go?"

Chase told him about the property he'd seen and about the owner's reluctance to rent short-term.

Grant looked thoughtful for a minute, then motioned toward the shady front veranda. "Let's go sit for a while. I have a proposal to run by you."

Chase followed, feeling—as he often did around Grant—as though he were headed for the proverbial woodshed.

"I'll get right to the point." Grant thought Chase looked nervous, and he wasn't sure whether his proposition would cure that or make it worse.

"Okay . . ." Chase leaned forward on the glider, hands pressed on the seat at his sides.

"Audrey and I were talking and we wondered how you and Landyn would feel about staying with my mother while you're here in Missouri. I've already talked to Mother about it and she'd love to have you for a month or two." He chuckled. "Now, you'd have to be out of there by March when it's her turn to host her bridge gals, but she said you could have the whole second floor to yourselves. There are two bedrooms and a bath up there, so you could set up your easels or whatever you need in the second bedroom."

Chase looked thoughtful. "CeeCee still lives in town—in Langhorne—right?"

"That's right. On the east side of town, so it's a quick jog over to Cape."

"I don't think I've ever been upstairs in her house, but . . . I'll talk to Landyn and see what she thinks. We're still trying to figure things out. I do appreciate the option, but I'm kind of liking the idea of renting that loft."

Talk about looking a gift horse in the mouth . . . Grant felt his jaw clench tighter and he tried to keep the frustration from his voice. "Well, I don't know what price my mother has in mind, but I can tell you it won't be six hundred dollars. I'm not sure you guys have the luxury of *not* taking CeeCee up on her offer."

"I think we can handle it. I'll talk it over with Landyn. But don't worry. We'll get out of your hair here. I know it's been an imposition and I apologize."

Grant waved him off. There was a twinge of . . . was it sarcasm? . . . in Chase's voice. Grant wasn't certain enough to call him on it. And he really was trying to keep the peace with his daughter's husband. For her sake. "It's not that it's an imposition, Chase, but we had those bookings set up a while back and we need to honor—"

"I understand. And we'll be out of your hair here—" Chase motioned in the direction of the upstairs room he'd been occupying.

The movement caused Chase's shirt collar to fall open enough to reveal that awful tattoo on his collarbone. Grant was just thankful it was usually hidden under his clothes.

"We'll get out of your hair as soon as we possibly can," Chase said again. "For sure, long before your guests are due."

The sarcasm was thicker now, Grant was pretty sure. He had half a mind to kick the kid out right now. See how sarcastic he'd feel if he was homeless. But he held his tongue. Audrey was always reminding him how far Chase had come—and what odds he'd had to overcome to get to where he was now. So today Grant would write off the sarcasm to poor parenting and let it go.

18

"Seriously? With CeeCee?" Landyn exited the subway turnstile. "Hang on, Chase. You're cutting out." She hurried down the platform and trotted up the stairs into the street. A brisk wind blew her scarf into her face and she adjusted it tighter around her neck as she walked. "Can you hear me now?"

He laughed. "You sound like a commercial. And yes, I'm serious. Would that be a bad thing? Staying at CeeCee's?"

"I don't know. I guess it never crossed my mind as a possibility. You like my grandmother, right?"

"Sure. She's cool."

"That doesn't necessarily make her easy to live with."

"I haven't talked to CeeCee yet, but your dad said we'd have the whole upstairs to ourselves."

"That's not a whole lot of space . . ." Still, probably twice the square footage of the BedStuy studio. "Did he say how much CeeCee would charge us for rent?"

"He said it would be under six hundred."

"Six hundred? That's an odd number. I wonder where she came up with that."

"I'm—not sure. But if it really is that cheap, we could afford to keep the studio while we're deciding."

She slowed her pace. "So you're still thinking that's the way we should go?"

"I just want to keep our options open."

"Would you try to sublease it though? I just don't know where we're going to get that kind of money, babe." *And we're going to need more money than ever a few months from now.* She was getting in deeper and deeper, not telling him. It wasn't fair to be making decisions like this when Chase didn't have all the facts. But things were complicated enough without her throwing the baby news into the mix. Besides, she wanted to tell him in person.

This wasn't at all the way things were supposed to be. She'd always imagined when the day came that she had news like this to share, she would set a romantic table with candles and roses, and she'd sit on Chase's lap and whisper in his ear, "You're going to be a daddy!"

Her dreams were always more like an old Doris Day movie than anything resembling reality. But it was what made her good at what she did—or at what she used to do. She wondered if her career was over before it ever got started.

She crossed the street, cutting it close, and a fast-approaching yellow cab honked at her. She couldn't read the cabbie's lips, but she could guess what choice words he was spewing.

"Wow," Chase said, "It's weird to hear the city in the background. I'd forgotten how quiet it is here."

"Too quiet?"

"I don't know . . . I kind of like it. It's just—two different worlds."

"Well, don't get too comfortable there. I don't think there are a lot of job opportunities for me in Langhorne, America."

"No, but—Cape Girardeau might have some. Or St. Louis."

"Whoa! Wait a minute. Where's this coming from? You're not really thinking of moving back to Missouri? And definitely not St. Louis." She did *not* want to raise her baby in St. Louis. But then, she'd never dreamed of raising a family in New York either.

"What do you want me to tell your dad—about staying at CeeCee's?"

"I guess I'm game if you are. It doesn't sound

like we have the option of staying at my house—I mean, at the inn."

"No. I think your dad is about fed up with us. With me anyway." Chase's tone said more than his words.

"Why do you say that?"

"It's nothing. Don't worry about it."

"No . . . What did he say?"

"Nothing. Just that they have guests booked next week that will fill the whole inn. So there's not a room for us there."

For some reason that hit her hard. And it hurt. She swallowed hard. "I guess I know where I'm not wanted."

"Well, you can't really blame them, Landyn. They didn't know we were going to create this comedy of errors and—"

"Yeah, I guess we should have booked a room sooner if we ever wanted to see my parents."

"They're just trying to make a living, same as we are."

It sounded like he was trying to convince himself as much as her.

He said something else but his phone cut out briefly.

"What was that, Chase?"

"Hey, baby, Miles is on the other line. I've got to go. I'll call you tomorrow, okay?"

"Okay. See you." She hung up. "Love you," she whispered.

She and Chase hadn't spoken those words to each other in too long. She couldn't remember when, but not since before the day he'd told her about renting the studio.

But she *did* still love him. And she thought he loved her too. Why else were they jumping through hoops trying to figure out their life *together?* Trying to figure out where to be together. It was what they both wanted.

Wasn't it?

"Miles, I don't have that kind of money." Chase gripped the phone, still stunned at the bombshell his agent had just dropped. So much for a relaxing weekend. He slumped against a column on the back deck of the inn, hoping the gaggle of middle-aged women he'd seen checking into the inn earlier didn't decide to spend the pleasant November evening out here.

"I warned you about this at the outset, remember?" Miles's patronizing tone reminded Chase too much of Grant. "We talked about it when you signed the contract, remember?"

"No, I don't remember. I don't have a clue where I'll get that kind of money." How could he owe that much in taxes? Surely he would have remembered if Miles had said anything. But then, in his excitement over getting a rep, he'd only skimmed the contract he'd signed with Miles's agency. Just enough to see that his percentage was fair, which it was. This news, however, was anything but fair. He felt like God had him on puppet strings, jerking him one way, then another. Miles's news on the heels of the good news about a place to stay at CeeCee's was too much. "So what do I do?" he said—too loudly—into the phone.

"If you can't come up with the money by the next tax time, you can always file an extension."

"Yeah, and then I pay even more in interest, right?"

The back door opened, and the chatty guests spilled onto the deck, swaddled in jackets and scarves, drinks in hand.

"Hang on a sec, Miles." Chase gave what he hoped passed for a friendly wave and walked around to the side yard.

"You there?" Miles said.

"Yeah. Go ahead."

"I've got a couple interested in that still life you just finished. No guarantee, but that would help . . ."

"I'd have to sell four or five of those just to pay taxes!" For lack of a wall to punch, Chase kicked at the grass, leaving a gouge in the manicured lawn. Great. One more reason for Grant to hate his guts. "What are Landyn and I supposed to live on in the meantime?"

"I'm sorry, guy, but like I said, it was in the contract. You didn't think this income would be exempt, did you? If you haven't already, you might want to set up quarterly estimated payments so this doesn't happen next year."

"Quarterly? Let me tell you how excited I am about that."

"Hey, welcome to real life." There was zero sympathy in his agent's voice.

"I just didn't think about it at all. I was too busy trying to make ends meet."

"Well, there's time to sell plenty of paintings before those taxes are due. And I can try to expedite your next commission check if you're short on cash right now, but I don't really have any other tricks up my sleeve."

Chase could tell his rep was seconds from inventing an important phone call from an imaginary client. He swore under his breath. "It's not your fault, Miles. I should have thought of it. I . . . I'll figure something out." He clicked off the call before Miles could beat him to it and tucked the phone in his pocket.

Standing in the middle of the lawn, he felt like he'd been sucker-punched by somebody twice his size. "God, what are you doing to me here?"

He immediately felt guilty. He was only cursing his own stupidity. God had nothing to do with it —unless God was in cause and effect. His stupidity had caused a big problem. And right now he couldn't see any way out.

19

"Come in, you two. Get out of the cold!"

Cecelia Whitman opened the door to her tidy home at the east edge of Langhorne's Main Street and received hugs from Chase and Grant. A cold wind blew in behind them, and the elderly woman stooped to gather up a few stray leaves that had followed them in.

When they reached the kitchen, CeeCee turned and winked at Chase. "This son of mine dragged you out of bed on a Saturday morning? Dirty trick that."

"I don't mind. It's good to see you again."

Landyn's grandma—Grant's mother—had to be one of the most interesting women Chase had ever met. The first time he'd been introduced to CeeCee, she was trudging up the hill from the creek behind the Whitmans' house, fishing pole over one shoulder, blue-white curls framing the Cardinals baseball cap perched backward on her head, and muddy Nikes accessorizing her bib overalls. If not for her petite feminine build, Chase might have mistaken her for a man.

When he'd seen her next, at Danae and Dallas's wedding, CeeCee had been strawberry blond, the epitome of elegance in a pale blue gown, her wrists and earlobes dripping with rhinestones—or maybe they were real diamonds.

Today, her hair was a coppery shade and piled high on her head.

"So I hear you and Miss Landyn are going to move in with me for a while."

"We're thinking about it, ma'am. If that's okay with you."

She winked at Chase. "It's okay with me as long as you heard the 'for a while' part of my invitation."

"Oh, yes, ma'am. We really appreciate it and we'll only be here until we can decide what we're supposed to be doing."

"Well, now . . ." A spark came to her blue eyes. "For some people that could be fifteen years. That's just a hair longer than I meant by 'a while'. I trust you and Landyn will have your act together a bit sooner than that."

Chase looked to Grant for a cue as to whether CeeCee was joking.

But his father-in-law only walked to the dining room and looked out the window. "We need to get those trees trimmed, Mother," he said. "An ice storm and you'd have big trouble."

"Well, come and trim them, then. Or maybe Chase can help me with that. You any good with a chainsaw?"

"I've used one once or twice. I'd be glad to trim things up." He hoped she understood that he would need to be working on his art while he and Landyn were here. He wouldn't have time to be a maintenance man.

"If you wouldn't mind helping out a little around here, we can probably see to it that you don't get charged any rent." CeeCee looked pointedly at Grant. "Right, son?"

Grant held his hands up, palms out. "I'll leave that between the two of you."

"Sounds like a good deal to me," Chase said. "We sure do appreciate you letting us stay here—"

"For a while," she reminded him. "Stay here for a while."

"Right. Just for a while." He grinned. CeeCee was outspoken and a little outrageous at times, but Chase liked that she said what she meant and meant what she said. And if he could pay the rent with a few hours of yard work, this could be a real answer to prayer.

"Now Grant told you I host my bridge club here in March, right? The fifteenth, I think it is."

"Yes, ma'am, he did. Don't worry, we'll be out of here long before then. Hopefully by Christmas." He wasn't sure where that had come from. He didn't have a clue how this was all going to play out. They didn't have any plans firmed up yet. They hadn't set any deadlines.

But it looked like he just might have committed them to one.

As soon as they returned to the inn from CeeCee's, Chase dialed Landyn. He wanted to put off telling her about Miles's call, but he might as well get the bad news out of the way. Maybe he could temper it with the good news about her grandmother's offer of letting him work off the rent.

Landyn picked up on the first ring. "Hey, baby. How's it going?" The smile in her voice made Chase feel worse.

"I have good news and I have bad news. Which one do you want first?"

"What happened?" She wasn't playing.

"It might not be as bad as he thinks, but Miles reminded me that we're probably going to owe a huge chunk in taxes. Because of all the art I've sold."

A long pause, then, "Define 'huge chunk' please."

He cleared his throat. "Probably around seven thousand."

"What! Chase, we don't have that kind of money." She sounded on the edge of panic.

He didn't tell her that was just for income from art commissions. It didn't include any liability they'd have from their regular jobs. And they'd made sure they kept as much of each paycheck as possible.

"I know," he said, "but April's a ways off. And Miles said we could file an extension if we need to."

She made a noise that was a cross between a moan and a growl. "Don't we have to pay even more if we do that?"

"Probably some interest. But we'll be okay, baby. Remember what Pastor Simmons said? All newlyweds struggle with finances the first few years."

"I don't think he meant to the tune of ten thousand dollars in the first six months."

"Once you're working again, we'll be fine. I can pick up some work on the side, and we can raise a lot of the cash just by selling my car." *Ha!* They'd be lucky if his beater brought a grand. That thing had been at least ten years old when he'd bought it from their next-door neighbor, but low mileage. Mr. Granger had been packing to move into a retirement home at the time and had sold it to him for five hundred dollars. The deal of the century, Chase now realized. But Frank Granger had died before Chase could thank him.

"Not if we have to drive it back to Missouri to sell it."

"Would you quit being such a cynic?"

"Besides, I thought we were using that money to fly one of us home—wherever home is now."

"Home is wherever you are, Landyn."

"Well, it just so happens I'm in New York, so you'd better get your tail out here."

Not exactly the response he was hoping his romantic line would get, but at least she'd implied that she wanted to be with him. It was a start. And he needed to take advantage of it.

The screen on his phone changed, and he realized Landyn had hung up. Without asking what his good news was. Had she given up hope?

If it took their last dime, he had to figure out a way to get to New York.

Landyn slipped her phone back into her purse and walked back to Chase's studio in a daze. When she unlocked the door, she realized her hands were trembling. They were in deep and getting deeper.

She *had* to tell Chase about the baby. He needed to know that she would not be finding a decent job anytime soon. Because she was having a baby. Their baby. And she would be showing before long. This morning, studying her figure in the mirror of the studio's tiny bathroom, she would have sworn she was already showing. But maybe that was just the effects of one too many deli breakfasts. Which, it seemed, she could no longer afford to buy. She tossed her purse on the counter and slumped into the lumpy futon. How were they ever going to make it?

She tried to sleep—not because she was tired, but because sleep seemed to offer the only acceptable escape from her circumstances. But after an hour of restless tossing, she went to get her phone and—before she could come to her senses and change her mind—dialed her father. She'd only spoken to her parents once since driving away from their house a week ago. She wouldn't blame them if they told her to take a hike. But she couldn't go on like this. Something had to give.

Dad answered on the second ring. "Landyn? Everything okay?"

"I'm fine, Dad."

"You're feeling okay? Everything okay with the baby and—?"

"Dad. I'm fine. Don't worry about me."

"That's a father's job, Landyn. So when are you coming back? Have you figured that out yet?"

"I haven't figured anything out." Tears threatened. "That's . . . why I'm calling. I—I don't know what we're going to do, Dad."

"What do you mean?"

"We're both just . . . confused, I guess. We just don't know what we should do."

"What does Chase want to do?"

"I'm not sure. I don't think *he's* sure. I thought he was set on Bed-Stuy—that's what started this whole mess. But now he's talking about—" She gave a frustrated sigh. "I don't even know."

"Well, you two had better figure something out. You can't keep playing games with each other—"

"That's what I'm saying. But I don't know what to do. And Chase just found out our taxes are going to kill us and—"

"Taxes? How does he know that already?"

"For the art he sold. I guess that's all taxable and they don't take anything out of his commission checks." She explained what Chase had told her.

Her dad was silent on his end and she imagined him fuming—whether at Chase or her, she wasn't sure. Probably both of them. And she couldn't really blame him.

"Landyn," Dad said finally. "I don't want to interfere, but you guys need to make some decisions and I don't mean next week. Do you want me to talk to Chase?"

"No. And—Don't tell him about the baby. Please, Dad. Let me talk to him first."

"I won't tell him, but you *have* to, Landyn. You can't keep pretending this will all go away. And you're just getting in deeper and deeper—financially, I mean—with every day that goes by."

As if she didn't know that.

20

"I'd like to surprise her and fly out there. But . . . we're pretty strapped right now."

Grant shut off the weed-eater he wielded and studied his son-in-law. Apparently plans had changed since he'd talked to Landyn Saturday. These two had changed their minds more often than his mother changed her hair color. "Couldn't you put airfare on your credit card? Pay it off when you sell the car?"

Chase shifted from one foot to the other. "We're kind of maxed out right now. On the credit cards."

"Kind of?" How much could a one-way flight to New York be?

"We *are* maxed out . . . sir."

Lord, help me keep my cool. "I probably don't have to tell you that I've already helped Landyn out more than her share. Are you aware she asked me to loan her the money to fly home?"

"Recently?"

"Yesterday."

Chase's eyebrows went up. "I . . . I didn't know that."

He placed the weed-eater on the edge of the sidewalk, then wiped his brow with his shirttail. "Are you thinking of going back to New York?"

"We're not sure, but—"

"No, I mean *you.*"

"Oh. Well, I think it's best we bring the cars back here to sell one of them, so I'll probably need to make another trip."

Grant wasn't sure he liked that idea, but he was keeping out of their business as much as possible. Besides, he didn't have a better option to offer. "Fine, but you two had better get your schedules synchronized before you end up crossing wires again."

"We will." Chase stretched and the thin white T-shirt he wore pulled taut over his chest. His tattoo showed through like an ugly bruise.

The thing was the size of a bagel. He didn't care if it *was* a cross. How anyone could do that to themselves, Grant didn't know. He looked away. "So you're wanting a loan for airfare, I take it?"

"Yes, sir."

"When a man has five kids, he needs to be careful he doesn't play favorites." He paused, letting his son-in-law sweat a little. "But I guess I could make you a temporary loan if you'll pay it off from the proceeds when you sell the car."

"Yes sir. I can do that."

Grant didn't correct Chase calling him sir. He was glad to see this hadn't been an easy request to make. He didn't want it to become a habit. Although it crossed his mind that he might be on the asking end someday soon if things kept going the way they were with the inn. He would be grateful when these kids got their differences worked out. So far it had been like watching a couple of bumbling circus clowns. "Did you say you wanted to *surprise* Landyn?"

"Yes, sir."

Grant cleared his throat. "Diamond necklaces are good surprises. Bouquets of roses are good surprises. What you are planning would be a surprise, but I'm not so sure it would be a good one." That line might come back to haunt him once Chase found out the surprise waiting for *him* in New York. But much as Grant was tempted, he wasn't going to be the one to spill the beans on

Landyn's "surprise." That news was for her to tell.

He only hoped she did it soon. And that Chase would take the news like a man.

Chase wiped damp palms on his jeans and rang the doorbell. It felt strange to be ringing his own doorbell, but it would have felt even more strange to walk in on Landyn.

He heard rustling inside, and then the door opened and suddenly, she was standing in front of him. His wife. Today, Friday, was the soonest he'd been able to get a reasonably priced flight—and it had now been over four weeks since he'd seen her face to face. It felt more like four years.

"Hi." She swung the door wide open, not smiling, but looking nervous and a little breathless. And beautiful. She was wearing one of those long swishy skirts with a T-shirt, and her hair was the way he liked it—wild and curly like she'd just crawled out of bed. Yet he knew how long it took her to get it looking that way. He thought it was a good sign.

He hitched his duffel up on his shoulder and entered, looking around the small space. "The place looks good."

She shrugged.

The apartment was tidier than he'd left it, and there were slightly droopy flowers in a Styrofoam cup on the lone counter by the sink. He wondered where they'd come from. Knowing Landyn, she'd probably talked a street florist out of day-old flowers. Even wilted, they cheered up the space. Or maybe it was Landyn who cheered it up.

He wanted to wrap her in a hug, but she was hugging herself and standing as far away from him as she could get in the twenty-by-twenty-foot studio.

"Have you eaten?"

He tossed his duffel by the door and shrugged out of his jacket. "I had a burger at the airport. Why? You hungry?"

"No. I had something already."

They stood awkwardly staring at each other until Landyn looked away and went to the sink. "I'm thirsty. You want some water?"

"Sure."

She filled two glasses and offered him one.

"Thanks." Her hand brushed his as he took the glass from her. He caught a whiff of the familiar scent of her favorite body lotion. An intoxicating mix of flowers and fruit.

They drank in silence, Landyn looking out the window to the street. Him watching her. It was going to be a long couple of days if somebody didn't break the ice. He took a deep breath. "So . . . You have everything you need here?"

"It's fine. I met your super."

"Yeah, you said . . . Ray's a good guy."

"He let me park in some guy's spot while he's out of town."

"I wondered what you were doing about that. Have you seen the prices the garages are charging now?"

"I know. It's crazy. So, Dad loaned you the money to fly out?"

He nodded. "I don't think he was too happy about it, but I told him we'd pay him back when we sell the car."

"How much do you think we'll get for it? It's still your car you want to sell, right?"

"I don't know. Maybe we should see how much the Honda would bring."

She tensed, and he waved off his comment. "Whichever you think. I don't know . . . We may not need a car at all."

"I thought of that. But I thought you said you wanted to stay in Langhorne for a while."

"Just till we figure things out."

She looked at the floor, tugging at a long curl, then winding it around her finger—a signal he'd learned to recognize.

"Can we just put everything on the table, Landyn? Do some pros and cons lists like we learned in counseling?" Without waiting for her to respond, he went to the taboret near the easel and pulled out two sheets of scrap paper. He rummaged in a mug for two pens that worked and put paper and pen on the bar counter in front of each of the mismatched stools.

"Pros and cons for what?"

He studied her, trying to get a feel for where she was emotionally. "Maybe I shouldn't have put it that way. Maybe what we need is a list of possibilities."

"Okay." She pulled out a bar stool and moved it up close to the wall before hiking herself up onto it. Her skirt rustled as she tucked shapely legs beneath her, resting her chin on one knee. She slid the paper and pen across the bar and clicked the pen.

Chase put the other stool at the far end of the bar and straddled it, mesmerized by her movements, remembering how her silky skin felt beneath his fingers. He wouldn't push her, but man! He wanted her.

It had been too long. Far too long.

21

Once they started tossing out ideas to write on their papers, Landyn began to feel a little more at ease with Chase. His hair was longer than he usually wore it and he looked like he'd gained a little weight. It looked good on him. Funny how a person could change in only four weeks.

Or maybe she was just remembering him wrong.

Chase wrote something else on his paper, then clicked his ballpoint pen and picked up the sheet. "Okay. Remember how Pastor Simmons said to do it? I'll read my list and if there's anything on it you absolutely aren't willing to do, we'll cross it off. Then same thing with my turn."

"Okay." She tried to sound more enthusiastic than she felt. But she could have predicted what was on Chase's list of possibilities.

"Okay . . . The obvious," he started. "Coming back to New York and living together here." His arm swept the small apartment with a wide gesture, as if he could make the place appear larger than it was. "Number two, moving back to Langhorne, and sort of"—he shrugged—"starting over. Number three, moving back to the Upper West Side and me commuting to Bed-Stuy."

"Really? You'd do that?"

"Well, it's not my first choice—"

"Or second."

"No. But . . . I'd consider it. If that seemed like the best thing for both of us."

"Okay." He'd managed to surprise her. "What else?"

"That's about it. Except maybe . . ." He pressed his lips together as if he'd changed his mind about telling her something on his list.

"No, we have to put it all out there."

"Okay. But remember, you can nix it, too."

"Okay."

"Well . . . I found this loft in downtown Langhorne that would make a fantastic studio."

"Langhorne? I thought Miles said you needed to live here."

"He did. And he might not be too happy about me leaving, but he doesn't own me."

"Maybe not, but if you're not making him any money, he might *disown* you."

He shot her a droll grin. "Then I guess I'll just have to be sure I'm making him money."

"And us."

"If I'm making him money, I'm making us money."

"I know," she said quickly, sensing his impatience. "You said we could live a lot cheaper in Langhorne." What he'd said was that they could live on one income in Langhorne. But she wasn't sure if he'd meant *her* one income, or his. She didn't see any way his art could generate enough income for them to make it. Anywhere.

"So? Anything on my list that you want to cross out?"

She thought a minute. "Your number one is the one I'm most tempted to cross off." She watched him closely, trying—and failing—to read his reaction. "But I'd leave it on there with some caveats."

"Like?"

"Like we'd have to be sure we could afford it." *And that there'd be room for a crib and a stroller.* She *had* to tell him. Her news changed everything, and here she was pretending to herself that any of these choices could work with a baby.

"I wouldn't do it unless I was sure." He shifted

on the stool, propping his elbows on the counter. "Okay. Your turn. What's on your list?"

She looked at her list and knew she couldn't read it until after she'd come clean. She slid off the stool. "Are you hungry yet? Can we take a break and go get something to eat?"

He seemed taken aback, but he hopped off his stool and ran a hand through his hair, combing it back from his face. Looking like the Chase she'd fallen in love with. That seemed so long ago. She felt a shiver of excitement about him being here. About them being together again. Just the two of them.

There was a line at his favorite deli. Chase had offered Landyn his leather jacket while they walked from the apartment. It was cold and she hadn't dressed warmly enough for the November evening. She'd declined, but she didn't refuse him now as he unzipped his jacket and pulled her close, wrapping half of the coat around her shivering shoulders.

The line progressed, and finally they were inside. But Landyn stayed close to him, burrowed in one side of the jacket. Having her so close aroused stirrings in him that were . . . *encouraging* —and decidedly disconcerting. Especially since he suspected she was feeling the same.

They ordered and took their food to a corner table. Watching the neighborhood come to life on a Friday night outside the plate glass window, they talked about everything and nothing at all. Just like they had when they were dating. Relishing just being together.

She took a big bite of the sub sandwich she'd ordered and he reached across the table to wipe a spot of mayo off her upper lip. Their eyes locked and he saw in the tilt of her head, the haze of her expression, that she was feeling the old attraction. Maybe they'd needed to go through this harsh time to truly appreciate what they had together.

They finished eating in silence and Chase gathered their trash and waited by the door while Landyn used the restroom. Outside the wind had died down and the lights in the storefronts twinkled appealingly. Some of the shops even had their Christmas decorations up already.

Chase held his jacket out for her again, and this time, she hooked her arm around his waist beneath the coat. He drew the leather close around both of them, smelling its richness, thinking about how well they fit together. And again, how much he desired her. "Do you want to do something tonight? A movie, maybe. Or we could find a bookstore, get some coffee?"

"Do you mind if we just go home?"

He didn't miss that she'd called his place home. And he hoped her thoughts were going the same direction as his. "You still need to read your list to me."

"Chase—I need to talk to you about something."

"Something else? Besides our lists, you mean?"

"Yes."

His steps stuttered as he tried to get a look at her expression, tried to gauge her mood. But with her tucked at his side, all he could see was the top of her curly head. "Okay, I'm all ears . . ."

"Not till we get home."

He was curious, but not overly concerned. Judging by the way she leaned into him, whatever she wanted to talk to him about wasn't anything to be worried about.

Back at the apartment, he gently untangled Landyn from his coat so he could unlock the door. He let her in first and followed her inside. But before he could even get the door shut behind them, she turned to look up at him, and in an instant they were in each other's arms.

Struggling to restrain himself, aware of how tender she needed him to be, he kissed her forehead, her cheeks, her fingers that were now stroking his lips, his face. But she was as hungry as he was, and her mouth found his like a homing beacon.

"Chase," she groaned. "We need . . . we need to talk." She was breathless, the way she'd been on the wedding night they'd both waited for. Waited so long for.

Her urgency was a gift, and he pulled her closer, shushing her with a palm to her lips. "Shh, whatever it is, it can wait, baby. Come here." He pulled her to the other side of the darkened room, shedding his jacket as he went. She did the same.

They moved in a beautiful frenzy—one they already knew by heart, but that somehow felt brand new tonight. He pulled her closer, feeling her heart beat hard against his.

"I love you, Chase." The words spilled out as if she'd been holding them in for eons.

"I love you, too, baby. So much . . ."

She pushed back his collar and kissed his neck, then tenderly traced one finger along the blue-inked knots in the Celtic star on his collarbone. "We're gonna be okay." Her voice rose on the end, making it sound like a question.

But he answered as if it was truth. "I know . . ."

He slid his hand to the tiny buttons that closed the front of her shirt, his fingers as clumsy and fumbling as they'd been the very first time.

With a light in her eyes that he hadn't seen in so long . . . so very long . . . she touched his face, then tucked her warm hands beneath his and helped him loosen the buttons one by one.

An hour later, spent and drowsy, they languished in each other's arms, sprawled across the futon, tangled in the thick quilt—and in each other.

22

Landyn awoke to the sun streaming through the window. She opened her eyes and immediately thought about what had happened last night. She felt certain the wave of nausea that followed had little to do with the child in her womb. All her good intentions to withhold the news from Chase until he could choose her apart from a sense of obligation because of the baby had been obliterated—by hormones. Both of them.

Yes, they were married. Yes, they had a right to enjoy each other in that way. And she loved him. Loved him desperately. But would Chase have wanted to make love to her if he'd known she was pregnant? That she'd kept this huge secret from him?

She would never know now. And still, she had to tell him.

She heard the shower running and her husband whistling. Oblivious to the news she would—must—tell him today. *This morning.* Fear consumed her at the thought. Maybe she could wait. Even tell him she only got pregnant last night.

The absurdity of the idea almost made her laugh. She could never hope to pull off such a deception—or pretend that an eight-pound baby was four months early. Besides, hadn't she determined to start being truthful? To quit playing games with her husband?

If there was one thing her parents had drilled into her, it was the fact that apart from the truth— apart from hard honesty—a marriage couldn't survive. And she wanted hers to survive.

She knew that now. Not just because of last night—though making love to Chase had bound her to him in a way she'd never experienced, and certainly not expected last night.

But she also knew she'd gone far astray of living honestly within her marriage. She *had* to tell him.

Chase appeared in the door between the bathroom and the studio wrapped in a towel, his hair damp and spiky. He saw her watching him and smiled. "Good morning, beautiful."

She studied him through hooded eyes.

"Let me start the coffee," he said, "then I'll come back to bed for a few minutes and cuddle."

She'd often complained that he didn't cuddle with her enough. *Oh, Chase.* He was trying so hard.

He whistled while he made coffee, then slipped under the quilt with her, his skin still warm and damp from the shower. She pushed down the new wave of desire that rolled over her. *Tell him. Now.*

"Chase . . ."

"Hmmm?" He nuzzled her neck, tickling her with a day-old beard. No doubt trying to start something again. She couldn't let that happen.

She inhaled, steeling herself. "I—I'm pregnant."

He went still, searching her eyes. And he must have read the answer there because he lurched away from her, rising up on his knees on the mattress. He clutched the quilt around his waist. "What did you just say?"

The horror in his eyes was far worse than what she'd expected. She tried to smile. "We're going to have a baby."

He grabbed his head as if he had a sudden migraine. "You can't be serious."

"I wouldn't kid you about something like this."

"No. Oh, dear God, Landyn. Are you serious? We can't have a baby right now. No way."

She tried to laugh. "I don't think we have a choice."

"How far along are you?"

"I—I haven't been to the doctor yet, but probably—almost four months."

"You haven't been to the doctor? Then maybe you're not really pregnant."

She hated the hope she heard in his voice. This was so far from the way she'd wanted this milestone in their marriage to play out. "I am really pregnant, Chase. There's no question." She'd had the same thoughts in the beginning. That maybe she wasn't pregnant, despite the home pregnancy test's positive results. Going to the doctor would have made it all too real, made it that much worse in Chase's eyes that she hadn't told him yet.

But she hadn't been able to live in denial for long. There were too many signs now. And from the beginning there'd been something . . . *intangible*. She just knew. In her heart. She'd even begun to feel flutterings that she suspected were the baby moving inside her.

Chase nodded, staring at the section of the quilt that hid her belly. "I thought—I thought you seemed—"

"Fat?"

"Not that. Just . . . different. Voluptuous." He actually grinned.

"Well, I guess that's good."

His grin faded as quickly as it'd come. "It's *not* good. The baby, I mean. When did you find out? How long have you known?"

She didn't answer, but he didn't seem to notice.

"How are we going to do this, Landyn? We can barely make it just the two of us."

"I don't know, babe. But we will. Somehow. Everything will be okay."

"How can you say that? We can barely pay the rent. How are we going to afford a baby on top of everything else?"

"I don't know, but it will work out. God will provide."

"That sounds so nice in theory, Landyn. But where exactly has God been providing lately?"

She hated the bitterness in his voice.

He eased his legs over the side of the futon

frame and groped on the floor for the jeans he'd shed there last night.

"Every couple struggles."

"Not like this they don't." He grabbed his wrinkled T-shirt, snapped it right side out, and slipped it over his head.

"What do you mean?"

"We've had to scrape for every dime. We've had to borrow from your parents, max out our credit cards—sorry, but I'm starting to wonder . . . Where is the provision in that?"

"What if we hadn't had that line of credit, or parents who were willing to help us out occasionally? Why can't God provide in those ways? Isn't that legit?" She knew conviction was missing in her voice. She'd wondered too why they'd had to struggle. Why things hadn't come easier. And yet, she *was* grateful for the help they'd received.

He shook his head and raked his hands through his hair. "I don't know. I—I don't know what I believe anymore."

She went to him, and put a tentative hand on his back, surprised to be overwhelmed with love for him—a measure of love she wasn't sure she'd ever felt for him—or for anyone else. "Babe, it's going to be okay. We—we'll work it out. We will." She wished she could make her heart match the conviction she'd managed to pump into her voice, but if hope meant anything, then they were good.

Chase slid from beneath her touch and went to look out the window. "I can't even figure out how to make a living for the two of us. How am I going to support a kid? Never mind be a good dad?" He put his forehead against the window pane.

"Chase, stop it. You know that's not true." Landyn hadn't seen this cynical, unconfident side of Chase for so long, she'd almost forgotten he could be this way. But she did remember that her instinctive reaction—to chide him and shame him—had never been well received. She reached deep to find words that would comfort and lift him out of his . . . despair. It was hard. She didn't like this Chase very much.

"I don't know the first thing about raising a kid. I'm sure no shining example."

"Chase, you'll be a great dad. You will."

"You can't know that."

She risked touching him again, laying her palm on his shoulder.

At least he didn't flinch.

"You'll be a wonderful father, Chase. And—I'm sorry if I've made you doubt. Doubt what you believe, I mean." It scared her to see him having this crisis of faith. And it did feel like it was somehow her fault. Maybe that was conviction.

He turned to face her, pressing his back to the window now. "I don't know what a dad does— and doesn't do. I've never had an example. Or anyone to tell me—"

"But you do! You've got my dad and Jesse and Pastor Simmons. And lots of other men who I know will give you advice and answer your questions."

"From a thousand miles away?" He shook his head.

"I don't know how to be a mom either, Chase. I think it's just one of those hands-on things. You have to jump in before you know how to swim and all that."

He shook his head. "I don't know. I've heard your parents talk about what a natural Jesse is. And they're right. Look how he is with those three little kids."

"Yes, but Jesse's had five years to practice. He probably wasn't like that right off the bat." She honestly didn't remember since Corinne and Jesse's kids had started coming along right when she left for college.

"Still . . . Jesse grew up in a good home. And his parents are around to help out even now. To show him how it's done. Somehow I don't think your parents are going to be saying that about me. What a good dad I am."

"You don't know that." But she was afraid he might be right. "Everything will be fine. You'll—"

"Landyn." He shook his head. "Listen to yourself. You say it will be fine, but you couldn't even tell me. You're four months pregnant and you couldn't even get up the courage to tell me."

He hung his head and when he looked back up, what she saw in his eyes frightened her. "Is that why you left? Is that why you wouldn't follow me here? Is that why you went back to Missouri?"

"No! Chase, no. Of course not. Is that what you think? No! I didn't even know for sure I *was* pregnant until after you'd already moved."

He glared at her. "Don't lie to me."

"I'm not lying, Chase. I swear." How could he think such a thing? *Oh, Lord . . . Please. Somehow help me help him.*

23

The traffic on the street below the apartment seemed louder and smellier than usual and Chase rolled off the futon to shut the window. It would be stuffy in the room again ten minutes from now and he'd just have to get up and open the window again. But what difference did it make? He'd seen every half hour on the clock since he'd gone to bed at midnight.

Landyn snored softly and curled against him the minute he got back in bed. How could she sleep so peacefully? He wasn't sure how things could possibly get more uncertain in their lives. Had he heard God wrong? Did he even recognize the voice of the God he'd claimed to follow for the last eight years?

Yet, even now, when he remembered that day, and Miles's offer of this studio, he couldn't shake the feeling that he'd been divinely led. Still, thousands of people followed false prophets and misguided leaders—to the death sometimes. Why did he think he was any less susceptible?

But he'd prayed. Miles had made the offer, and told him of the urgency of signing for the place before someone else claimed it. He'd informed Miles he needed a few minutes to think it over and discuss it with Landyn. His agent had looked skeptical, but he'd allowed Chase the time he needed. Now Chase wondered if maybe he'd been rushing God. Maybe he should have given Him more time.

And despite her accusations, he had tried to consult Landyn. But she had been at work, in a meeting. And besides, he'd thought she would be happy for him. That she'd want this opportunity for him. For both of them.

But he *had* prayed about it. And the peace that came over him then . . . A person couldn't just manufacture that of his own will. Could he? All he knew was that it felt right. It felt like an answer to his prayers. And even now, when he examined his motives, he felt no guilt. He only wanted to use the gifts God had given him, and to provide for Landyn—and now, for the child that was on the way. Whether he was ready or not.

He rolled over onto his back and stared at the

ceiling. The fan in the corner droned and squeaked, and the refrigerator kicked on, humming in a key that just might drive him up the wall.

He punched his pillow and flipped it over to the cool side.

I'm going to be a father.

He'd spoken the words aloud to his image in the bathroom mirror while getting ready for bed tonight. It had looked like a stranger staring back at him. He hadn't dared to face this day in his imagination. How could he face it in reality?

Landyn kicked off the sheets and rolled over on her belly. Her favorite way to sleep. How much longer would she be able to do that?

Looking back, he'd known something was different when they were making love. Her figure had . . . changed. Filled out in all the right places. But he'd never imagined the reason. And now it caused a cold sweat to break out on his forehead and palms. He crawled out of bed—again—and went into the bathroom. Splashing cold water on his face, he tried to pray.

It struck him that he might pray Landyn would lose the baby. But that thought struck true terror in his heart. What kind of a man prayed that kind of prayer? *I didn't mean that, Lord. Forgive me.* He would never forgive himself if anything happened to the baby now. Or, God forbid, if anything happened to Landyn.

He went back out to where she slept and watched her, wondering again how she could sleep so soundly, when their world was utter chaos. He went to the easel and turned on a floor lamp, illuminating the large watercolor he'd been working on. He'd been happy with it when he left the studio. Now it looked like something a kindergartner had slopped together. In a flash of frustration he ripped the heavy paper off the pad and wadded it up, making a noise like a thunderstorm.

"Chase?" Landyn sat up in the bed, rubbing her eyes. "What time is it?"

He looked at the clock. Four thirty in the morning. "Sorry I woke you. Go back to sleep." He reached to switch off the lamp.

"Are you okay?" She pulled the sheet around her shoulders.

"I'm—no. I'm not okay." His heart hammered in his chest. "I don't know what we're going to do. I don't know what I was thinking getting us into this mess."

"Chase, don't—"

"I'm going out for a while." He hurled the giant paper wad into the corner and crossed the room in two long strides. He scooped up his jeans and flannel shirt and dressed quickly, not looking at her. "I'll be back in a little while. Go back to sleep."

"Don't go, Chase. It's the middle of the night.

You're upset." She started to get out of bed.

"I'll be fine. Go back to sleep."

He turned his back on her, unlocked the door, and opened it. "Go back to sleep," he said again.

He didn't wait to see if she'd try to stop him.

It was after eight and Chase still wasn't back. He'd been gone almost four hours. Landyn peered out the window, but from this fourth floor vantage point, it was still too dark to make out faces. And every person on the street seemed to walk with the hunched over posture she imagined Chase would have.

He'd taken the news of her pregnancy even harder than she'd expected. And now he'd been gone too long—far longer than he'd implied. She couldn't imagine him doing anything . . . *stupid*. But then, he'd been pretty upset.

His phone was lying on the windowsill, so there was no reaching him that way. As far as she knew, he didn't have any friends in Bed-Stuy except his agent—who probably didn't even live in the neighborhood himself—and she doubted Chase would go there this early in the morning anyway.

She turned away from the window and went to make coffee. There was no decaf in the apartment, so the baby would just have to understand. She needed coffee. She got it brewing and went back to the window to watch for Chase. She'd give him until nine o'clock and then—

Then *what?* She knew better than to go looking for him. With their track record lately, the minute she got on the elevator to go down, he'd no doubt be coming up the other one. But she didn't think she could sit up here doing nothing much longer.

She eyed the refrigerator. She should probably eat something for the baby's sake. Especially if she was going to tank up on coffee. She found some bread that wasn't moldy and popped two slices in the toaster. Dry toast had been a staple in weeks past, but thankfully, the morning sickness had lessened over the past few days.

She really needed to make an appointment with a doctor to make sure everything was going as it should. But that could wait till they were back in Missouri and she could see Dr. Gregory in Langhorne. He'd delivered all of mom's babies except Corinne, and all of Corinne's babies. She wasn't sure how long her insurance was good beyond her quitting date. She'd barely gotten off her three-month probationary period to *start* her insurance. But they'd need to find a way to keep health insurance at least until the baby came. One more thing to worry about.

She buttered the toast and took her plate to the window to watch again. She picked up Chase's phone and tried to turn it on. Nothing. Apparently the battery was dead. No wonder he hadn't taken it with him. She found his charger in his backpack, which he hadn't taken either. Surely if he'd intended to be out this long he would have taken both.

She plugged in the phone and waited.

At nine o'clock, fighting images of Chase bleeding in some alley or lying dead under a subway train, she called home.

Her dad answered the phone. "Landyn! How's my girl? Everything good there?"

"Hey Dad, and . . . no. Things are not so good." Hearing his voice only encouraged her tears. "Chase went out early this morning and—he hasn't come back yet."

"Went out? Where to?"

"I don't know."

"He's not answering his phone?"

"He didn't take his phone. Or his backpack."

"And you don't know where he was going?"

"Just . . . for a walk. I—I told him about the baby, Dad. He didn't take it very well."

"Oh, honey . . . I'm sorry. Was he angry . . . at you? Or just—"

"Not at me, I don't think. He's just worried how we'll handle a baby on top of everything else. He doesn't think he'll be a good dad . . . since he never really had a dad."

"I can understand that. But he'll figure it out."

"That's what I told him, but I just think it's too much with everything else we have going on. I've never seen him like this, Dad. I'm worried."

"How long did you say he's been gone?"

She glanced at the clock. "He left here about four thirty." A splash on the windows made her look out again. "Great. It's starting to rain now and—"

"He's been gone since four thirty this morning?"

"Yes."

"That's a long time." Worry was thick in her dad's voice. "But . . . He probably just needs some time to think, honey. Work things out in his mind. Let's give it another half hour or so. If he's not back by then, give me a call and we'll figure out what's next. Mom and I will be praying. You know we will."

"I know. Thanks, Dad. I'm sorry about all this. I'm so sorry." Her voice broke. She didn't want to cry. Not on the phone. She hated when people cried on the phone with her. There was nothing you could do, nothing to say that would bring comfort.

But her dad seemed not to notice. Or pretended not to. "Nothing to be sorry about, honey. I'm glad you called so we can be praying. Just—" He hesitated. Then started again. "Listen, Landyn. Don't you go looking for him, okay? That won't help anything. And we need to be able to get hold of you."

"I have my cell phone. I'll take it if I have to go out."

"I think it would really be best if you just stay put. Give Chase some time . . . as much time as he needs. Besides, you don't want to be gone when he comes back. He'll need you there. I'm not trying to tell you what to do. Just . . . making a suggestion."

She put a smile in her voice. "Okay. I'll take it under advisement."

That made him laugh, which turned her smile genuine.

"Bye, Daddy."

"Bye, sweetheart. You keep me posted."

"I will."

She'd no sooner hung up when a quiet knock came on the door. Chase must have forgotten his keys. *Thank you, Lord, for a swift answer to prayer.*

She hurried to open the door, but took a swift step back when it wasn't Chase standing there, but a stranger in a trench coat and fedora.

He looked over her shoulder into the apartment. "Is Chase here?"

She pushed the door forward a few inches, ready to close and lock it if she needed to. "Um . . . He went out for a minute. He should be back any minute. May I tell him who's asking?"

"Sorry"—he extended a hand—"I'm Miles Roberts, Chase's rep."

"Oh! Of course. I'm Landyn . . . Chase's wife."

"Nice to meet you. I've heard a lot about you. All good, of course."

She wondered, but didn't argue. "Could I give Chase a message?"

"I'm really sorry to bother you so early on a Sunday morning, but I've been trying to call Chase, and he wasn't picking up."

"Oh. He . . . forgot to charge his phone. Sorry."

"I wanted to let him know I'll have a commission check for him tomorrow—probably won't get them cut till afternoon, but anytime after three or so it should be there."

"Oh . . . that's great. We could use the money." She wished she hadn't said that, but then, an art rep was no doubt accustomed to that kind of response—the whole starving artist thing . . .

"That's what Chase said." Miles smiled. A genuine smile that helped dispel her first impression of him as a smarmy con man. "I may be able to get another one for him by the end of the week, too. Or early the following week. He said you guys might be making another trip back to Missouri?"

"He said that?" She was surprised Chase had told his art rep that, knowing how strongly Miles felt about Chase living in Bed-Stuy. Even Manhattan hadn't been close enough for the rep, to hear Chase tell it. "We may go back for a while—a few weeks," she added quickly, then worried she'd said too much. She didn't know what Chase had told Miles Roberts.

He frowned. "Well, don't stay away too long. That husband of yours is on a roll."

"What do you mean?"

"He's got a lot of talent, and he's doing very well with it."

"That's . . . great. That's great," she said again, trying to pump conviction into her voice. She didn't know whether to take the art rep seriously or if he was just giving her a hard sell, trying to use her to keep Chase in New York. Chase had sure never made it sound like he was doing so well.

"In fact, we're not far from being able to raise the prices on his work. He's got a bright future if things keep going the way they are."

"Does . . . Chase know that?"

Roberts looked puzzled. "That he has a bright future?"

"No . . . I mean, does he know you're going to be able to raise the prices on his paintings?"

"I'm sure I've mentioned it. Maybe he didn't want to say anything until we knew for sure. But after his last show in the gallery here, I'm pretty confident."

"Well, that's good news. I'll tell Chase to give you a call. I appreciate you stopping by." She felt like she should invite him in and ask him to wait, but she had no clue when Chase would be home. For a minute, she was tempted to tell Miles that Chase was "missing." But she didn't want him to think her husband was irresponsible or in trouble of some kind. Especially after he'd sung Chase's praises.

The agent tipped his hat to her. "Nice to meet you, Landyn. I'm sure I'll be seeing you around."

She gave a noncommittal nod and closed the door after him.

Was Miles Roberts on the up and up about how well Chase was doing? Why hadn't Chase said anything? Had he been lying to her about how broke they were? And if he hadn't, then where was all the money he was supposedly making?

24

Landyn literally had her hand on the phone to call the police when she heard keys in the lock.

She hit End on her phone and went to the door, half afraid it wouldn't be Chase there. Half afraid it would.

The door creaked open and he stepped inside, looking five shades of sheepish.

"Where have you been? I've been worried sick, Chase!" She didn't dare let herself go to him, for fear she'd pummel him.

"I'm sorry. I didn't mean to worry you." He shrugged out of his jacket and hung it on a hook by the door.

"You didn't just worry me. You scared me to death. I thought you were dead, Chase."

He walked toward her, and she saw that he looked like death warmed over. His hair was matted to his scalp as if he'd just run a marathon, and his complexion was sallow around dull eyes. She wondered for a minute if he'd been drinking—or worse.

But when he spoke again, his voice was clear, his words even. "I'm sorry," he said again. "I . . . lost track of time." He regarded her as if to determine whether it was safe to get within arm's reach of her.

She took a step back so he wouldn't be tempted. "You lost track of time? Are you kidding me? You've been gone for six hours and you expect me to believe you just lost track of time?"

"I had—a lot of things to work through. I was just walking. And sitting in the park. I really am sorry." He touched her arm, still tentative.

She didn't pull away, but she didn't reciprocate either.

"Landyn, can we talk for a little bit? Please?"

"I think we'd better talk. Miles was here." She studied his expression, watching for some sort of clue in his face.

"Miles, my rep?"

She nodded. "He said he'll have a check for you any time after three tomorrow."

"Really? That's great."

"He said you're really doing well with the gallery. That he'll probably be able to raise your prices soon."

"He told you that?"

"He did."

He grunted. "I'll believe it when I see it."

"He said you have a lot of talent."

Chase only shrugged.

"Babe, has he told *you* this? Why didn't you tell me all that?"

"Would it have made any difference?"

"Well, sure it would!"

His eyes narrowed. "So you believe in me when someone else says I'm worth trusting? Is that it?" His tone grew taut. "I don't want you to believe in me because someone else says I'm worth believing in. Worth trusting. I want you to trust me because . . . because you believe I'm trustworthy."

"Chase, I do believe in you."

He shook his head. "No. You don't. You treat me like I can't be trusted with anything breakable." He pierced her with his eyes. "Don't think I don't know that I married out of my league. But I'm trying here, Landyn. Can you see that?"

"That's ridiculous, Chase. I don't know what 'league' you're talking about, but please don't ever say that again. And I do believe in you."

"If you believed in me, you wouldn't have questioned my judgment about taking this apartment. About trying to make it with my art. You would have supported me. If you believed in me—"

"That's not true. And what does that even mean—believe in you?"

"I made a decision—granted, a major decision—but I made it because I felt like God was leading me to do so. I didn't make it lightly. I prayed about it. I truly did, Landyn. I asked Miles to excuse me, and after I couldn't get hold of you, I prayed. I could show you the exact awning I stood under outside of Miles's building. I asked God to stop me if I was making a mistake. I prayed, Landyn. Hard."

"You never told me that." She thought it might have made a difference. But there was too much water under that bridge now.

"I did tell you, Landyn. You just didn't want to hear it. But it was a once-in-a-lifetime opportunity. And I had to make a snap judgment. You never believed I heard from God. And maybe you're right. Maybe I just made it all up. You have a different idea of what 'success' is. You think it's all about money and being 'someone' but it's more than that, Landyn. Don't you think God wants us to do what we enjoy? What He's gifted us to do?"

"Sure, babe . . . Sure He does. But sometimes if you can't do what you enjoy, you just have to suck it up and learn to enjoy what you do."

"Please . . . Let's don't hash this all out again."

She held up a hand. "I know. We might have to . . . agree to disagree on this one. I don't know what else to say. It all happened too fast, and *I* didn't have a chance to even pray about it before it was done. That still doesn't seem fair. But it's done now, Chase. We can't go back and undo it, so can we just—go on from here?"

"I don't know . . . *Can* we? Are you willing? To go on with me?" He looked down, scuffing his toe on the dingy carpet.

"I—"

"And not just because you're pregnant and you have no choice."

She eyed him through a thicket of bewilderment. "Is that what you think? That I only came back to you because I'm pregnant?"

He shrugged. "What am I supposed to think?"

She couldn't help it—she laughed. And went to sit on the futon beside where he stood. "Oh, babe. That's why I didn't tell you about the baby. I didn't want you coming back to me because you felt obligated."

"I never left you, Landyn. Don't you get that? You never lost me."

"I know." A lump clogged her throat. "I realize that now. I'm so sorry, babe."

"Come here . . ." He pulled her up beside him.

She went willingly, resting her head on his shoulder, pressing her fingertips on the upper point of the knotted cross inked on his collarbone like a touchstone, remembering what that cross meant for Chase. Praying that God would remind him again. And at the same time, remind her.

After a few minutes, she looked up at him,

tears in her eyes. "Can we agree that we're in this together? Not just because of the baby, but because—we promised each other."

"I'm willing if you are."

She nodded against his chest. "We have a lot of things to figure out."

"Yes, we do."

"This is not what we agreed on, Chase." Miles paced the length of his office wringing his hands. "I hope you know what you're throwing away."

Chase's chest constricted, and he sat up straighter on the chair in front of Miles's tidy desk. It crossed his mind that this might be what a heart attack felt like. He and Landyn had talked late into the night last night and finally decided they would go back to Missouri to regroup. Stay with CeeCee while they tried to sell one of the cars, get Landyn to the doctor, smooth things over with her dad. Beyond that, they didn't know what the future held, but it seemed best to get away from the city for a while.

But Miles was not a happy camper.

"Are you telling me you won't represent me if I leave New York?" Chase braced for his agent's answer.

"I didn't say that." Miles furrowed his forehead. "But you're not going to sell as well remotely. You can bank on that."

"Or not," Chase said wryly.

Miles didn't seem to see the humor. "You're leaving at exactly the wrong time. We just had some momentum going." He turned and paced the other way. "This is crazy. And now you want to give the apartment up too? I went to bat for you on that, man. I had people standing in line for that place. I gave you the first crack at it because I saw promise in you."

"I know you did, Miles. And—I appreciate it. I do. Maybe we can find a way to keep the studio. It'd be good to have a place to stay whenever I come back. Someplace I could work a little bit, too." Purely wishful thinking. He doubted he could afford airfare to come back to New York once, let alone the once a month Miles had talked about. Never mind hotel and food and cab fare.

But the notion seemed to calm Miles down a little. He stopped pacing and came around to stand behind his swivel chair, resting his forearms on its high back. "I'll see if I can move a few more pieces in the next week or two. Give you a little extra rent money."

"That'd be great." Maybe they could keep the studio after all. The thought buoyed him.

"At least don't sublet the place until after the first of the year. Unless you can find someone short-term. That'll give us some time to see if your stuff is going to keep trending."

So he was trending now? "Then, you'll give me a chance to prove I can do it? From Missouri? At least a few weeks? I think it would be good for my wife to spend Christmas with her family." *Maybe New Year's, too.* But he didn't tell Miles that. He hadn't mentioned the coming baby either. Mostly because he didn't trust his voice not to betray his emotions on that subject.

Miles shook his head and all but rolled his eyes. "We'll give it a go."

Chase stood and extended a hand. "Thank you, Miles. You don't know what that means."

The art rep waved him off. "Don't thank me yet. And don't hear promises I'm not making, Chase. We'll see how it goes. That's all. But"—he looked at the floor—"I know you're a praying man. Don't be surprised if I say a few prayers myself about where you end up. And about how well things go in Missouri." He raised an eyebrow. "Or not."

That made Chase laugh. Then sober. He didn't remember ever mentioning to Miles that he prayed. But he was glad the fact had apparently come through in their dealings. He hated disappointing his agent, he really did. And he was glad Landyn hadn't been here for this meeting. No doubt she would have found it far more discouraging than he did—and that was plenty. Still, Missouri seemed like a better place to try to stitch things back together with Landyn.

He felt for the commission check in his pocket, then shook Miles's hand. "I'll be in touch."

"And you know where to find me." Miles

gripped his hand. "Best of luck to you. Don't forget to drop those inks off before you leave town."

Chase tapped his phone. "On my to-do list. And—thank you, Miles. I mean it."

25

"You're sure we got everything?" Chase stood between their two vehicles, both packed almost to the ceilings, with only a sliver of space cleared so they could see out the back windshields.

He'd turned in the keys to the studio to Ray last night—interrupting the super's family Thanksgiving feast—so he and Landyn could get on the road before the sun came up. They were leaving behind only what furniture they couldn't fit in the cars.

Ray had made an exception to the sublet policy after Chase told him Landyn was pregnant, and at the last minute, Miles had rustled up someone—another client—to sublease the place for a month, which helped immensely. And gave them some time to decide whether they could afford to keep the studio—or whether they'd even need it.

When Chase had told the super their news about the baby, Ray had clapped him on the back and beamed. "That's great news, my friend. The best!" The super's reaction gave Chase a glimmer of hope, but he tried not to think too much about what his life would look like a few short months from now. Less than five months if Landyn's math was right. Her pregnancy was half over. Maybe it was a good thing he hadn't had to carry this burden for a full nine months.

"Chase, let's go." Landyn's voice broke his focus. "You're the one who wanted to be on the road at this ungodly hour. If we forgot something, it won't be the end of the world."

He rolled his eyes at her. "You say that, but if it's your blow dryer or your makeup we forgot, I'll hear about it all the way to the Missouri border."

He hated that they were traveling in separate cars. Time together in the car for the long drive home would have been a gift. But they'd given up trying to sell his car in New York. He shot up a prayer that they could sell it quickly in Missouri. They needed the cash.

Chase had a feeling they might not be coming back to New York as soon as either of them imagined. And he fleetingly wondered if he should bid the city farewell forever. But he was grateful—he was taking the most important thing with him. He bent to kiss her through the open driver's side window. "Okay. You ready, baby?"

"Hey, I'm an old pro at this, remember? But next time we make this trip, *you* are driving, you hear? The whole way."

"You have your phone on for sure?"

She patted her purse in the passenger seat beside her. "On and fully charged."

"Okay. Let's do this." His breath came in puffs of steam in the chill, early morning air.

She gripped the steering wheel at ten and two, and revved the engine of her Honda. He gave a little salute, kissed her again, and went to get in his car.

Landyn seemed almost excited about the trip, and he had to admit, he was too. Except for the fear that loomed over him because of the baby, these days together in Brooklyn had been good ones. Days that had reminded them both, he thought, of why they'd gotten married in the first place. He'd said as much to Landyn and she feigned a disgusted look. "It's always all about the bedroom, isn't it?"

He smiled, remembering. Well, that hadn't hurt matters, he had to admit. But it was so much more than that. For the first time he felt like he could finally talk to her and that she *heard* what he said. The secrets they'd kept from each other had put up walls between them. Getting them out in the open, painful as it was, had worked a small miracle.

There were still hard decisions to be made. And their financial situation was precarious at best. He was terrified his sales at the gallery would drop off once he left the city. Out of sight, out of mind, and all that. But as unhappy as Miles was about his decision, the agent seemed resigned to helping Chase make it work long-distance.

Landyn pulled onto the street and led the way out of the borough and across the bridge. They'd agreed they wouldn't worry too much about trying to stay together until they got on the Interstate outside the city. Even at five a.m., traffic was too crazy going out of the city, and they were more likely to have a wreck trying to keep up with the same lights and turns. Besides, they had their cell phones to stay in touch.

They managed to not get separated all the way through the Holland Tunnel and back onto I-78 headed west. Chase thought it was a good omen.

He watched Landyn's Honda in front of him and whispered a prayer for her safety. Unbidden, on its heels came a prayer for their child.

Seeing the lights of the city recede behind them he felt a little like he had the first time he'd jumped off the high dive at the Langhorne Municipal Swimming Pool—brave, daring, exhilarated . . . And scared out of his mind.

Audrey dusted powdered sugar over the scones, then checked the sausage-and-egg casserole in the oven. After making Thanksgiving dinner for fourteen yesterday—including Bree's parents— then getting the rooms ready for guests to check in that evening, baking was the last thing she was in the mood to do. Especially for guests who wanted breakfast at seven a.m.

But hey, at least they *had* guests. And the kitchen was clean. Her daughters, and Bree and her mother, had helped her clean up after their turkey dinner yesterday. Never mind that while they were cleaning up, the little girls were turning the family room upside down—right under the noses of the menfolk, who apparently could not watch football and babysit at the same time.

She let out a sigh. Next year, they would *not* book the inn on Thanksgiving weekend at all. She didn't care how much money they lost. She wondered what their family would look like next year. Landyn and Chase would have a baby. But would they be here or would they be living in New York? It had been hard not to have them here for the holiday. Since Tim's death, it seemed all the more important to have the whole family around the table for holidays.

She heard someone rolling luggage across the hardwood floors in the foyer. Wiping her hands, she went to greet them. "Them" turned out to be one man. One very noisy man.

"Good morning. Did you sleep well?"

"Slept okay, I guess," the forty-something, burly man said. "That is, once the guy in the next room quit snoring."

"Oh, dear. I'm so sorry," she said in a stage whisper. She didn't tell him there hadn't been anyone staying in the room next door to him last night. She had a feeling it was Grant's snoring the guy had heard—in the room above. She hadn't slept so hot herself. "Well, breakfast will be ready in a few minutes. Do you need help with your luggage, Mr. Larmont?"

"Nah. I got it." Larmont shouldered the screen door and dragged another suitcase across the threshold and through the door. Did people not have any concept of being careful of shiny wood floors and expensive doors? She was beginning to wonder.

The woman, Becky, who'd checked in with Mr. Larmont—his wife, she assumed, though they'd adopted an "ask no questions" policy—trotted down the stairs.

"Oh, hey," Becky said when she spotted Audrey. "Did you see where Mike went?"

Audrey pasted on her hostess smile. "He just took a bag out to the car."

The woman spit out a curse. "I told him I wasn't finished with my bag." Brushing past Audrey, she stood at the screen door and hollered across the lawn. "Mike! Bring my bag back in here right now!"

Becky ran toward the car just as Grant came in from the back porch.

He shot Audrey a questioning look as their irate guest swept past him. "I hope nobody was trying to sleep in this morn—"

An ear-splitting crash sounded from the front yard.

Grant and Audrey exchanged wide-eyed glances and raced each other to the front door.

Audrey gasped. "Grant! That guy just backed over the fence!"

Grant shot out the door and down the steps.

A nauseous feeling settled in the pit of Audrey's stomach. *There went another thousand dollars. Or more.* This place—her dream—was turning into a money pit. The thought had barely formed when she heard Grant's frantic shouts—and then the sickening crunch of tires on wood.

The fence had somehow lodged in the under-carriage of the car and yet the man kept gunning the engine, grinding fence, lawn, and car to a pulp with every rev of the engine.

Grant bounded off the porch and ran around to the driver's side. He yanked the car door open. "Are you okay?"

Their guest hopped out like his seat was on fire. "Why didn't you tell me there was a fence back there? Just look at my car!"

"Just look at my fence," Grant yelled back.

"You ought to have a sign or something posted."

"And you ought to check your rearview mirror before you back up."

As if things couldn't get worse, Huckleberry came dashing around the side of the house, muddy from the creek. Audrey knew that look in his eyes. He was going to defend his master against the evil stranger. "Huck!" she yelled.

Too late. The Lab charged toward Mike, barking like he'd treed a squirrel.

The man scrambled onto the hood of his car. "Call off your dog!"

"Huck!" Grant took up the call and lunged for Huckleberry. He managed to get a grasp on his collar and calm him down. The man on top of the car hood was another matter.

Their guest ranted for a full five minutes, alternately informing Grant that he had a lawyer friend they'd be hearing from—and blaming his wife for the fact that he didn't see the six-foot tall, bright red fence on which he'd impaled his vehicle.

To Grant's credit, not one curse word left his mouth. But to Audrey's chagrin, the civil words that did leave her husband's mouth were delivered with such velocity they may as well have been curse words. Not that the rude guest didn't deserve them, but this would not end well.

"Lord, don't let them kill each other," Audrey whispered. "Please help Grant control his temper."

Ten minutes later, after exchanging insurance information, the man assured Grant he'd be hearing from an attorney. The man paid their bill under protest—and with a refund for the breakfast they didn't eat—and, with his testy wife in tow, roared down the driveway.

Audrey stood behind her husband, watching as the car disappeared down the drive in a whirlwind of dust. The chill November breeze whisked across the porch, sending leaves whirling as she followed Grant into the house.

Red-faced and breathless, he paced the length of the kitchen. "This wouldn't be a half bad business if it wasn't for people like that." He pointed out the window where the mangled fence rested. "Tell me, how could you miss a fence like that? Big as life and he backs right into it. And then blames the fence? The gall of some people—"

"Grant. Just calm down." She didn't dare suggest Grant check his blood pressure right now, but if she were a betting woman . . . He was going to put himself in an early grave if he didn't settle down. "It could have been worse."

"I don't see how."

"Well, for one it could have been another guest he ran over."

"Too bad somebody didn't run over him. The world would be a better place—"

"Grant! You don't mean that." She put a hand on his arm, trying to stop his pacing. "Whatever happened to 'the customer is always right'? I thought that was going to be our business motto."

"Like blazes it is."

"Besides, you know what they say: 'When you're right, you can afford to keep your temper; when you're wrong, you can't afford not to.' "

"Well, I *was* right," he huffed.

"So you didn't need to lose your temper."

"And what I can't afford is a new fence," he shot back.

"Okay, okay . . . Please calm down. I suppose our insurance will cover it."

"Oh, they'll cover it all right. Happily. And then they'll happily raise our rates through the roof, which by then will probably need repairing because some guest decided to go shingle-climbing."

Audrey couldn't suppress the giggle that came at the image.

But Grant didn't seem to share her humor. "I doubt it would even pay to file a claim after figuring the deductible." He picked up a soggy dishtowel and threw it back down again. "This place is going to nickel and dime us to death."

"It will be okay, babe."

Grant brushed her off, then lifted his head and sniffed. He looked around the room. "Do you smell that? Something's burning."

"My casserole!" She reached the oven in two strides and opened the door. Thick smoke billowed out, and a second later the smoke alarm in the entryway began its high-pitched blare.

Audrey held a hand over her mouth, coughing.

"Shut the door!" Grant took her by the shoulders and moved her aside, slamming the oven door shut, then punching the controls.

"Everything all right down here?" The bath-robed woman from the second floor suite—Ms. Jennings, if memory served—looked down at them from the staircase landing.

Audrey pasted the smile back on and went to the bottom of the stairway. "So sorry. We had a little issue with the oven. Everything's fine, but breakfast might be a little late this morning."

The woman didn't reply but, apparently satisfied that everything was under control, padded back to her room.

"Grant," she hissed. "I have to get that casserole out of there. What am I going to serve for breakfast?"

"Well, it's not going to be that hunk of charcoal."

Teeth gritted, she scoured the fridge for the makings of a second breakfast. There were no guests scheduled for the next two nights so she hadn't stocked up on groceries.

She carried a carton of eggs to the counter while Grant gingerly set the blackened casserole dish in the deep apron sink on the island. Before she could stop him, he turned the water on.

"Grant!"

Cra-ack! The casserole broke like a hunk of ice, a wide fissure dividing it into two pieces. Steam hissed upward.

Grant gave her an "oops" look. "Well,"—he

shrugged—"you weren't going to salvage that anyway, right?"

He had a point. There went another twenty bucks down the drain. Literally.

The phone rang.

"Oh, good grief!" Audrey threw up her hands. "What now?"

"Can you get that?" Grant asked, doing his best to look busy. The stinker.

She went to the hall table and picked up the cordless.

Grant mumbled something she couldn't hear.

"Hello." She hadn't meant to sound so curt.

A missed beat. "Whoa. Did somebody wake up grumpy?"

"Landyn!" Audrey laughed. "Sorry. We've had a beyond-crazy morning. Already. Everything's under control though. I think. What's up?" The whole family had Skyped with Chase and Landyn after dinner yesterday, so she hadn't expected to hear from her so soon.

"I just wanted to let you know we're on our way." She sounded happy and excited.

"Already? I thought you guys weren't leaving until this weekend."

"We got everything taken care of, so we decided to beat the weekend traffic. We're in Pennsylvania already."

"Wow . . ." They'd be here tomorrow. "You're making good time."

"We left at five."

"Oh. Did you sell the car?" *Please, Lord, they need that money so badly.*

Landyn sighed. "No. We decided since all the paperwork is in Missouri it would just be easier to sell it there."

"Where are you staying tonight?"

Silence on Landyn's end.

Audrey gripped the phone. "Please don't tell me you guys are going to drive straight through."

"We'll stop if we get tired, Mom. I promise."

"Stop where?"

"I'm—not sure."

"And don't say a Walmart parking lot."

"Okay, I won't say that."

"Very funny."

"Well, we can't exactly afford a hotel, Mom. But we'll be fine."

"I know." Guilt pierced her, and it was all she could do not to offer to pay for the hotel. But they simply did not have the money to spare. Especially after this morning's fiasco. And as much as she hated the kids being on the road for sixteen hours —probably longer since they were driving two cars—they were adults, after all. They could . . . *should* make these kinds of decisions for them-selves.

But Grant would be none too happy about the situation, thinking they were foolish trying to drive two vehicles home from New York.

And now she had to go tell him that the kids were arriving a couple of days early besides. And Landyn's old room needed to be cleaned and ready by tonight. Grant's mother's offer for the kids to stay with her still stood, but Audrey selfishly wanted the kids to themselves for a night or two. Actually, in retrospect, she and Grant were both having second thoughts about the kids living with Cecelia. Her house was tiny, there was no Internet connection, and as much as they all loved CeeCee, she tended to be rather— high maintenance.

Audrey had wasted her time worrying about the kids taking up a room at the inn that could be earning income. It was a moot point given that, until last night, they hadn't filled all the rooms in the inn since—well, never. At least not with *paying* guests. Yes, they had future reservations— the inn was booked solid over the winter holidays, including Valentine's Day, and they already had May filled with graduation guests— and a waiting list to boot. But right now, they were squeaking by. And just barely. She pushed the thought aside. For now, she would try to see it as a blessing that they had a room to offer Chase and Landyn.

She went to find Grant. This early arrival would be fun news to deliver. Her sweet husband's blood pressure was getting a whale of a workout this week.

26

Landyn felt like Sacagawea leading the way west across the country. She saw familiar landmarks along Interstate 78 from her previous trips and called Chase on her cell several times along the way to point out things she wanted to be sure he saw.

"Landyn, you're going to have an accident," he'd scolded on her third call. "Talking on the phone and driving is a bad idea. Cut it out. Besides, I have eyes. I think I can see the sights for myself."

"I'm being totally safe. Besides, it's legal to use cell phones on the road in Pennsylvania."

"Are you sure about that?"

"Positive. No texting, but phone calls are fine." She didn't tell him she knew because she'd Googled it on her phone. Hands-free though . . . Well, mostly.

"Listen, I'm asking you not to do it. And I'm hanging up now."

She laughed and disconnected the call. That man could be so bossy at times.

They drove through for coffee around eight, just outside of Harrisburg. Pennsylvania had experienced a late autumn, and despite the morning's near freezing temps, the trees still bore some of their glory.

They stood between their two cars in the convenience store parking lot, fresh lattes warming their hands. Chase put a warm palm on her cheek. "You sure you're awake?"

"Wide awake. You?"

"I'm good. You let me know if you get sleepy and we'll stop, okay?"

She nodded and lifted her coffee in a toast. "This will keep me alert."

"Okay. Ready to hit the road again? Only thirteen more hours."

"Not funny."

"Just keepin' it real." He tweaked her nose and leaned in for a kiss. "You feeling okay?"

She gave him a puzzled look.

He touched his fingertips to her belly. "The baby, I mean."

She grinned. "The baby feels fine." But it moved her that he'd touched her that way. Maybe he would come around after all.

Chase rubbed his eyes and rolled the window down, trying to stay alert. He'd just called Landyn, and she sounded perky and wide awake. They'd made it through Pittsburgh and were about an hour from Columbus, Ohio, where they planned to stop and get something to eat—and maybe grab a short nap in a parking lot. That would give them a shot in the arm and hopefully get them the rest of the way home.

The radio station he'd been listening to faded to static and he tried to tune in another one, but when his search produced nothing but talk radio and classical music, he turned off the radio and let his thoughts hold sway. In the days since Landyn had told him she was expecting their baby, he'd started deflecting the arrows of fear by counting his blessings.

The fact that yesterday had been Thanksgiving Day wasn't lost on him. "Lord, thank you for bringing Landyn and me this far. I don't know what you have in store for us, but I know it will be good, and I'm grateful." He prayed aloud, his own voice echoing back to him in the confines of the car.

He listed, one by one, the things he'd seen God accomplish in their lives over the past month. "Thank you for letting me be an artist for however long you'll allow it. Help me not hold on to my plans too tight but to be willing to hear your voice—and then obey."

Guilt had nagged him ever since that night he told Landyn he didn't think God provided very well for them. He'd asked forgiveness—of God. But he knew he needed to apologize to Landyn too. He'd failed to recognize all the Lord had done to carry them through, and he'd thrown God's goodness to him and Landyn back in His face. He felt sick about it, but he couldn't exactly take it back.

He remembered an illustration Pastor Simmons had used in youth group one night—having a couple of the kids squeeze all the toothpaste out of a tube onto a paper plate. And then, when the tube was empty, asking them to put it back in the tube.

The message of that illustration had made an impression on him then. But he thought he understood the point better now than he ever had. It was a lot easier to never make a mistake in the first place than to try to mend the damage after the fact. He had so many regrets in his short life. But he'd told God more than once since he and Landyn were back together that he intended to adopt a new habit, one of living a life without regrets. It was easier said than done. He'd discovered that quickly. But still, he'd made it a goal.

On the road in front of him Landyn changed lanes to pass a pickup hauling a trailer. A fast approaching car wouldn't let him over, but he kept an eye on the Honda and passed as soon as he could.

Landyn was driving almost ten miles over the speed limit according to his speedometer. He'd tell her to slow down a little next time they pulled over. He didn't mind going five miles over, but the last thing they needed was a speeding ticket.

She was probably trying to make up for lost time for all the bathroom stops they'd made. Man, it was no joke, that thing about pregnant women having to go all the time. They'd been on the road ten hours and had already made four bathroom stops besides the gas and lunch stop. Those extra stops had probably cost them an hour or more. He hoped she could at least make it to Cincinnati without having to stop again.

As much as he was trying not to worry about it, Landyn's pregnancy was at the forefront of his thoughts. Because it terrified him to think about being a dad, yes. And because he had no idea how they were going to afford the doctor bills and baby expenses. But for another reason, too.

Sometime in the middle of one of his "dark nights of the soul," he'd done some quick math and been disturbed to realize that Landyn had already been pregnant the day he'd stood on that Brooklyn street praying for God's direction. It made no sense that God would have led him to a tiny Brooklyn studio when He already knew there was a baby on the way. Why would God have led him to do something that, now that Chase knew their true circumstances, seemed utterly foolish?

How could he continue to hold onto his belief that he had sincerely been seeking God's guidance, that God had answered, and he had followed in obedience?

Either he had been mistaken—sincerely mistaken, but mistaken nonetheless—or God had misguided him. He was pretty sure God didn't work that way, but it bothered him that he'd been so far off base. How could he ever trust his own instincts—that he was truly following God's will—when he couldn't trust himself to hear God's voice correctly?

But *God* knew. At least that's what he'd been taught. That God was omniscient. That He knew everything before it happened. Would a loving God who cared about him, cared about Landyn, cared about their baby, let Chase make the decision he'd made? He'd even prayed that God would *stop* him if it was the wrong decision.

God, did I hear you wrong? I need to know. Because I can't ever make a mistake like that again. I can't ever risk losing her again.

His troubled mind tried to pray. And faltered. Yet, somewhere in the depths of his heart, there was a thin thread of peace. He clung to it for all he was worth.

At least his wandering thoughts had kept him awake.

He saw a sign ahead for the Columbus exit and flashed his headlights at Landyn, their signal to turn off. He wished she was in the car with him so he could hash out all these questions and doubts with her. And so he could look in her eyes and find assurance that she loved him even when he fumbled blindly to live as he should. To believe as he should.

But maybe it was better that he wrestle it out with God first. Sometimes it seemed to him that the Almighty was easier to reckon with than his wife.

27

"You still awake?" Landyn asked Chase as they stretched in the parking lot at a Taco Bell in Buckeye Lake, Ohio, outside of Columbus.

"I was getting pretty sleepy there toward the end." He stretched his arms over his head and twisted his torso like an athlete getting ready for a race.

They still had a full day's drive ahead of them—eight hours—but Landyn felt surprisingly alert. She was hungry though, and ready for a break.

"This okay?" Chase angled his head toward the restaurant.

"Sure. About anything sounds good right now. We should have brought more snacks."

They went inside and ordered, then took their food to a corner booth.

"Could you find any decent radio stations?" she asked him over a mouthful of taco.

He shook his head. "I gave up and quit looking a couple hours ago."

"So what are you listening to?"

He shrugged. "Nothing."

"Don't you have an audio book or something on your phone?"

"I do, but I'm good."

"Aren't you going bonkers without something to listen to?"

"No. I'm fine." He shrugged again, and she thought he looked a little sheepish.

She studied him with a furrowed brow. "What?"

"I've been having a good conversation."

"Conversation?"

He grinned and pointed up.

"With the light fixtures at Taco Bell?"

"No silly. With God."

"Really?" That wasn't at all what she'd expected to hear.

"So how is He? God?"

Chase looked instantly worried. "You not on speaking terms or something?"

She laughed. "No, we are. I just meant, how are you and He getting along?"

"Better, I think. He's pretty much got things figured out. I, on the other hand, am a little slow on the uptake."

A swell of love for her husband filled Landyn up, and she leaned across the table and put her hand over his. "Hey, baby, I know the feeling. I'm glad . . . you're talking. You and Him."

"I'm getting things untangled. One mile at a time."

She squeezed his hand. "Well, shoot, by the time we get back to Cape you ought to be tangle-free."

That earned her the smile she loved. "Might take a trip to California and back for that." He took a swig of his iced tea and started wadding up empty food wrappers and gathering things onto the plastic tray. "You about ready to go?"

"Yeah. Let me use the restroom one more time."

He rolled his eyes. "Big surprise."

In the parking lot Landyn buckled her seatbelt while Chase waited. She looked up at him. "I'm fine. You can go. And don't worry too much if we get separated. After making this trip three times in the last month everything is familiar now."

With one hand still on top of her car, he shaded his eyes and looked up at the graying skies. "I'd feel better if we stayed together. I don't trust your car, and it looks like it could rain."

"Okay. Let's stick close then." She was not a fan of driving in the rain.

"We will. I don't think it's cold enough that the roads will be icy or anything. Just watch the white line and stay to the left of it."

"Well, there's some great driving advice. Thanks, Professor."

Laughing, he kissed her and dug into his pocket until he produced his car keys. "See you in . . . what? About twenty minutes?"

"Twenty minutes?"

"Bathroom break."

"Ha ha. Very funny." But probably not far from the truth given the huge glass of iced tea she'd drunk in Taco Bell.

"Be safe, baby." He kissed her again.

"I will."

Eight hours, nine at the most, and they would start the next chapter of this crazy life. And only God knew what those pages would look like. But she was beginning to like the story quite a bit. She was beginning to think it just might have a happy ending.

The next hour went quickly as traffic thinned out and they ate up the highway. Landyn snacked on red licorice and listened to a rather boring novel on her iPod. At least it helped pass the time. Late in the afternoon on a particularly lonely stretch of the four-lane Interstate, when the hours left in the trip started to get to her, Chase started an impromptu leap-frog game, waving and grinning as his old Toyota passed her, then making a defeated face when he let her pass him in the Honda. They took turns passing each other for the next forty miles, and Landyn marveled that such a simple thing could lift her spirits so.

As they got closer to Cincinnati, traffic picked up a little, and Chase let her back in the lead. "So if you have car trouble I can help you," he'd said before they started out this morning. She'd reminded him that he was the one driving the clunker.

Already, New York felt like another lifetime. In her heart, she suspected they'd be back. But as much as she'd once been infatuated with the city, there was a part of her that was ready to put New

York—and the not-so-happy memories it now held—behind her. Still, the time there this week had been good, a time of healing. A time of growing up for both of them.

The gray clouds had followed them since Pittsburgh, but they proved a blessing when the sun dropped in the sky, keeping it from being constantly in their eyes as they headed west. They made it through Cincinnati before sunset and stopped to gas up outside of town.

Thirty minutes later, it began to sprinkle. That turned into a nice shower, but a few miles farther, it looked more like a downpour.

Landyn switched on her headlights and turned her wipers on high—for all the good it did. Rain veiled the car in sheets, and Landyn leaned over the steering wheel trying—without much success —to see that white line Chase had lectured her about. Every few minutes the jarring jackhammer sound of the rumble strips would scare her back onto the road. But after a passing semi deluged her car, she decided she'd rather risk the ditch than a head-on with a one of those monsters.

She turned on the radio and tried to tune in to a weather station. She finally got something she could hear over the static. The DJ had an edge to his voice. "Folks, we have a line of highly dangerous thunderstorms moving east, northeast across Carroll County."

Landyn sought in vain for a road sign that would

tell her where she was. She had no clue what county she was in, or even what state Carroll County was in.

"Again, a severe thunderstorm warning is in effect for much of the state. These storms could produce damaging winds, heavy rain, and large hail. If you are in the vicinity of these storms you need to move to shelter immediately." The DJ rattled off a list of towns and counties, none of which Landyn knew of.

Tiny beads of ice hit the windshield and piled up in the recess between the wipers. Every few seconds, a larger chunk of ice hit the hood with a *thunk*.

She checked her rearview mirror, trying to spot Chase's car, but all she could see were a few spots of hazy light in the deluge behind her. Thank goodness there wasn't much traffic on the road right now.

They needed to find someplace to get under cover. She could barely make out the taillights of the cars in front of her, let alone the terrain surrounding the highway.

Without taking her eyes off the road, she groped for her phone in the passenger seat but before she could call Chase, her phone was ringing his tone.

"Hey? You okay up there?" He sounded as worried as she felt.

"I can't see a thing, Chase!"

"I know. We need to get out of this. Pull over

under the next overpass you come to. But be careful. Don't slam into another car. Everybody's going to be trying to get over and—" He cut out.

She hit End and tucked the phone under her leg on the seat.

A few seconds later, a shadow passed above her, but by the time she realized it was an overpass, it was too late.

She tapped the brakes, then worried that she'd get rear-ended by the car behind her.

Another mile and the hail pelting her car turned the size of marbles. Her phone rang again. Chase. She didn't dare take her eyes off the road, but she desperately needed to hear his reassuring voice. She held the phone up near the top of the steering wheel long enough to press Answer. "Chase?"

She heard his voice—heard him say her name—but he was cutting out every other word.

The hailstones grew larger. Some of them looked as big as golf balls, and the noise pounding her from every direction was deafening—like someone had set off a whole package of fire-crackers at once. "Chase, I can't hear you! I missed that last overpass, but I'm pulling over under the next one. The car is getting totally hammered. Can you hear me? Chase?"

The racket on the roof of the car was so loud she couldn't tell if he answered or not. And things were likely even noisier in his junker. At least the hail couldn't make his '79 Toyota worth less than it already was. But they couldn't afford to lose both their cars. She wondered what the deductible was on the Honda.

She shouted into the phone, not having a clue if Chase could hear her, since she could barely hear her own voice. "I'm pulling over the next chance I get."

She tucked the phone back under her leg and risked a quick glance in the rearview mirror. The headlights in the mirror seemed too close and she sped up slightly. Blinking, she tried to focus on the road, desperately hoping to see the shadow of another overpass ahead.

The hail came down harder—if that were even possible—and Landyn could see the dents each icy stone left on the hood of the car. Without warning, red and yellow taillights loomed immediately in front of her. She screamed and slammed on the brakes, clutched the steering wheel with both hands.

The lights disappeared as quickly as they'd come but suddenly the sensation of falling was strong. She held her breath, trying to get her bearings. The pounding hail continued, only now it sounded like it was coming on her left side. Her head felt heavy, as if she were hanging upside down. Stomach churning, she grabbed in vain for something to hold on to with her left hand. But her right hand went instinctively to her belly, cradling the baby—her and Chase's baby.

Oh, Lord, save us! Save my baby!

28

Chase frantically scanned the horizon, but all he could see was a wall of water and the hailstones that continued to batter his car. Landyn had sounded terrified on the phone. She hated driving in the rain, but this was beyond any rain he'd ever seen.

The rubber on his windshield wipers was almost threadbare, and they grated and screeched across the glass at their highest speed. But for all the racket they made, they couldn't seem to clear more than a thin swath for him to view out.

He could make out a string of red lights in the mist ahead. He slowed his car and the dark shadow of an overpass loomed above him. It took a minute before he realized the cars were piling up beneath it trying to get out of the storm.

He braked and pulled as close to the next car as he could, but he still felt the jolt of an occasional hailstone hitting the back end of his Toyota. He put an arm over the back of the passenger seat and maneuvered as close to the edge of the road as he could get without going off the shoulder. He turned on his hazard lights and prayed he didn't get rear-ended.

And he prayed for Landyn. And their baby. With no view and no sense of where they were he felt disoriented. His phone said five fourteen, but he couldn't remember how long ago they'd left the gas station at their last stop.

He dialed Landyn again but five rings and it went to voice mail. He tried to tell himself it was just the weather messing with reception. But he had a bad feeling.

They'd gained some daylight traveling west, but it would be pitch dark soon—although sunset couldn't make the sky any darker than it was right now.

The shoulder and median under the overpass filled up with vehicles. Drivers parked six abreast and at least as many deep, trying to get beneath the shelter of the bridge. Chase couldn't see more than a halo of light at the other end of the overpass, but with all the parked vehicles, the highway was already down to one lane. If they kept narrowing the road with this jam of cars, somebody was going to get hit for sure. He thought about getting out of the car and trying to direct traffic so he could get through to find Landyn, but when he saw the dent a stray golf-ball sized hailstone left in the hood of his car, he realized it could be suicide to get out of the car now.

He inched forward as the cars in front of him did the same, trying to make room for more vehicles under the overpass. All the while he dialed Landyn again and again, willing his eyes to find the only thing he cared about seeing right now—her Honda.

After the longest three minutes of his life, the hail began to let up in the reverse of how it had begun, thinning to marble-size, then ice pellets, until finally nothing but the incessant clatter of rain pelted the back half of his Toyota.

The driver of the car in front of him revved its engine and inched forward, tacitly urging the cars ahead of them to do the same. Finally people seemed to trust that they could leave their makeshift storm shelter. They filed out in a stream of uncertainty.

He tried Landyn again. Why wasn't she answering her phone? He had four bars, so they were in range of a cell tower. Going no faster than thirty-five or forty miles per hour, the little caravan drove through the rain. Chase kept one eye on the slow traffic in front of him while constantly panning the ditch for any sign of the Honda.

He followed the ragtag group of travelers under another overpass where they picked up the stragglers who'd apparently been too frightened to leave the temporary shelter of the bridge and buttresses.

No more than a mile past the second overpass the rain lifted a bit and visibility improved. Chase tried Landyn's phone every couple of minutes, with the same result.

Another mile and he saw a knot of vehicles and flashing lights. Emergency crews directed traffic around another clump of cars. No doubt someone had been rear-ended in the storm. *Lord, don't let it be Landyn. Please, God—*

The car ahead of him slammed on its brakes and Chase did likewise.

A glimmer of waning light shot through the clouds on the western horizon bathing everything in a greenish gold light. Broken branches dangled from trees like broken human limbs, and mounds of hailstones were piled like snowdrifts along the edge of the road as far as the eye could see.

Despite the muted chatter of the emergency personnel, the squawk of a police radio, and the murmurs of the bystanders, everything seemed eerily quiet—as if he were hearing it all from the depths of a tunnel. Then the distant wail of a single siren crescendoed toward them. The air smelled . . . odd. A musty mixture of earth and rain, and something else. Acrid, like rubber burning.

The small crowd gathered by the edge of the road craned their necks, looking down into the northern ditch. Chase got out of the car, stood on tiptoe, and strained to see what they were looking at, but his line of sight was blocked by half a dozen cars parked on the side of the road behind two fire service vehicles and a sheriff's SUV.

He threw the car in Park and jumped out. Rushing toward a group of men at the edge of the knot, he shouted, "What happened? Anybody know?"

A man pointed. "There's a car rolled over. Down in that ravine."

"Did anybody see the car that rolled over? I'm looking for my wife!" Chase shouted to anyone who would listen. "She was ahead of me in her car. She drives a white Honda."

A white-bearded man put a hand on his shoulder. "Can't see anything from up here, son, but they've got guys down there now working around some car."

Chase strained to see through the brush and rock below. His mind raced with scenarios he wasn't willing to entertain, but the possibilities shoved their way into his mind unbidden. He shouldered through the crowd and scrambled down the steep ditch, somehow knowing before he even saw the car, that it was hers.

And knowing that if it was, he was getting what he deserved. He hadn't taken care of Landyn the way he should have. He hadn't wanted the baby she was carrying. Hadn't been grateful for everything he'd been blessed to call his.

Still, when the workers pushed the brush aside revealing a glint of white-painted metal, his stomach lurched.

29

"That's my wife! That's my wife in there!" Chase could not get enough air in his lungs to be heard. He yelled again.

The car was flipped on its side in the ravine. And though it was crumpled beyond recognition, there was no doubt it was Landyn's Honda. His breath snagged again when he saw rescue workers pulling a body from the wreckage. Out of the passenger side door. A body he knew as well as his own.

"Landyn!" He slid the rest of the way down the slippery ditch.

"Sir, we need you to get back! Get back." A uniformed woman raised a hand in warning.

"That's my wife!" he said again. Couldn't they hear him?

"Okay. Calm down. We're getting her out."

Chase craned his neck and saw them hoist her limp frame onto the stretcher. "Landyn! Oh, God, no! Landyn!"

He shoved through two emergency workers and scrambled for the gurney. When he got closer, he saw her eyes flutter. And his heart started beating again.

"You know this woman?"

Chase looked up to see a Highway Patrol officer. "Yes, sir. She's my wife."

"Chase?" Landyn's voice was barely a whisper, but he heard it and charged forward, relief rushing over him.

"Landyn? You okay?"

"Oh, Chase. The baby! I . . . I wrecked the car! It's—"

"Everything will be okay. You're safe now." Apparently they'd already encased her neck in a bulky brace, which sent alarm surging through his veins, but he did his best to hide it and leaned over her so she could see his face. He pushed sodden curls from her forehead and swiped at the swath of mud and blood streaking one cheek. He turned to the EMT. "She's bleeding. Where's the blood coming from?"

"Am . . . am I bleeding? Chase? The baby!" She reached for him, and he saw that her finger was bandaged.

"It's just your finger." An EMT restrained Landyn, telling Chase, "That finger will need sutures. We bandaged it best we could, but it does look like a lot of blood." The worker touched Chase's arm, nodding toward the road above them. "Sir, we need to get her up to the ambulance."

Chase nodded, but stayed and helped the men as they hauled the stretcher up the treacherous incline.

"I tried to get out of the rain, but I couldn't see and"—her voice turned frantic—"the hail was hitting the car . . ."

Chase wondered if she was in shock. "Shh. It's okay. Just relax. Everything is okay."

"It was so loud, Chase, and I—I tried to call you." She strained, trying to look down the length of the stretcher, the only direction the neck brace afforded her except for straight up. Apparently she caught a glimpse of the bloodied bandage on her left hand again. "I'm bleeding!"

"No . . . No, remember, you just cut your finger. The baby is fine. You're going to be fine, Landyn." He wished he felt as certain as he tried to make his voice. "Does anything hurt?" Other than her finger, she didn't have any visible wounds. But he glanced over at a female EMT with a questioning look.

Her eyes told him nothing.

Chase turned to the technician. "She's pregnant. Did she tell you?"

"Yes, sir. We got it."

"Be sure they don't give her anything—"

"No, we won't. But we don't want her to go into shock. How far along is she, sir?"

"Almost five months."

"Five months," Landyn echoed, struggling against the straps on the gurney, which was now angled as they carried her head-first up the steep ravine. "Please help me."

"Shh." Chase put a hand on her shoulder. "You just rest. They've got everything under control."

"I'm fine. I'm okay. But Chase, don't let

them give me anything that will hurt the baby."

"Don't worry. We won't give you anything, ma'am," the male EMT said. "Are you in any pain?"

"I—I don't know. I don't think so."

For one awful second Chase wondered if she'd been paralyzed in the accident. But a moment later Landyn was struggling against the restraints again, all her limbs flexing with purpose. He sighed with relief.

"I'm okay," she said. "Really, I'm okay. Just . . . let me get off of here. Please!"

"Ma'am, we need to have you checked out. I think it would be best if you let the ambulance take you to the hospital. There's a good one just a few miles from here over in Carrollton."

"No . . ." Her eyes went to his, wild. He knew instantly that she was worrying about the money.

Guilt hit him like a three-hundred-pound tackle. "I don't care. You're going to the hospital."

"Chase. We can't af—"

"Stop, Landyn. You need to let them check you out. Think about the baby."

She sank back against the stretcher. Then immediately fought the straps again, trying to sit up. "My purse! Chase, all my stuff is in the car. You have to get it. All our stuff . . ."

"Ma'am, don't worry about that." The EMT looked at Chase. "The vehicle is stable, but be careful. The driver's side door is wedged shut. We had to bring her out through the passenger side."

"I'll be right back, okay?" He patted Landyn's right hand, then turned to the EMT. "Can I ride with her in the ambulance?"

"You have another vehicle up there?" He motioned toward the road. "Is it drivable?"

"Yes."

"It might be best if you follow us in your car . . . Get it off the road."

As much as he hated to leave Landyn, Chase saw the wisdom in the advice. Otherwise he'd have to get a ride back out here—or have the Toyota towed. That could be a while given the number of damaged vehicles this storm had likely produced.

The EMT pointed. "Just follow the signs for the hospital. It's north off the interstate, down by the river."

"Okay. Thank you, sir." He leaned to kiss Landyn. "I'll see you at the hospital. I'm right behind you. You cooperate with them, you hear me? Don't worry about the money. We'll figure something out." He pulled back and studied her. "You're sure you're okay?"

She nodded, her eyes drooping, as if she were getting drowsy. She'd said she wasn't in any pain, other than the cut on her hand—probably from the airbag deploying, he'd overheard one of the emergency crew surmise.

Chase scrambled back down the embankment.

When he got a closer look at the Honda, his chest constricted. Landyn's car looked like someone had put it in a can crusher. How had she survived inside that mangled hunk of steel? He ran his hand along the concave metal that used to be the passenger door. The door they'd had to bring her out of because the driver's side door was demolished. He stood in mute shock, feeling Landyn's life—their life together—passing before him. *Oh, God.*

He felt desperate to see her now. Desperate to know she was truly all right. Moving quickly, he pried the door open far enough to pull out a few of her belongings. Her purse was wedged behind the driver's seat, but he managed to extricate it from the wreckage. He surveyed the contents of the car, most of which were pinned in the back-seat by the roof of the car, which was compressed to half its height. Her phone charger hung empty from the cigarette lighter, but no phone attached. Maybe it was in her purse.

He grabbed what he could carry and scrambled back up the ravine.

The crowd along the highway had thinned, but there were a couple of other cars that hadn't fared well. Two with windshields decimated by the hail were being hooked up to tow trucks.

Feeling guilty for not offering help to those still stranded, yet feeling he didn't have a minute to waste, he climbed into the battered Toyota and started the engine. He began to back up, but feeling lightheaded, he shifted back into Park, then gripped the steering wheel. He took a deep breath and held his hands out in front of him. They were shaking like Jell-O.

He didn't have time to fall apart now. He put the car in gear, pressed the accelerator, and crunched over the ridge of hail that was already starting to melt. Landyn needed him.

And he needed her.

30

"I can walk just fine. Please, can't you just let me walk in?" Landyn tried to get up again but felt like she was in a straitjacket. She felt ridiculous letting them roll her in on the gurney, like she was headed to surgery.

But the stout orderly pressed her shoulder just firmly enough to get his message across. "Sorry, miss. Hospital regulations. You need to wait until after the doctor has looked you over."

"Is my husband here yet?" She tried to turn her head to the side to look past the orderly toward the ER entry they'd just wheeled her through. But her prone position and the stupid neck brace they had her in limited her view and made everything look skewed and out of context.

"Is he supposed to be here?"

"Yes, but he doesn't know where the hospital is . . . We're not from around here. We were headed to Cape Girardeau when I rolled the car."

"You're a ways from home."

She nodded. "Chase—my husband—was going to follow the ambulance but—"

"He'll find you then. Don't worry. Carrollton is a small town and there are signs for the hospital. I'm going to take you on back now so the doctor can check you over."

"Will you be sure and let my husband come back when he gets here?" She'd seen the worry in Chase's face.

After a blur of X-rays and lab work, they finally let her get out of the neck brace and wheeled her into a large tiled area where they pulled a curtain around her, creating an exam room. They transferred her from the gurney to another "bed" that looked more like a table. A nurse helped her into a hospital gown and asked Landyn many of the same questions the EMTs and lab techs had asked.

Shortly, the nurse left the room with the chart. But within a few minutes, a man who didn't look much older than Chase pulled back the curtain.

"Mrs. Spencer?"

"Yes?"

"I'm Dr. Meier." He pulled a rolling stool away from a desk just outside the curtained area and pulled it up beside the exam table. "I hear you got caught in the hailstorm. Rolled your car?"

"Yes." She turned her head, trying to see past him. "Do you know if my husband is here yet? He was following the ambulance." Surely Chase had had time to get here by now.

"I'll let the nurse know to watch for him." He pushed off with one foot and rolled the chair against the heavy divider curtain.

Landyn heard him tell the nurse to send Chase back when he arrived. She relaxed a little.

Dr. Meier looked at the clipboard with the list of questions the nurse had filled out. "So you're five months pregnant? Have you felt the baby move since the accident?"

She shook her head, sobered by what the question implied. "But—I'm not really sure I've felt movement at all yet. I *think* I have but—"

"What is your official due date? The date your doctor gave you?" He waited with pen poised above the chart.

"I . . . don't exactly have a doctor yet."

"You haven't seen a doctor since you got pregnant?" He looked taken aback. "So . . . you're just going by your last period for your due date."

She nodded, feeling like some backwoods country hick. "I used a chart I found online. We're kind of in the process of moving so we just haven't . . . found a doctor yet," she finished lamely.

"You would probably have felt quickening—movement—if you really are five months along."

"Well, maybe I have. Felt it, I mean." She described the fluttery feelings she'd experienced in the past few weeks.

The doctor nodded. "Yes. It sounds like you are feeling quickening. Well . . . Let's take a listen and just make sure everything is okay with the baby." He called the nurse back into the curtained area. "You're sure you don't have any pain or anything unusual going on since the accident?"

"I'm sure."

"Sounds like you are one lucky lady."

She wanted to tell him that it was anything but luck but decided against it. She did shoot up a huge prayer of thanks while the doctor listened to her heart, then he had her lie back and moved a Doppler stethoscope to her belly. She suddenly had an urgent need to see Chase. If anything had happened to the baby . . . She couldn't even let herself finish the thought.

The doctor moved the stethoscope to various spots on her stomach.

Her gaze intent on his eyes, she tried to decipher what he was hearing. What he was thinking.

Finally, on the third try, he smiled. "There it is . . . good and strong."

Landyn released a breath she hadn't realized she'd been holding. *Thank you, Lord.*

The divider curtain parted behind Dr. Meier,

and the orderly who'd brought her in appeared. "Someone here to see you, Mrs. Spencer."

He pushed the curtain farther and Chase stepped in. He immediately went to Landyn's side.

"Ah, this must be Dad." The doctor greeted Chase. "Everything looks fine," he assured. "We've got a strong heartbeat for the baby and—"

"Is Landyn okay?" Deep creases furrowed the spot between his eyebrows.

"She's fine. Just a little shaken up. And very lucky from the sound of it."

Chase nodded and swallowed hard. Landyn thought he looked like he might cry. She reached for his hand. He knit their fingers together and squeezed so tight she winced.

"What's wrong?" Concern carved lines in Chase's forehead. "Are you hurting?"

"Yes, but—" She wriggled loose from his grip. "Only because you're about to break my fingers, babe." She laughed and Chase looked sheepish.

"I think we should keep her overnight for observation," Dr. Meier said, still moving the stethoscope around on her belly. "But she can probably go home in the morn—" He stopped mid-sentence and frowned.

Moving the stethoscope again, he listened. Then moved it again. Then back to where he'd first heard the baby's heartbeat.

Landyn couldn't read his expression.

"We can wait until tomorrow, but I think we

might want to schedule an ultrasound while we have you here. Especially since you haven't seen a doctor yet."

"Why?" Landyn sought Chase's eyes and saw in them the same fear she was feeling.

"Is something . . . wrong?" His voice strained, Chase squeezed her hand again.

Dr. Meier shook his head looking at Chase, then at her. "No, no . . . Nothing's wrong. I'm hearing strong heartbeats." A smile bloomed on the doctor's face. "For *both* babies."

"Are you sure?" Chase stared at the doctor, wishing there was a chair he could sink into or something to hang on to besides Landyn—who looked as shocked as he was.

"You're not serious?" Landyn's eyes were wide. "Two . . . ? You mean like—twins?"

Dr. Meier and the nurse both laughed, but the nurse quickly sobered. "You both look like you could use some water. This kind of news takes a while to sink in sometimes."

"Water, yes. And . . . maybe some Valium," Chase said, not sure where he found the strength to joke about something like this. He hadn't thought anything could surprise him more than the news that Landyn was pregnant. But twins? It was so far out of his scope of possibility, he didn't even know how to start processing it.

Dr. Meier rose and pushed the stool he'd been

sitting on over to Chase. "You look like you need this worse than I do."

The nurse reappeared with two small bottles of water. She handed one to each of them. Landyn opted to place hers, unopened, on her forehead. That looked like a good idea, and Chase followed suit.

They stared at each other in bewilderment until Landyn started laughing. Or at least he thought it was a laugh. "Oh, Chase. I'm so sorry," she finally said.

Moved, he touched his water bottle gently to Landyn's cheek and kissed her hand. "Hey, don't I get a little of the credit here?" he whispered. Then he started laughing too.

If he didn't laugh, he might cry.

31

Audrey plumped the pillows in the parlor for the third time and checked her phone again. She'd expected to hear from Landyn and Chase when they got close. The last they'd heard anything was around four. It was already past nine o'clock. If they were still on schedule, they'd be here in about an hour.

She'd be glad when those two were safely back in Langhorne, but just knowing they were back on familiar territory let her breathe a sigh of relief.

If she'd voiced as much to Grant, he would have reminded her that most accidents happen within twenty-five miles of home—or whatever the latest statistic was. Sometimes she thought he *liked* to see her worrying.

They had three rooms booked tonight and all but one party was in for the night. The others had gone to a concert on the campus in Cape Girardeau and probably wouldn't be in until late. Meaning they'd probably want a later breakfast in the morning. She made a mental note to fix something that reheated well. Chase and Landyn would no doubt sleep in too.

She put her phone on the counter and went to get some bacon from the deep freeze in the garage. When she came back, her phone was ringing. She deposited the bacon on the counter by the refrigerator and grabbed her phone. Good. It was Chase.

"Hey, Chase. You getting close?"

"Hi, Audrey. Sorry to be calling so late but—we've decided we're going to stay here—stop for the night, I mean."

"Oh? Where are you? I figured for sure you'd come on in tonight. But that's fine," she added quickly, knowing her disappointment was evident in her voice. "I'd rather you be safe and not push it. Is the trip going okay?"

"We're both pretty beat and . . . It just seemed like a good idea to stop for the night. We'll see you in the morning. I'm not sure what time."

Chase sounded—she couldn't put her finger on it, but he didn't sound like himself. She hoped he and Landyn weren't having an argument. Surely they could manage to get along since they were traveling in two cars. "Where are you guys, anyway?" she asked again.

"Oh. We . . . We're in a little town . . . just off the Interstate."

Well, that told her exactly nothing. "What town? Which route did you take? Grant will ask . . ." She wasn't trying to be snoopy, but Grant *would* ask, and she was curious how far they had to drive in the morning. "Will you get here in time for breakfast?"

"We're in—Carroll County, not sure what the town is—hang on just a second."

Audrey heard him talking to someone. Did he not know where they'd pulled off? He must really be exhausted. And if he was, how must Landyn feel? Traveling that far—and driving the whole way, since they were bringing both cars—was hard enough when you *weren't* pregnant. But if they'd been on the road since five, they had to be so close to Langhorne.

Still, disappointed as she was, if they were that tired, it was better that they stop and get some sleep. "Chase?"

More muffled discussion. "Yes? I'm here, Audrey."

"Can I talk to Landyn for a minute?" Chase still hadn't told her where they were. Maybe she could get more information out of her daughter.

"Oh . . . Um . . . Landyn's not here right now. She's actually—in the bathroom. Again." He chuckled, but it sounded stilted.

Audrey shook her head. They must be fighting. She gave an inward growl. *Those two* . . . Sometimes she just wanted to smack their heads together and tell them to grow up. "So . . . everything's going okay?"

A pause while he talked to whoever he was talking to. "Oh, and we're in Carrollton, Audrey. That's the town we're staying in tonight. But we'll be back there tomorrow . . . I'm not sure what time, but we'll let you know. I need to run. See you guys tomorrow."

He hung up before she could ask him where Carrollton was. She'd never heard of the town.

It was still dark outside the hospital window when a nurse came in and woke Landyn to take her vitals. "You've got quite the shiner going there," the nurse said, adjusting the blood pressure cuff on Landyn's arm.

"Do I?" Landyn put a hand to her eye. She hadn't looked in a mirror since she got to the hospital.

Chase stirred in the recliner beside her bed. After they'd moved her to a regular room last night, Chase had called her insurance company, and then had gone out to check on her car—after he'd finally tracked down where they'd towed it to.

He'd transferred as much as possible into his car, but he seemed discouraged after he returned to the hospital. "I think we can safely say your car is totaled."

He described the accident scene, but Landyn had a feeling he wasn't telling her just how bad the damage to her car was—and how much of their stuff had been destroyed. She tried to remember what was in her car that was so important. Chase had retrieved her purse and the EMTs had found her phone. Those were the things that would have been hard to replace. They would worry about the rest later. Maybe that was one nice thing about being so poor—they had nothing to lose.

She'd heard Chase get up and putter around the small room several times during the night. She hadn't slept well either with the bright lights and constant noise at the nurse's station outside her room. But at least they had a room to themselves.

She put a finger to her lips now, asking the nurse to let Chase sleep, then eased her legs over the side of the hospital bed. She felt like she'd run a marathon. Every muscle cried out in pain, and when she got into the bathroom and looked in the mirror, she saw the bluish shiner that had developed under her right eye.

"I'm fine," she told the nurse, who was hovering over her like a mosquito. "I'm going to get cleaned up and try to do something with my hair."

"Okay. I'll be back to check on you in a few minutes. Here's the call button if you need anything." She placed the cord on the bed near the pillow.

Landyn washed her face and wet down her curls enough to try to get them to cooperate. Gazing at her image in the mirror, the events of yesterday played in her mind like a fast-paced movie. She and Chase had talked briefly after he got back from unpacking the Honda, but mostly they'd just looked at each other and said again and again, "Can you believe this? Can you get over this?" Mostly they meant the news about the babies. *Twins!* It still hadn't quite sunk in. But also they were exclaiming over her wreck and the damage the hail had inflicted on their cars.

Surprisingly, Chase didn't seem as worried about that as she was. "I don't care about the cars," he'd told her last night. "The only thing that matters is that you're okay."

She knew he felt bad about hedging with her mom when he'd called her parents last night, but Landyn hadn't wanted him to tell them about the wreck. They would only worry, and there wasn't anything they could do from Langhorne.

She went to the window and pulled back the heavy curtain. Dawn had begun to paint the horizon in tinges of pink. Feeling suddenly weary, she went back to the hospital bed. She'd made Chase promise not to tell her parents about the babies. She wanted to tell them in person. And there was still a chance—she was holding out *hope,* if she was honest—that the ultrasound would prove the doctor wrong. He'd seemed pretty confident about those two distinct heart-beats he'd heard in the ER, but if he was wrong, she had to admit she would heave a sigh of relief.

She felt guilty for hoping he was wrong. The novelty of twins was a fun thought. But the reality of what it would mean for her and Chase was *anything* but fun. If she was having twins, the studio apartment in Bed-Stuy was out of the question. And she couldn't even let herself think about the hospital bill, let alone diapers and day-care and trying to put two kids through college at once.

Landyn closed her eyes but opened them quickly. It seemed every time she closed her eyes, she felt that awful, helpless sense of falling, seeing the accident happen all over again in slow motion.

She finally dozed off only to have the nurse reappear, pushing a wheelchair. "They're ready for you downstairs. Your husband will want to be there for the ultrasound."

Chase struggled to sit up in the chair. "I'm awake." He groped for the lever and put the recliner upright, then rubbed his eyes and ran his fingers through his hair, giving it that spiky style Landyn loved on him.

"Let's go meet your babies," the nurse said, smiling like it was the best news possible.

The technician ran the wand across Landyn's belly again, then swiveled the screen toward Chase. Judging from the woman's smile, he was pretty sure she was confirming Dr. Meier's diagnosis of twins. But he couldn't make out— well . . . heads or tails of the image on the screen.

"Ooh, look, Chase!" There was awe in Landyn's voice and he strained to make the black-and-white pictures look like a baby. Or two babies.

"You can see the head here"—the tech circled a haloed area on the screen—"of Baby A. And here is Baby B."

"So . . . there *are* two? You're sure?" Landyn sounded a little breathless.

Chase took her hand and squeezed it.

"Oh, yes, definitely twins." The tech moved the wand again and the image shifted. This time the pieces all fit together and came into focus, and Chase saw the forms clearly. Two little heads and—"Is that . . . a spine?"

"Let's see . . ." She adjusted the screen and moved the wand again. "It sure is. That's a good shot," the tech said. "Come on, baby . . . Let's get a look at you." She pointed out an arm and five little fingers—distinct as his own—and she talked to the babies all the while, as if they were already real people.

And of course, they *were*. It took his breath away.

The tech smiled at Landyn. "Pretty amazing, isn't it?"

"Can you tell if they're identical? Or their gender?"

Chase hadn't even considered gender yet. What if it was two little girls? He couldn't even imagine living with *three* Landyns.

"It's a little early to determine gender," the tech said. "And we can't conclusively determine zygosity—whether they're identical or fraternal—via ultrasound. As you can see"—she pointed to the screen—"there are two placentas, but that's just one factor for fraternal twins. I'm sure Dr. Meier will want you to see your regular physician right away."

Chase couldn't help but see dollar signs, but he pushed the thoughts to a back burner.

Landyn blew out a breath, her eyes glued to the screen. "Twins, Chase. *Twins,*" she whispered.

"I know. That's wild. I—can't quite wrap my mind around it."

Landyn turned to look at him, and he knew she was trying to gauge how he was feeling about this confirmation. He gave her a smile that came easy. "Looks like we've got our work cut out for us."

And it looked like a lot of work to him. But something had happened—something had changed in that moment when the image on the screen became clear. For the first time those babies were *real* to him. A little Chase. Or a little Landyn— maybe one of each. And while he couldn't honestly say he loved them already, he felt . . . responsible for them. In a good way.

They were *his* babies. Two little someones were going to call him Daddy. And it was a gift. A gift from God. He didn't have a clue how they would manage, how he would provide for his family. But God had seen fit to give him a family. The one thing he'd never really had, the one thing he thought he didn't deserve. And God was giving it to him. In spades. He would be grateful. He *was* grateful.

And though he knew he had a long way to go, and a lot to learn, he promised God then and there that he would do everything in his power to be a good father to these two little people waving their tiny fingers at him from the screen.

32

It was after nine o'clock before Dr. Meier finally made his rounds and dismissed Landyn to go home. But not before they'd signed a stack of papers promising to pay an amount they hadn't even seen yet. She'd heard horror stories about ER bills in five figures. She just prayed her insurance from Fineman & Justus would cover most of it.

She buckled her seatbelt and pulled down the visor to check her shiner in the mirror. There wasn't enough makeup in the world to cover the ugly contusion. Mom would go ballistic when she saw it.

Chase had somehow managed to cram all but a few of their belongings from the Honda into his car. The rest would be shipped to her parents' as soon as an adjustor had looked at the car.

She stretched her neck to look out the windshield at the pockmarks on the hood of Chase's car. "Won't our insurance pay to fix that?"

He shook his head. "It didn't make sense to pay for full coverage on this pile of scrap metal, so I only had collision on it."

"Well I'd say those hailstones *collided* with the hood of your car. Isn't that worth something?"

He laughed. "I'll let you plead that case with the insurance company. I'm just thankful we have full coverage on your car."

And that was thanks to her dad, who'd paid her insurance premium a year in advance before she got married. But of course she didn't say that to Chase. He felt bad enough as it was.

"And at least our cars are paid for."

"Thank the Lord for small miracles." He sounded utterly defeated.

"Chase—"

He shook his head in a way she knew meant "please spare me the platitudes." That hurt, but she knew him well enough to understand that sometimes he had to think things through on his own.

Because of their belongings—mostly Chase's from the studio—piled to the car's ceiling, he could barely see out the back windshield, so she had to be his eyes as he navigated the parking lot and got them back on the Interstate.

They'd driven in silence for twenty minutes when Chase—eyes glued to the highway—said, "I wonder how much more He thinks we can take."

He meant God, she knew. But she wasn't sure how to respond. Wasn't sure Chase even wanted a response. An image from when she was a little girl came to her mind, and almost without thinking, she started singing. A song CeeCee had used to sing when she had put them to bed the nights she babysat them while Mom and Dad were out on a date or away on business.

She sang softly, "Count your many blessings, name them one by one . . ." She sang a couple of lines but couldn't remember all the lyrics. But she did remember—for the first time in a long time—the warmth of having her grandmother's arms around her. And how CeeCee had encouraged her to list her blessings. One by one, just like the song said. Mom and Dad, a happy home, her brothers and sisters—two of each, though back then she hadn't always been so sure they were blessings. CeeCee had laughed when Landyn said as much, but then she pressed her to think of other blessings. A beautiful sunset. Recent rains. Supper on the table. A new litter of kittens MamaKat had delivered.

"What's that song?" Chase asked, sounding a little annoyed that she was singing when he was working so hard to be depressed.

"CeeCee used to sing it when I was little. I think . . . I think we should count our blessings, Chase. We've been through a lot, but—we *have* a lot too." Somehow speaking those words helped her see the truth of them more clearly.

Yes, she and Chase had been through a lot. Some of it—much of it, if they were honest—had been brought on by their own choices. But some of it was just—life. And she knew so many people who had suffered far more than she and Chase had. She thought of her boss at the PR firm in Manhattan whose little boy had drowned at three. And Carly, her friend in high school who'd lost both her parents in a car accident. Mom's friend Karyn, who'd gone through chemo. Twice.

Yes, she'd had her share of tragedy and trials. Losing her brother in Afghanistan was pretty high on the list. But she had a lot to be thankful for, too.

Chase pressed his lips into a thin line. She sensed he was praying. Probably praying God would give him patience with his wife's silly car games.

But after a minute he looked over at her with a boyish grin. "Okay. I'll go first. Number one. I'm blessed to have a hot wife."

She laughed. "Have you looked at me recently? I've got a black eye and my hair is out of control. I'm fat. I'm—"

"You're beautiful. And . . . Thank you."

"For what?"

"For making me realize . . . we *are* blessed. Okay, your turn."

She thought for a minute, wanting to hold tight to the hope she felt rising inside her. "I'm blessed that we own such a great car."

That made him laugh. "Ha! I'm blessed to have a four-hundred-square-foot apartment"—he winked—"and twins on the way."

She glanced into the backseat and wondered where on earth they would put two car seats. But she forced her thoughts back to blessings. "I'm blessed to have patient parents who are willing to put up with me."

"I'm blessed to have patient in-laws who—so far—haven't kicked me out of the family."

"And they never would, Chase," she said, making her tone serious, but quickly steering him back to the game. "Okay . . . I'm blessed that I've only gained twelve pounds in the last five months."

His eyes grew wide. "Seriously? Twelve? You're chunkin' out on me, woman!"

She slugged him in the bicep. "Hey, you try keeping your slim figure with two babies in tow."

"That's okay. You're doing a fine job." He gave her knee a proprietary pat. "All right, my turn . . . I'm blessed that you weren't—killed last night." Tears sprang to his eyes.

Landyn gave up on keeping things lighthearted. She scooted over as far as her seatbelt would allow and reached across the console to rub his shoulder. "Me too. It was kind of a close one, huh?"

He shuddered. "Too close. If anything had happened to you, Landyn, I don't know what I would have done. And . . . We might never have even known we were having twins."

It was a sobering thought. "I'm blessed that you're the daddy of our twins." How many more times would she have to speak such words before it seemed real that they were having two babies?

She looked out the window at the landscape rolling by, more familiar now that they were headed down I-57 on the Illinois side, not far from crossing the Mississippi River into Missouri.

Chase caressed her cheek, then captured a curl at her temple and slowly wound it around his finger. "I don't know how it's all going to work out, babe, but I've been thinking how strange it is when it seems like everything that could possibly go wrong went wrong, and yet—in spite of everything—I've somehow felt more sure than ever that God has everything under control."

"Yeah . . . I've felt that too."

"Mind you, I'm not saying I like everything that's happened."

She shook her head. "Me neither. But maybe . . . because we've *completely* lost control of our lives, God has no choice but to step in now."

"And maybe he can, now that we've finally gotten out of the way."

Oh, how she prayed that was true.

Audrey hung up the phone and rolled her eyes.

"So you finally got hold of them?" Grant put down his newspaper and waited for the rant he knew was coming. "Are they getting close?"

She sighed. "I do not know why a person owns a cell phone if they're not going to have it turned on. How on earth are they traveling in two cars with their cell phones off?" Audrey looked as peeved as he felt.

After last night's guests had checked out, he and Audrey had pretty much wasted the rest of the morning sitting around waiting to hear from Landyn and Chase. It was almost noon and Audrey had just now hung up from talking to them.

"They're still three hours from home. I don't know why they're taking their sweet time getting here."

"Well, maybe they ran into weather." He turned back to the weather report in the *Southeast Missourian*. "Where'd you say they spent the night?"

"I thought they said Caroltown or Carolville . . . Something like that. Landyn said it was a small town. I wasn't familiar with it."

"It wasn't Carrollton, Kentucky, was it?"

"Oh, I think it was. Because I was surprised they'd only gotten as far as Kentucky. Why?"

"They had a whale of a storm there last night. Hail and flooding."

"That's in the paper?" Audrey came to read over his shoulder, resting her chin on the top of his head. "Landyn said they ran into a storm, but it didn't sound like it was anything newsworthy."

"According to this, it was bad enough to make national news. Hit all along the Interstate. Cars piled up under the overpasses, several accidents. Thank goodness the kids missed that."

"Oh, Grant. Just think if they hadn't stopped when they did."

"I, for one, will breathe a sigh of relief when they finally get here. And I *am* anxious to see them again, but I'll sure be glad when those two figure out their plans."

Audrey blew out a breath that ruffled her bangs. "That makes two of us."

"We weren't ever that—*flighty,* were we?"

"Well, maybe we should ask your mother the

answer to that. I seem to recall coming home from St. Louis a few years ago to find CeeCee pacing the floor with a sick Corinne and wondering why on earth we were so late."

Grant cringed. "I'd forgotten all about that. We were at that big awards thing, right?"

She nodded. "With Kelvin and Mary . . . I've forgotten their last name."

He frowned, feeling appropriately chided. "Yes, but it's not like we had cell phones back then." They'd been having a wonderful evening dining with friends. CeeCee had agreed to babysit—and spend the night, as he recalled. He and Audrey had never given his mother—or the kids, for that matter—another thought.

"Maybe we should cut Chase and Landyn a little slack. But I'd sure like to give them a piece of my mind."

He laughed. "That makes two of us. But maybe we should hang on to all the pieces of our minds. You never know when we might need them."

33

The closer they got to the inn, the more jittery Landyn felt. She'd imagined her parents' surprise and excitement at learning they were going to be grandparents to twins. She'd imagined their relief to learn that she and Chase had made it through the storm safely. And their alarm at hearing what a close call it was. But the closer they got to Langhorne, the more unsure she was about how Mom and Dad would react to their news.

What if they blamed Chase? What if this last round of events was the last straw for her parents' generosity to them?

It was after four when they finally pulled up the long driveway to the inn. Like always, her parents hurried off the porch to greet them. Landyn wondered if they'd been sitting there since her last phone call right after they'd stopped for lunch and to gas up.

Mom held her arms open for a hug but raised them to her mouth when Landyn got close. "What happened to you? Oh, Landyn! Honey . . . What on earth happened?"

Dad came over and inspected her the same way, then he looked past her to Chase's pulverized Toyota. "What on earth happened? Where's *your* car?"

She held up a hand. "I'm fine. . . . I had an accident."

"What do you mean?" Dad narrowed his eyes at her, then at Chase. And for one awful moment, she saw blame in his eyes—that he thought this was Chase's fault.

"I wrecked my car. We got caught in a crazy storm—" She started laughing. Genuinely, because her parents' faces were mirror images of each other.

"A wreck? What happened?" Mom put a hand up to touch the shiner, but Landyn backed away, reaching for Chase.

"Where *is* your car, Landyn?" Her dad looked past them, down the driveway.

"We had to leave it behind," Chase answered for her. "It was totaled. Landyn is lucky to be alive." His voice cracked, and he pulled her into a hug, as if he could protect her after the fact.

"We spent the night in a hospital last night," Landyn finished quickly, seeing the alarm in her mother's eyes. "That's why we were so late this morning."

"Oh, Landyn. That just gives me the chills." Mom reached for her.

Chase let her go.

Her mother hugged her close, then pulled away to study her face. "You're sure the baby is okay? The doctor checked that?"

"Everything is fine. I promise."

"So where's the Honda?" Dad seemed more concerned about her stupid car than he was about her.

Chase explained that he'd already contacted the insurance company. "We're sure grateful for you having full coverage on Landyn's car," he told her dad.

"What about yours?" Dad said. "Looks like it took quite a beating too."

"Yes . . . Unfortunately, I—we only have

collision on it." He nudged at a hunk of gravel with the toe of his shoe.

Dad shook his head like it was a lost cause—like *Chase* was a lost cause. Landyn wanted to shake her father. Couldn't he see Chase felt bad enough about everything as it was?

But if Chase noticed, he didn't let it show. He squared his shoulders and injected a confidence in his tone that Landyn was pretty sure he didn't feel. "I have an appointment in Cape Monday to talk to the insurance guy so we can get things straightened out and hopefully replace Landyn's car."

Dad gave a noncommittal nod.

Landyn cleared her throat and shot Chase a raised eyebrow. This seemed like as good a time as any to share their news.

Chase shrugged.

Mom watched their exchange with eagle eyes and looked at Landyn with a question written on her face.

"Mom . . . Dad . . ." She looked between them. "You guys might want to sit down for this."

"This? What are you talking about?"

"Just come and have a seat. Chase and I have some news."

Her mom led the way to the porch and sat primly on the edge of an Adirondack chair. "What's this all about?"

"You asked if the doctor checked me . . . He did.

And when he listened for the baby's heartbeat, he found something."

"Oh, no . . ." Mom's face went gray.

"No, Mom." Landyn laughed. "It's good news—Well . . . it's not *bad* news."

"Would you just tell us," Dad snapped, "and put your mother out of her misery?"

By the way he plopped onto the porch swing, Landyn thought her dad might be experiencing a little misery too.

"The doctor heard two heartbeats." She glanced up at Chase to include him in the announcement. He was smiling, but she knew he was nervous about her dad's reaction. "We're having twins."

"Twins?" Mom's hands went to her mouth again, the way they had when she'd first heard about the accident. "Are you serious? I always thought we might have twins in the family. You know your great uncle Harold was a twin. But the other baby died at birth." She gasped, as if just realizing how her comment might affect Landyn. "Things were so different back then, of course. Babies were born at home and they didn't have all the modern—"

"It's okay, Mom." Landyn touched her mother's arm. "The doctor said things are fine with our babies. We want to get started with Dr. Gregory here, just to make sure everything keeps going like it should."

"Dr. Gregory? Does that mean you'll be staying

until the babies are born?" Mom's color was still a little on the gray side. "When are you due anyway?"

"Don't worry, Mom." Landyn patted her shoulder. "We're just staying at the inn tonight. We've already talked to CeeCee and she's ready for us to come out there tomorrow."

"And to answer your question, she's due April 2nd." Chase said.

"Actually, the chart the nurse had showed April 1st, but we're telling people April 2nd, so *no* April fools' jokes, please. We didn't exactly plan any of this."

Her dad actually laughed at that.

"So what do you think, Daddy? You haven't said anything."

He shook his head in that I-can't-believe-you-did-that way he'd always used whenever one of them did something stupid. "I've always told my kids I'd take as many grandchildren as you wanted to give me, but I didn't mean you had to double up on production. There's not a prize for the winner or anything, you know."

That made even Chase laugh.

Dad reached for her and squeezed her shoulders in a side hug. "I'm happy for you, kiddo. You guys have your work cut out for you, but if anybody can handle it, I believe you two can." He extended a hand to Chase, grinning. "Son, congratulations. I just hope you're prepared to become a money-making machine for the next twenty years or so."

"Thank you, sir. And yes, I'm prepared."

"Maybe you'd better prepare for thirty years, if these kids are anything like their parents."

"Hey!" Landyn protested. But she couldn't quit smiling. Chase, too. For once it was good to have happy news to share.

Audrey woke early on Monday to the sound of the washing machine running on the second floor. She left Grant sleeping and tiptoed downstairs to see what was going on. Landyn and Chase had slept in Landyn's old room, and the only other room occupied was on the main floor in the handicap accessible room—a couple here to celebrate their sixtieth anniversary.

She found Landyn stuffing sheets in the washer. "Honey, you don't have to do that. I can do the laundry after you guys leave. We don't need your room till the weekend. In fact, you and Chase can stay another night or two if you like."

"No, it's okay, Mom. We already told CeeCee we'd be there tonight."

Audrey had to turn away to hide the tears. Less than three short weeks ago she'd been near tears of anger over the same laundry. Maybe her little girl was growing up after all. She composed herself and cleared her throat. "Is Chase up already, too?"

Landyn nodded. "He's in the shower. He's going in to Cape this morning to see about the insurance. I don't know how soon we'll get a check, but if Chase can find out how much we're getting for my car, we might go car shopping this afternoon."

"Well, thanks for helping out with the bedding."

"I'll get them in the dryer later."

"Actually, I've been hanging them on the line to dry. I like the way they smell." That was true, but more true was the fact that it saved on electricity.

"Well, if you're sure . . ." Landyn filled the fabric softener dispenser and shut the lid on the washer.

Audrey studied her daughter. "Are you feeling okay today? Your eye looks a little better than it did last night."

"Does it?" She gingerly touched the spot under her eye. "I haven't even looked in the mirror yet this morning. It doesn't hurt. Everything else does, but my eye feels fine."

"You're bound to be stiff and sore after that. Your dad said Chase was pretty shook up when he saw your car."

Landyn looked surprised. "I haven't seen it yet. I mean . . . I guess I have, but I don't really remember. I don't think I was ever unconscious or anything, but it's all kind of a blur. But Chase said the insurance guy thought it was totaled."

Now Audrey let the tears come. "I'm so glad you're okay. I—" She couldn't finish.

Landyn reached for her. "I'm fine, Mom. It all turned out okay." She no doubt read Audrey's thoughts.

Audrey took a deep breath and forced herself to . . . *trust*. She'd survived the death of one child. She wasn't sure she could lose another one and be okay with it. With God.

She pulled away. "I need to go start breakfast. Will Chase be back in time?"

"Knowing him, he'll probably snag a donut in Cape. Don't worry about us. I'll just have some yogurt . . . if that's okay."

The tears were close again. "Honey, of course it's okay. I—I'm sorry if I've made you feel unwelcome here. I've been so worried about—"

"No, Mom. It's okay. You didn't make me feel unwelcome—" She stopped and gave a wry smile. "Well, maybe a little bit. But I wasn't a very thoughtful guest either. I'm sorry. I promise I'll do better at CeeCee's."

"Stop," Audrey chided. "I know you will. And Cecilia will love having you. And I'll miss you."

"Nah . . ." Landyn gave her a playful shove. "I bet you can't wait to get rid of us."

"Never." She started down the stairs. "Who would do my laundry?"

Her daughter's soft laughter followed her down.

34

Chase prayed all the way to the insurance agency in Cape Girardeau. They simply had to get enough money for the Honda to replace it with something halfway decent. His Toyota would get them around while they were back here in Missouri, but given that the car was older than he was, it was not a long-term solution. He doubted it would make it back to New York even one more time. But he also didn't see any way they could take on a car payment. They'd be doing good to come up with the money to rent a place and feed themselves.

Chase only had to wait ten minutes before Hank, their insurance agent, had news for him. "We'll be able to cut you a check in a few days. There's no question the vehicle is totaled." He swiveled his computer screen Chase's way and showed him the amount the check would be.

It was a disappointingly low number. Especially after the deductible. Sure, it could have been worse, but it wasn't nearly what they'd hoped. They would definitely be trading down. Or driving his Toyota till it died. Which wouldn't be long.

"You said you had damage to your vehicle, too?"

Chase gave a short laugh. "I did, but you

wouldn't be able to tell the difference from the dings it had in it before the storm." He reminded the man that they only had collision coverage on his car.

"You realize you could get a significant savings if you'd insured both of your vehicles with us."

Chase explained about his father-in-law paying Landyn's insurance in advance. "I don't know how much you could save us on an old beater like my old Toyota, but next time her premium comes due, we'll sure keep it in mind."

"That your car out front?" The agent pointed through the venetian blinds to where his car was parked.

"It is." Chase told him briefly about the car and how Frank Granger had sold it to him.

"That's a good vehicle. A '79, right?"

Chase nodded.

"That was a good year. Those things keep their value better than most. Yours is low miles, too. I can recommend a good body shop. Assuming you're wanting to get it fixed."

Chase winced. "Probably can't afford that. Especially now." He nodded toward the computer screen that held the anemic check information.

"Well, let's take a look." The agent walked him out to the sidewalk and circled the car. Twice. "You're not looking to sell this one, are you?"

"I wasn't planning on it. Figured it was pretty much scrap. Why?"

"I've got a friend at one of the body shops we use who's been looking for this make and model. I think he'd pay you pretty decent money for it."

"Seriously? As is?"

"He's looking for one to refurbish. If you're interested I can give him a call."

"Can you give me a ballpark figure?"

He shook his head. "No clue. I'd have to talk to him first."

Chase shrugged. "Sure. I guess it can't hurt to see if he's interested." He hated to get his hopes up, but if they could get any decent amount for his car, they might come out of this okay.

Hank, the insurance guy, called his buddy Rick and gave Chase directions to the body shop.

Rick came out and inspected the Toyota inside and out. When the mechanic ran his hands over the worst of the dings on the left front fender, Chase prepared himself for the letdown.

But Rick straightened and scratched his head. "I'd give you six thousand for it."

"Six thousand?" It was all Chase could do not to let out a whoop, but he managed to remain poker-faced. "Why—do you want it?"

Rick grinned. "It was a good year. Good car. I had one just like it when I was in high school. Same color even." He hooked a thumb toward the vehicle. "In fact, when I first saw you drive up in it, I thought it *was* my car. Sold that one when I

291

got married. Regretted it ever since. I could probably go sixty-five-hundred . . ."

"Yeah. Sure . . . I'd be interested in selling it for that." Wait till he told Landyn. She would freak.

He would have given just about anything to be able to tell Mr. Granger what a gift he'd actually bestowed back when he'd sold Chase that car for five hundred dollars. But then, even in his old age, Frank Granger had been a car whiz. Maybe he *did* know.

The thought brought a lump to Chase's throat.

"Are you serious? Oh, Chase. That's amazing!" She wanted to skip all the way down to the creek. "Sixty-five hundred dollars? That's—a fortune."

"It is." Chase beamed with a confidence she hadn't seen in her husband for a while. It did her heart good. Maybe they hadn't exactly turned a corner yet, but at least they could survive for a few more weeks.

Huckleberry trotted between them, then dashed off to chase a squirrel. It felt good to be out in the crisp morning air. And to get away from the obnoxious old man who was regaling her parents at the breakfast table. She made a mental note about future career choices: bed-and-breakfast? No. Never in a million years. Her mom was perfectly cut out for the job, and Landyn could see how much she enjoyed it. At breakfast, Mom had let Mr. Blowhard tell his stories, and she'd laughed in all the right places and been her gracious self.

The only thing that had saved Landyn from saying something rude—or at least pulling her hair out—was Chase's arrival home. She'd steered him away from the house and they'd gone on a nostalgic walk down to the creek and the climbing tree so he could tell her his wonderful news about the car.

"Are you kind of sad to be selling it?"

He shrugged. "Maybe a little. That car has been very good to me. And . . . it's got a lot of memories tied to it."

"Frank Granger?"

"And Landyn Whitman."

She smiled up at him. "Oh, yeah. Her. Shoot, now you're making *me* sad to see it go."

"Well, we could keep it."

"Not *that* sad."

He laughed. "So you think we can get by with one car—if it's a decent one?"

"I think that makes the most sense. But"—she patted her belly—"it might have to be a minivan."

He made a face that cracked her up.

Huck came running again and Chase found a stick and played catch with the Lab the rest of the way to the creek.

When they got to the climbing tree Landyn knelt to scratch Huck's neck. "Maybe we could get a dog."

"Let's not go crazy. That would eat up a good chunk of our windfall."

"Good grief, what kind of dog are you thinking about? I'm just thinking a mutt from the pound or something."

"I'm not talking about the cost of the dog. I'm talking about food and shots and vet bills and replacing chewed up shoes and—"

"Okay, okay . . . Point taken. Maybe we should adjust to having twins before we complicate things."

"Excellent idea, Mrs. Spencer."

"Chase—When that nurse told us the babies were due in April—"

"Maybe before. Remember Dr. Meier said twins can come early."

She nodded, sobered by the thought. "It just—it made me feel really bad that I didn't tell you sooner. We should have had nine months just enjoying everything about having our first baby, and I feel like I stole that time from you."

He reached for her hand and kissed it. "We'll never know for sure, but knowing me like I do, I'd probably have wasted all that time freaking out and trying to get used to the idea."

He leaned against the trunk of the massive Osage Orange tree and reached for her. Strong arms pulled her close, until her back was pressed against his chest. She relaxed in the circle of his embrace, and they watched the creek babble, carrying the last of fall's leaves on its crest.

"Tell you what," he said after a while. "Let's spend these next months making up for lost time. Sure, we have a ton of stuff to do—and a lot of big decisions to make. But let's celebrate being pregnant as if we had nine months to get used to the idea."

She looked up over her shoulder at him. "I like that plan. And boy, is it going to make time fly."

"Ah, it *is* a plan, isn't it? One thing we've decided."

She laughed and snuggled back against him.

But his demeanor was serious. "I want to do this dad thing right, Landyn. I don't want to mess this up. But . . . I'm going to need help."

"Every dad needs help, babe. Every mom, too. This stuff doesn't just come naturally."

"Yeah, well, it seems like it does to your parents."

"Baby, they'd been parents for twenty-some years by the time you met them. You'll be a pro at this too by the time our babies are twenty."

"Stop." He made a face. "I don't even want to think about having twenty-year-old *kids*."

She giggled. "I know. It's kind of freaky to think about, isn't it."

"Let's *not* think about it." He drew her closer, pushed a curl off her temple, and kissed the spot. "I can think of better things to occupy our thoughts."

"I got my first kiss from you right under this very tree."

"Don't think I don't remember. You made me work so hard for that kiss."

"I was playing hard-to-get, but oh, man, did I ever want you to catch me."

"And now that you're caught?"

She started to give a flirtatious answer, but Chase looked so serious she drew back and turned to face him. "Now that I'm caught I don't ever want you to let go."

He shook his head. "Me neither. I hated living alone in Brooklyn. It's . . . it's just not the same without you."

"I know. It really is kind of like missing your other half, isn't it?"

He held her tighter. "I never really got that Scripture until now."

"What Scripture?"

"The two shall become one. It's not just about sex."

"I've been trying to tell you that," she teased.

"Well, I get it now. Not that I don't appreciate the other." He wriggled his eyebrows.

That made her laugh. And earned him another kiss.

35

"Is everything going okay at CeeCee's?" Grant pulled another box of Christmas decorations down from the attic, trying to be casual with his question. But he was prepared to press Chase for an honest answer. An answer he was pretty sure he could predict.

The kids had been staying with his mother for almost a week now, and while *she* was beyond delighted with her house guests, judging by the stories CeeCee had told him and Audrey, those poor kids hadn't had a minute to themselves since they arrived.

Chase hefted a box onto one shoulder. "We're really grateful for a place to stay. And CeeCee's cooking is amazing."

"Chase." He cleared his throat. "I appreciate your diplomacy, but I know a hedge when I hear one."

Chase slanted a sheepish grin Grant's way. "CeeCee is—well, Landyn would say 'high maintenance.' But sweet as they come," Chase added quickly.

"That, she is. But the question is, have you been able to get any work done?"

"I—I'm working on a—" He slid the box to the floor and his shoulders slumped. "Honestly, Grant, no. I'm not getting much art done at all.

Between CeeCee and Landyn I feel like I'm on call every minute. Gotta love 'em both but"—he rolled his eyes—"let's just say 'high maintenance' is the pot calling the kettle black."

That made Grant laugh out loud.

"To be fair," Chase said, "all the stuff with the car insurance and shopping for another vehicle, plus Landyn's doctor appointments and dealing with the sublease on the Brooklyn apartment . . . All that stuff is a big part of it too—why I feel like I'm not getting anything done."

"I hear you. That extracurricular stuff is the bane of my life. And I hate to tell you, but it doesn't get better with age. If it's not one thing, it's another. But I'm guessing it's harder for you when you don't have an office building to hide away at." He hoped Chase didn't take that as an indictment of his work-at-home status. He still wasn't convinced Chase could make a living as an artist, but he truly hadn't meant his comment that way.

Grant cleared his throat. "Would I be prying too much to ask if you and Landyn have made any decisions yet? About where you'll live? Or . . . at least how you're leaning?"

"No, not at all." Chase picked up the box marked Twinkle Lights again.

"I'd really like to explore how far I can go with this art career. I feel like I had some momentum going and I hate to waste that. Landyn likes New

York, but I don't see how we can stay in the Brooklyn apartment with two babies." He panned the spacious attic. "I think you could fit two of those studios in here."

"Grant?" Audrey's voice lilted up the stairs.

Grant hoisted the heaviest box. "Let's get this stuff down to her before she comes looking for us." Audrey was eager to get the inn decorated for a couple of early Christmas parties that were booked at the inn. She'd taken down most of the autumn and Thanksgiving decorations and already had the living room decorated to the hilt for Christmas. It looked nice too. Very festive and warm—which Audrey excelled at.

Chase stacked a smaller box atop the one he was carrying and followed Grant down two flights of stairs. They deposited the boxes in the front hall where Audrey was perched precariously on a tall ladder.

Grant went to the bottom of the ladder and looked up at her. "What are you trying to do here, Mrs. Whitman? Besides break a leg . . ."

"I want this garland all along the woodwork here and the wainscoting below. Swooping like so—" She held tight to the top of the ladder with her left hand and swept the right dramatically, demonstrating.

"Why don't you let us boys take over here? If you trust us."

"I would gladly turn this over to you. I won't

even stay to supervise." She did, however, give them a few more detailed instructions about how she wanted it done, before climbing down and retreating to the kitchen, where something delicious-smelling simmered on the stove, filling the house with the heady aromas of cinnamon and apples.

Grant and Chase made small talk for a few minutes before Grant steered the conversation back. "I'm not trying to influence your decision at all, but I wondered if you've given any more thought to that loft you looked at in Langhorne."

Chase put down the strand of garland he'd been untangling and eyed him like he wondered where this was going. "If you want to know the truth, I think about that place every day." He looked as if he was embarrassed by the fact. "I know it needs a ton of work, but I can just picture what it would look like if it was finished out."

"Is that right?" Grant was a little surprised that Chase was still interested in the loft. But pleased, too. This might not be as hard as he'd thought.

"Obviously," Chase said, "I don't know as much as you do about that kind of stuff, but it just seems to me like the place has good bones. And the views, being along the creek like that. I can just see it becoming a really cool space if it was done right."

"I can too, Chase. Good bones is exactly what I would have said. That Colonial Revival architecture all along Main Street there was built to last. It's too bad somebody didn't take care of it."

They worked together in silence until Chase stopped and looked at him. "Can I ask why you were wondering about the loft?"

"I just wondered if you were still at all interested in the place." Grant had purposely—no, *purposefully*—broached the topic, but in retrospect, he felt a little guilty for steering the conversation the way he had. But as long as Chase was urging him on . . . "I—I don't want you to feel like I'm trying to push you one way or another—although you've got to know that a man is going to do everything in his power to keep his grandkids as close as possible to home."

Chase laughed. "Point taken, sir. I'd like to hear your ideas. About the loft."

Well, a man could hardly argue with an invitation like that. He took a deep breath. "If you were to put the proceeds from your car as a down payment, you could probably get a pretty decent loan. I'd have to take a look, but from the Realtor's information and what you've told me, it'd take probably twenty grand to get the place livable, but they've got it priced pretty fairly. And there'd be plenty of room for a nursery and even an extra room or two. You wouldn't have to finish the whole place off right away, of course, but I could see a gallery down below someday—open to the public."

Chase's eyes lit with interest, which only fueled

Grant's enthusiasm. "We could do a lot of the work ourselves—assuming you want help—but I'm going to have a lot more free time this winter without the yard to keep up." He steadied himself on the ladder, pounded another tiny nail, then looped the garland Chase handed up to him over it. "The thing is, even if you two decided to go back to New York—say, after the babies are born—you could probably turn that place around for a profit. Worst case scenario, you might have to rent it while it's on the market. But you could probably get your mortgage payment in rent."

"I like the way you're thinking." Chase beamed. "But—I wouldn't dare make any decisions without talking it over with Landyn. And praying about it, of course."

"Of course." Grant measured and pounded the next nail into the wall above the wainscoting. "While we're throwing out ideas, Audrey had one for Landyn."

"Oh?"

"We've got these Christmas parties coming up—right up Audrey's alley with what she wanted the inn to be. Anyway, she's thinking if we could get some kind of an ad campaign going we might be able to make a little extra money renting out the inn for holiday parties. Especially on the weeknights, or weekends when the place isn't booked. Landyn's been sitting right under our noses with all her PR experience. I don't know why we didn't think of it before. We could work out something—I don't know . . . maybe a percentage of the take?"

Chase's eyebrows lifted. "She'd be great at that. I know she would."

"You want to talk to her about it? She'd probably be more receptive if it came from you."

"I'll do what I can."

Grant climbed down from the ladder and they stood back and admired their handiwork. He thought Audrey would be pleased. With all of it.

Landyn peeked into the living room again. "She's out like a light."

CeeCee had fallen asleep in front of the TV—as seemed to be her habit—and she and Chase stood side by side at the sink finishing up the supper dishes.

This had become her and Chase's time—about the only time they had together without CeeCee tagging after them chattering a mile a minute.

She stepped away from the sink, arched her back and stretched. Chase smiled and pointed at her belly.

She looked down to see an elongated water stain on the front of her T-shirt where she'd rested her belly against the sink. It seemed like the ER doctor, by revealing that she was carrying twins, had somehow given the babies permission to make their presence known. Because in the two weeks since the accident, Landyn had "blossomed," as CeeCee called it. It was getting tricky to keep her belly out of the way of her tasks. She dabbed at her shirt with the soggy dishtowel, but soon gave up and resorted to fanning her shirt out away from her body.

Chase hung up the dishtowel. "It's pretty nice out. You want to go for a walk?"

Landyn gave him a look. "I know exactly where we'll end up."

"Where?"

"You *know* where. That loft you're so in love with."

He grinned. "Are you getting sick of talking about it?"

She went to him and put her arms around his neck. "I actually love seeing you so fired up about it. But . . . I'm worried you'll be disappointed if the deal falls through."

"Whoa . . ." He pulled back and shook a finger at her. "We haven't made any deals yet."

"I know, but I have a feeling you will be."

He ran his hands down her arms and circled her wrists with his fingers, gently pushing her arms' length away. "Not without you, I won't. Landyn—" He closed his eyes. "How are you feeling about things by now? I don't want to make another mistake. I promise I won't make an offer until you're one hundred percent onboard with this whole idea."

"I know. And I appreciate that, Chase." She kissed him, wishing she could give him her honest, full-hearted approval right now. But she wasn't quite there yet.

He'd approached her a few days ago with the wild scheme Chase and her dad had come up with to refurbish the loft on Main Street. She didn't tell Chase that having her dad's stamp of approval on the purchase made her feel far more confident in *Chase's* dream.

She didn't mean to be deceitful by not telling him. But they'd worked so hard to rebuild their trust in each other, she didn't think it was something her husband needed to know. And truly, it wasn't a lack of faith in Chase's judgment as much as it was confidence in her dad's years of experience that had given him wisdom Chase couldn't be expected to possess at his age.

But she'd been praying about their future and the decisions they had before them. And she was humbled to recognize that her prayers had matured. Maybe it was the fact that she was going to be a mother. Maybe it was going through the hardships with Chase. Whatever the cause, she was grateful.

It had *not* been fun in the midst of the battle. And though it had been barely three months of her life, it had seemed far longer. She'd hated being estranged from her husband. Hated feeling displaced from her apartment and her job—her identity. And going through the accident, fearing she'd lose her baby—and then discovering that she was carrying twins—those things had enabled her to grow up in ways she never could have apart from hardship and pain. She didn't want to ever go through those trials again, but neither would she trade what she'd gained in the process. Not for anything.

She leaned in to kiss him. "Let me leave a note for CeeCee. Let's go for that walk."

The smile he gave her put her that much closer to her answer.

36

"Is CeeCee coming with Landyn and Chase?" Audrey spoke to Grant over her shoulder while she peeled potatoes at the kitchen sink.

"As far as I know. I think we'll all be here." Grant sounded like a little kid on Christmas morning.

Which reminded her . . . "I wonder if we shouldn't take those presents out from under the tree. Hide them in the hall closet maybe?"

"Why?"

"You know those little girls are going to want to open them."

Grant shook his head. "We didn't put things away for our own kids. I don't think we need to for the grandkids."

"Honey, two weeks is a long time to wait. How are you going to explain that to Simone?"

"That's not my job. I'll let Jesse and Corinne explain. If they want to put them up, they can."

"Okay, but don't say I didn't warn you." She cubed the potatoes and put them in the pot to boil. Link had requested *real* mashed potatoes for their first family dinner night.

Grant had declared Tuesday nights family dinner night. He'd written TUESDAY FAMILY NIGHT on the calendar in all caps in the squares for the Tuesdays between now and the end of the year. And he was already bugging her to hurry up and buy a calendar for next year so he could do the same.

Though it'd felt like a burden when he first suggested the idea, given all the Christmas events on the inn's calendar, Audrey loved how intentional her husband was about making sure family didn't slip through the cracks of the business of running an inn. And these few weeks' worth of Tuesdays would be especially precious if Chase and Landyn ended up moving back to New York.

Now that the twins were on the way, Audrey could hardly bear the possibility of having them so far away.

She went to the window and looked out over the driveway. She hated how early it got dark these days, but it had snowed last night—the first real snow of the year—and the white-blanketed lawn reflected the last crimson stains of the setting sun and illuminated the yard. Corinne had brought the girls over earlier this afternoon for sledding, and Audrey had to admit it had felt like the old days when the Chicory Inn was just a humble family home.

A wave of homesickness swept over her. She recognized it for more than just nostalgia for the years they'd had all the kids at home. The holidays had been hard—lonely—since they'd lost Tim. No matter how many Whitmans they squeezed around that dining room table, it always felt like there was an empty chair where Tim should be. Three Christmases without him . . . soon to be four.

She wrapped up the potato peelings and took them out to the compost bin. The frigid air felt good and helped her slough off the melancholy. She had too much for which to be thankful to dwell on things she couldn't change. And she knew Tim would tell her as much too, if he could. She took a deep breath and gazed up into the velvety blue canopy overhead and—as she'd done countless times before—she whispered a prayer of thanks for her son, who was already Home. *We all still miss you so much, Tim. So very much. But we're taking care of your precious Bree, loving her as if she was our own.*

She breathed deep and exhaled, so grateful

that this life wasn't all there was. Far from it.

Back in the kitchen she pulled two pans of lasagna from the oven and put foil-wrapped loaves of homemade French bread in to warm. The doorbell rang and Grant went to answer.

Within ten minutes the house was a crazy, chaotic, wonderful hive of noise and activity. Her daughters and Bree helped her get food on the table while Grant hung up coats and entertained three of the sweetest little girls on earth. Audrey could hardly wait to see how two little cousins fit into the mix.

"Hey, Mom"—Landyn plopped on the bar stool across the counter from her—"I've got some ideas to run by you after supper if you have time—publicity stuff for the inn. Chase said you'd mentioned it."

"Oh! That'd be great. I can't wait to see what you came up with." Audrey loved the passion she heard in Landyn's voice. For the first time since her youngest had pulled up the driveway with that U-Haul in tow, she felt like she had her Landyn back.

From the corner of her vision, she saw the longing in Danae's eyes as she surreptitiously watched her sister move about the kitchen, Landyn's pregnancy more apparent every week. Audrey sent a silent prayer winging, that Danae and Dallas would soon have happy baby news to share too.

It seemed impossible that there would soon be four Whitmans—Corinne's two youngest and Landyn's twins—that Tim had never known. And who would never know him. Not this side of heaven anyway.

She felt Grant's hand on her neck. "You okay, babe?" he whispered. And she knew he'd read her thoughts in her expression.

"I'm fine." It came out more brusque than she'd intended, but when he was so tender with her like this, tears were never far behind. She did not want to start this happy evening with tears.

Too late. Not hers. But Simone's angry screams came from the family room. And Jesse's stern voice. "No, baby girl, I told you not until Christmas. Does Daddy need to put you in time out?" More Simone screams.

Audrey shot Grant daggers. "Didn't I tell—"

He shut her up with a bear hug and a full-on-the-lips kiss.

"Whoa, Parents! Get a room!" Link laughed and sampled a finger full of mashed potatoes on his way through the kitchen.

Sari and Sadie came running to see what all the excitement was.

Sadie's towhead cocked to one side, watching them. "Why do Poppa and Gram have to get a room?"

To the cacophonous music of her grown children's laughter, Audrey squirmed out of Grant's embrace and straightened her clothes. "As long as you're all in here, you may as well get to the table. We're just waiting on the bread to warm."

Grant tossed her a self-satisfied wink and went to the broom closet to retrieve the high chair for Simone and a booster seat for Sadie. Like a well-choreographed dance, once they were all seated, hands went up on the table and everyone, young and old, clasped the hand of the loved one next to them.

Grant prayed—too long, in Audrey's opinion since Sari's hand was sweaty and the green beans were already growing cold—but she wouldn't begrudge him a single minute.

Landyn held her breath and chewed the corner of her bottom lip, more nervous than she'd ever been with a high-dollar client at Fineman and Justus.

The rest of the gang was in the family room watching a movie with the little girls—part of Dad's grand TUESDAY FAMILY NIGHT plan—but Mom had curled up on the couch in the living room with Landyn's proposal in hand. The proposal she'd worked on for three solid days before she felt it was ready to present. Her P&L on this job would not have cut muster at Fineman and Justus, but thankfully, Mom wasn't keeping track of profit and loss.

After what seemed an eternity, Mom turned to

the final page and shook her head, her mouth pressed in a thin line. Landyn's heart fell. But when her mother looked up, the smile that came looked more like a wow-I'm-impressed sort of smile. Landyn scooted to the edge of the couch. "So, you like it?"

Leafing absently through the six-page document one more time, Mom looked thoughtful. "I think your ideas might be a little more elaborate than our budget can handle right now, but I like the way you're thinking." She uncurled, crossed her legs, and picked up the ballpoint pen from the coffee table. "Let's talk about which of these we could implement right away."

Landyn smiled and the familiar adrenaline rush she always got when a creative project was coming together surged through her. "Look at the top of the second page. I think we could do that on a barebones budget."

Mom chuckled. "That would be ours." But then she studied Landyn as if seeing her for the first time tonight. "Just look at you! So professional and competent. I can see why you loved your job. You're a pro, sweetie!"

Warmth flooded her. And then doubt crept back in—about the decision she was so close to. "Mom, do you think—Do you think I'd be sorry if I gave this up?" She waved her copy of the proposal.

"The marketing?"

"My *career*."

"Oh honey . . . You're the only one who can answer that question. But don't think that just because you gave up your career now that you couldn't have it back again one day."

"I know, but—I'd be so far behind the curve. I've only been away from Fineman and Justus for three months, and already I feel like I'm in the dark. Marketing is a high-tech industry. It changes every day and—" She stopped, closed her eyes, and breathed deep. "Why is this so hard?"

"Maybe you're making it harder than it needs to be," Mom said softly. "What does Chase think?"

A few months ago that question would have raised her hackles, but she knew her mother didn't mean it the way Landyn would have been tempted to interpret it in the past—that Chase's opinion was more important. Or that she should just be a little doormat and do whatever her husband said without question. Even though it did seem like that was the way her mother sometimes handled things in her marriage to Dad. But then, she couldn't argue that it worked for them.

"Chase is pretty excited about the possibility of buying the loft in Langhorne." Landyn riffled the edges of the proposal. "If we did that, I know it wouldn't be forever, but it would be pretty long-term."

"Chase is trying to do the right thing, Landyn. He's never had anyone to show him how to be a husband—how to lead his family. But I think he's doing a pretty fine job. Just something to consider . . ."

She'd seen that look on her mother's face many times. And hadn't always been thrilled with what followed. "I'm listening." She was learning.

"This might be a good time—with the babies coming and the opportunities you've both been given—to let Chase make the call. To give your blessing for whatever it is he feels God is calling him to. Trust him. And trust that if Chase makes a mistake, God has his back."

"I—I know He does. But it's hard. It's hard to trust someone else when"—she gave a sheepish grin—"when I'm so sure I could make better decisions."

Her mother smiled and raised a brow. "I happen to know a certain girl who has learned quite a bit over these last few months, and I've seen quite a change in her. For the better, I might add. But I don't think she's ready to be God yet." Mom reached across the couch and patted her cheek.

"Mom . . ."

"I'm not saying you were unbearable before—" She looked toward the ceiling. "Actually, maybe I *am* saying that . . ."

Landyn laughed. "I'm sorry. I know I'm not always the most pleasant person to have around. These last few months have been so hard, Mom." And they had been. But they'd also been good in a way she'd never imagined.

"You know, honey, your dad took a pretty big risk and made a huge sacrifice—of finances, and of his own desires—when he agreed to open the inn. I feel a little guilty about it, if you want to know the truth. But I also felt—*feel* so much love in his decision. It—" Tears sprang to Mom's eyes. "I can't ever thank your dad enough for letting me explore my dream. I can say without reservation that you'd be giving Chase a wonderful gift if you allowed him the same."

"I know." She looked at her lap.

"And here's the thing, sweet girl . . . This B&B thing has *not* been all it's cracked up to be. We've faced some pretty tough challenges already. And there are no guarantees that we won't be trying to sell the place in a year or two—"

"What?" Surely she wasn't serious.

But her mother held up a hand. "I'm not saying we've talked about that. It's just that we don't know what might be down the road. The economy could go south—"

"You mean farther south?"

Mom gave a humorless laugh. "Our health could go south, the house could burn down . . . There's a lot that can go wrong when you're trying to make a dream come true. I'm just saying that if you do allow Chase his dream, you have to do it with no strings attached. Dad has done that for me. And it's been the best thing about the whole venture."

"I didn't know all that."

"I know you didn't. Dad's not one to toot his own horn. And sadly, I'm not given to much humility." Mom rolled her eyes. "I'm working on that. And speaking of working on that, what about this Valentine's Day giveaway idea you had?" She flipped back through the proposal.

Landyn took her cue and outlined her ideas in more detail.

She was in the midst of fleshing out another idea when Chase drifted in from the family room and sat on the arm of the couch, kneading the muscles in her neck.

A minute later, Dad and Link wandered in too and plopped down across from them in over-stuffed chairs.

"That film must have been pretty boring for you to choose our company over a movie," Mom said. "Hey, but this is great. You guys can give us your input on Landyn's ideas."

Landyn presented them in a nutshell, and for the next half hour, the five of them brainstormed the way Landyn used to with her team at Fineman and Justus. With input from her three favorite men on the planet, she wasn't sure she'd ever had so much fun on a project.

"Shoot, sis," Link said, "you could open your own firm in Langhorne. I'm serious."

She'd dared to entertain that very idea over the last few minutes, but to hear her brother say it—in front of the rest of them—made her believe it might be possible.

"I just might do that. Who knows," she said, with an exaggerated wink. "If this goes over well, I might even hit up Lawna and Fred Farley to see if they want me to design some folders."

"Folders?" Link's brow knit.

"You look flummoxed, brother. Did you forget?"

"Forget what?"

"Folders for Farleys Family Fun Friday at Tease, Tan 'n' Tone?"

"Oh, that's right." The glint in Mom's eye told Landyn she was in on the joke. "That's the fourth Friday in February . . . How fantastically fitting."

Deadpan, Link rolled his eyes and lumbered out of his chair. "I'm finished with you foolish females."

Chase and her dad got up to follow Link, but not before Dad threw his best effort over his shoulder. "Finished . . . f-forever."

The men retreated in the wake of their girlish giggles, and even Chase and Link groaned over that one.

But Landyn's heart swelled with love for her family, and without warning, her laughter turned to tears.

"Honey?" Alarm colored her mother's face. "What's wrong?"

"I'd miss all of this so much . . . If we moved back to New York, I mean."

"Is that how you're leaning? Toward a move?" Her mother's voice was so soft she could scarcely hear, and she suspected Mom was holding her breath for the answer.

"I don't know. That's the hardest part—not knowing. I just wish this was settled." She laughed through her tears. "I'm sorry . . . I think I'm just emotional. Too many hormones running through my veins."

Mom leaned to hug her. "You'll figure it out. God will show you what to do. I'm not worried."

"Thanks, Mom. I hope you're right."

37

"I just can't quit thinking that if—" Chase wrung out the dishcloth and took another swipe at CeeCee's spotless kitchen counters, wishing he'd never started this conversation. But he had, and he knew Cecelia Whitman wouldn't let him abandon it now. "If I missed God's leading by such a long shot, how can I ever know when I do get it right?"

Landyn's grandmother—still in bib overalls from her "evening constitutional" around the block—regarded him with a questioning look. "Who says you missed it?"

"Well, it's pretty obvious I did. I thought God was saying one thing, but at the very moment I was supposedly hearing His voice, Landyn was already pregnant. I didn't know that, but God surely did. There's no way He would have led me to take that stupid studio apartment when He knew we had twins on the way. So . . . I couldn't have heard Him right."

"Chase, my boy." She made a *tsk tsk* sound with her tongue. "Quit beating yourself up over this. If there's one thing I've learned, it's that God rarely works in ways that make sense to us while they're happening. All too often, it's only after we look back, sometimes many years later—often, truth be told, peering over heaven's balcony—that we can make sense of the way He was working."

"I appreciate that, CeeCee. I really do." He wasn't sure why he was so filled with doubt today. It had been a good day. He'd finished a painting and gotten a check from Miles. A decent one. But between the emergency room and the deductible on Landyn's car—never mind babies coming!—bills were piling up and doubts assailed him. "How many times can I mess up without—"

"Son, God isn't a three-strikes-you're-out kind of guy." CeeCee handed him a platter to dry. "Who knows? Making that decision about that apartment in Brooklyn might have been the only way you'd have ever gotten Landyn to come with you. God knows"—she rolled her eyes heavenward—"that girl is stubborn enough the

Lord likely has to come up with some creative ways to get her to do His bidding."

"Boy, can I sympathize with Him on that one."

CeeCee gave an impish grin. "I can still see that girl—she must've been four or five at the time—with her feet dug in hard, and her mama pushing and her daddy pulling, trying to get her to go on the merry-go-round at the Clemens County fair. They never did get her on there. And she's still that little girl sometimes, refusing to go wherever it is God—or anyone else, for that matter—is trying to lead her. Even if there's a merry-go-round ride waiting on the other end."

Chase laughed out loud. It wasn't hard to picture a stubborn little Landyn. But he got CeeCee's point, too.

She leaned her head closer to his. "And if you tell Landyn about this conversation, I will deny it with my dying breath."

He feigned a sigh and shook his head slowly. "And I wonder where she gets it."

CeeCee looked proud enough to pop the buttons off her bib overalls. But she sobered. "I'm going to say this once, Mr. Chase. And if I have to say it a dozen more times I will, but it would behoove you to hear me this first time."

"I'm all ears."

CeeCee thumped an arthritic finger at his chest, but the expression on her face was pure love. "Don't let this bog you down. If you made a mistake, fess up and move on. If you're not sure whether you made a mistake or not, give it to God. He's not going to strike you with lightning if you thought you were doing the right thing."

Could she be right? This thing had been eating him up ever since the possibility of refurbishing the loft with Grant had come up. But he wasn't sure he could just let it go. It felt too important.

"Are you two up for a rematch?" Landyn popped her head around the corner from the laundry room. They'd been playing a marathon of Mexican Train Dominoes in the evenings and Landyn was low man on the totem pole. "I'm feeling lucky tonight."

"Yeah, well, I'm feeling lucky too." Chase gave Landyn "that" look over the top of CeeCee's head.

Her smile said she got his meaning. He'd have to find a way to end the game early tonight.

"Don't think I'm so blind I don't see those googly eyes you two are giving each other." She shook a finger at them. "And I'm not so old I don't remember what 'getting lucky' means." She yawned. "I am pretty tired."

A fake yawn if Chase had ever seen one.

"I believe I'll just go on to bed." She winked at him, then slipped off her apron and hung it on a hook. "You two enjoy your evening."

Landyn covered a smile with her hand, and Chase felt his face heat. "Goodnight, CeeCee."

When her door was safely shut, Chase turned to

his wife, arm outstretched. "Are you as tired as I am?"

She laughed and accepted his hand. "Why, I do believe I am."

Hearing her husband's even breaths, Landyn slipped out of bed and went to the window. The clouds blew across the night sky parting a curtain on a sliver of bright December moon.

Landyn stood there in her nightshirt, just as she had as a little girl spending the night at CeeCee's little house in town. That fathomless sky had always held such mystery for her, and tonight was no different.

She and Chase had lain atop the nest of quilts on the bed in CeeCee's house, spent, entangled in each other's arms.

She wasn't sure how long she'd been standing there watching the moon—and praying—when she heard Chase stir in the bed behind her.

"You okay, baby?"

"I'm fine. Go back to sleep. I'll be there in a minute."

But he climbed out of bed and came to stand behind her, wrapping his arms around her, cupping his hands beneath her expanding belly, and nestling his chin atop her head. "What are you thinking about?"

"Nothing . . . Everything. Just trying to figure some things out."

"Yeah," he whispered. "Me too." He told her about his conversation with CeeCee earlier tonight while they had done the dishes together. "I wish it was so easy as your grandmother makes it sound."

"I don't think she meant to make it sound easy. But maybe it's true that it's always easier looking back." She leaned back into him and pulled his arms tighter around her like a blanket, filling to overflowing with love for him—a love she'd once been afraid she'd lost forever. "Chase, we may never know why everything has happened like it has. Why we had to go through this to get where we are. But does it really matter? We're just—imperfect people trying to follow a perfect God. We try to be obedient to all we know of Him. And we have to trust that He'll take care of the rest."

"And He will." Gently, he turned her around and folded her into his embrace. "He's proven that over and over again. And the more we see Him work in our lives, the easier it will be to trust Him. At least . . . I hope it will be."

She relaxed against him, happy to be in his arms, to be carrying his babies. She glanced over at the clock on the nightstand. The numbers glowed red in the darkness. Just past midnight.

The beginning of a brand new day.

And just like that—in the twinkling of an eye, as if a switch had been flipped—she knew what she wanted. Beyond a shadow of a doubt. And she knew that now was the time to tell him.

"Chase?"

"Hmm?" He sounded drowsy. Or maybe he was just feeling as content and relaxed as she was.

"What if I told you I want to stay?"

He stilled. "Stay?"

"Yes."

"Here?"

"Well, not at CeeCee's. But in Langhorne. I think we should buy the loft and fix it up. I think we should raise our babies here, close to Poppa and Gram and CeeCee and all the aunts and uncles and cousins."

He was quiet, too quiet.

But a heartbeat later he said, "I'm listening."

"You can have your studio and we'll make a room for the babies. We can take getaways to New York, to the galleries, and to meet with Miles. I love the city. I do. But—this time back here—back *home*—has reminded me of what I grew up with. I want that for our babies, Chase. I do."

He tipped her chin. "Are you sure?"

"I'm sure."

He nodded against her cheek. "Me too. I want our kids to have what you had growing up. What I . . . didn't have."

She hated the sadness and longing in his voice.

But when he spoke next, there was a lilt of hope

there too. "I sort of feel like I've been given another chance, you know?"

"You have, babe. And you'll be a great dad, Chase. I have no doubt."

He tensed. "I'm going to need help. I know your dad has his doubts, but I feel like even he is giving me another chance—offering to help me renovate the loft. That's one of the reasons I most want to stay here. I want to get to know him better, too. To . . . learn from him." His hands moved over her abdomen, over the place that nestled their children. "It'll be slow going. I'll have to work on the paintings for Miles during the day and do the remodeling after hours. But if you can handle living in a dump for a few months . . ."

"Oh, Chase . . . As long as you're there with me, as long as we're in this *together*"—she covered his hands with hers—"I think I can handle just about anything."

38

"Hey, Chase. What do you think?" Grant held an unwieldy sheet of corrugated tin up to the wall of the loft where Chase's worktable was to go. The metal was aged and rusted to perfection.

"Looks good."

"It'll take some doing to get this cleaned up, but I'll take it home and work on that tonight."

"Cleaned up? Um . . . I was thinking about using it just like that. It has a nice aged look."

"Probably because it's sixty years old."

Chase could tell Grant was having to work to keep from rolling his eyes. He leaned the metal up against the wall in question, took a few steps back, and squinted. "I guess it does look okay like that. Got that grunge thing going. Gives the place some character, that's for sure."

Chase grinned. "Exactly." He was frankly surprised his father-in-law seemed halfway enthused about what he kept referring to as "the grunge look." Chase had to curb a smile every time.

"Looks like the Chipotle restaurant in Kansas City . . . you know, the Mexican place. Except theirs is shiny. Nice and new. Real clean look, you know?"

He nodded. "Yeah, Landyn was showing me something similar in one of her design magazines the other night—it was in a SoHo loft. She says they call it Industrial Chic."

Grant made a face. "Let's just stick with industrial and leave the 'chic' to the girls," Grant said, chalking quote marks in the air.

Chase chuckled. "Sounds good to me. But I do want to keep the rust and crud on for my studio."

"Rust and crud it is." Grant pulled a tape measure from his pocket and stretched it out, handing Chase one end and dragging the other across the length of the loft. "So you think you want this on this whole wall?"

"If there's enough."

Grant nodded. "Lots more where that came from." He stopped at the window that overlooked Langhorne's Main Street. "You've got a pretty nice view up here, I'll give you that."

Again, Chase had to hold back a grin. Grant hadn't "given him" much since he and Landyn had come back to Missouri. But working together on the loft these past two months had made him appreciate Landyn's dad in a different way than before. And he felt pretty certain that was starting to go both ways.

Grant arched his back and stretched before picking up the sheet of metal again. "If we get on it, we can get this up yet tonight. These longer days are in our favor."

"Good. I'm a little nervous about making CeeCee's deadline," Chase ventured.

"Deadline?"

"She hosts her bridge club two weeks from today."

"That's right. I forgot. Two weeks, huh?"

Chase nodded, frowning.

"We'll make it." Grant reeled in the tape measure and stuffed it back in his pocket. "And if we don't, we'll figure something out. Looks to me like you could move in downstairs any time if you needed to. The girls finished all the painting didn't they?"

"Yes, but Audrey thinks Landyn should wait another week to give the paint fumes a chance to dissipate."

"Oh. Sure. Hadn't thought of that. Well, we could get the furniture moved in at least . . . Get the babies' room set up."

He nodded, but every time the subject came up, he felt a little lightheaded. Landyn's mom and sisters had spent three days painting the entire apartment below the loft. There was plenty they still wanted to do to the place, but a coat of paint had made a huge difference, and Landyn had been combing Craigslist and eBay for stuff for the babies' room.

He was still getting used to the idea of having a baby in their lives—let alone two. But then, he was getting used to a lot of ideas he'd never considered before. Being part of a large family for one.

It wasn't perfect—was just flat messy at times—but one thing he knew: he wanted that for his children. Comparing their lives in New York to their lives intertwined with Grant and Audrey's, CeeCee's, and all of Landyn's siblings and their families, had made him ache all over again for what he'd missed growing up. Living these weeks at Landyn's grandmother's house, he felt like he'd made up for some of the nurturing he'd been deprived of as a child. He didn't want his own children to ever know anything other than this warm, loving, crazy family he'd gotten himself mixed up with.

"What's so funny?" Grant was studying him with an odd expression on his face.

He startled, unaware that he'd let his expression give his thoughts away. "Sorry. Just thinking about—something your mother said." That was the truth, if not the whole truth.

"I'm sure you two are ready to get out of there and have a place of your own. I know Mother can be a pistol sometimes, but I hope—"

"No, she's been great. She's a lot of fun actually. Keeps me and Landyn in stitches most of the time. She's probably the one who's ready to have her place to herself again."

Grant looked stunned to hear the sentiment from Chase.

Chase started to ask him what was wrong, but before the words were out of his mouth, it struck him that his "attitude of gratitude," as CeeCee called it, probably *was* shocking to Grant.

He felt bad that he'd taken everything Landyn's family had done for them for granted. For too long. He decided then and there that he would try to make it up to them however he could.

A lump formed in his throat, and he turned away and knelt on the dusty floor, pretending to be intent on picking up a few stray nails he'd missed when he swept earlier. When he gained his composure again, he straightened and turned to

Grant. "What would you think about using corrugated tin on that opposite wall too?"

Whether Landyn's dad caught on to his show of emotion or not, Chase couldn't tell, but he was grateful when Grant played along.

"I don't know," Grant said. "I'd be careful about overdoing a good thing. Maybe live with it on this one wall and see what you think. You could always add more later."

"Yeah." Chase rubbed at a paint stain with the toe of his work boot. "Good point. Besides, it won't cost as much if we do it the way you suggested."

"Mom, I can't get this stupid thing to thread right." Landyn bent her head, trying to see where she'd misrouted the thread in her mother's old sewing machine.

Mom came into the dining room where Landyn had fabric and cotton batting spread over every flat surface, including the floor. She leaned over Landyn's shoulder. "Hmm . . . It looks right. Here, scoot over. I can't tell unless I sit in the driver's seat."

"Yeah, and even though I'm sitting in the driver's seat, I can't get close enough to see because of this stupid huge belly."

Mom placed a palm over the mountain of Landyn's stomach. "It's getting close. I can hardly wait!"

"I can hardly wait to have my figure back." Landyn rolled her eyes. "I'm not so sure about the four a.m. feedings and dirty diapers, and—"

"Times two," Mom joked. "Everything times two."

"Thanks for the reminder," she said wryly.

"Happy to help."

Landyn slid off the chair and her mother slipped behind the sewing machine. In half a minute, she had the machine rethreaded and purring like a well-fed lioness.

"How about if I trade you? I could do laundry or something . . . whatever you need done, if you'll finish up the hems in those curtains."

Mom gave her a look that said, you-little-Tom-Sawyer-you. Landyn laughed and put on her best pouty face. But in that moment she felt overwhelmed with joy and with gratitude that they'd made the decision to leave New York. She had loved working with her mother on some advertising for the inn. It had paid off, too. The inn was booked for most of the summer.

Chase was enjoying being back in Missouri, too. He'd made a trip to New York to meet with Miles. His work was selling reasonably well and "gathering steam" according to the rep. Even better, Chase was beyond passionate about the studio he was creating over their apartment in Langhorne—with plenty of help from her dad. She had to admit the place was shaping up nicely, and she was eager to begin this next chapter, imagining what their small-town life would look like.

"There's plenty of laundry in the baskets upstairs, and a bedroom to make up."

Her mother's voice interrupted the swirl of day-dreams. "Okay. Thanks, Mom. You're the best."

Mom gave her a watery smile that hinted she, too, was grateful for where life had carried them all.

Landyn lumbered up the stairs—lumbering seemed to be her only speed these days—and found clean sheets for the guest room. She unfolded the fitted sheet and smoothed it out over the mattress cover, then added the flat sheet, tucking in the corners hospital-style like Mom had taught them all from the time they were old enough to make their own beds. She still got homesick for the house she'd grown up in, but having her own nest to feather in downtown Langhorne had eased the pangs considerably.

And she was beginning to realize how transforming this house had been a necessary thing for her mother. As Mom liked to say, "if you do your job right as a mother, you soon put yourself out of a job."

Landyn unfolded a pillowcase and reached across the king-size bed for one of the feather pillows. She gasped as something gave way and a contraction—far stronger than the Braxton Hicks ones she'd been feeling regularly—rolled over her. She wasn't due for another month. This couldn't be the real thing.

She sat on the edge of the mattress waiting for the contraction to subside. It did and she rose to resume making the bed. But not five minutes later, another one began its crescendo.

"Mom!" Her voice seemed to come from somewhere outside herself. She called again, but she was trembling so hard she needed to sit down. She half-sat, half-rolled onto the clean sheets and waited again for it to pass.

When it did she called again for her mother. This time Mom must have heard, for Landyn heard a rush of footfalls on the stairs, and her mother appeared in the doorway of the bedroom. "Landyn?"

"I—I think I might be in labor."

"Oh, my goodness." Mom grabbed the pillow Landyn had been reaching for when this all started and plumped it behind her. "Stay right there. I'll get your dad."

"And Chase," she called weakly. "Don't forget Chase . . ."

But Mom was already halfway down the stairs.

39

"It's too early . . . too early." Landyn hadn't quit trembling since Chase had walked in and found her curled on the bed in her childhood bedroom.

He'd received a frantic call from Audrey, and he and Grant had raced home from the loft, leaving a concrete countertop halfway poured and likely sitting off-level this minute. He shouldn't care. This was an emergency. Landyn wasn't due for another month and although the doctor had told them to expect her to go into labor early, this seemed too early.

He sat on the edge of the bed and stroked wisps of her curly hair away from her forehead. "It's okay, baby. Everything's going to be okay."

But why couldn't she seem to quit shaking?

When three contractions came exactly five minutes apart, they decided it was time to get to the hospital. Better to get there and find out it was false labor than to wait too long and not make it to the hospital in time. At least Audrey was here. Chase gave a silent sigh of relief. He'd had more than one nightmare about having to deliver the babies himself.

Grant and Audrey had guests arriving any minute and Audrey was on the phone downstairs trying to get hold of Corinne, hoping she could come and help out with the inn.

He leaned down to look Landyn in the eyes. "Do you think you can get up and walk to the car?"

No answer.

"Baby?" He repeated the question.

"I don't know. I'll try." But she made no effort to sit up. She seemed unfocused—and terrified.

Audrey appeared in the doorway. "Aren't you going?" Her harsh question was aimed at Chase.

"Yes. We . . . I'm waiting for her to get up." He checked his watch. "It's almost noon. Should you have some lunch before we go, Landyn?"

"No. She probably shouldn't eat anything until they make sure this isn't the real thing. Come on, sweet girl." Audrey gave a huff and pushed herself between him and Landyn. "Get up. You need to get yourself in the car."

Audrey and Chase manhandled Landyn until she was sitting on the edge of the bed.

He stuffed his wife's swollen feet into a pair of Toms and put her arm around his shoulder. "Come on, baby, don't make me carry all three of you."

That didn't earn him even a hint of a smile. He'd never seen her so scared.

Which scared *him*.

Despite Chase's protests that they could take their car—they'd replaced their cars with another Honda, which ran fine—Grant insisted they take his Highlander. He brought the SUV around to the front of the house and, between the three of them, they got Landyn in it and buckled in.

Audrey shut the passenger side door and turned to grab Chase by his T-shirt. "You drive safe, Chase. But drive fast. This is the real thing. Those babies are coming."

"And you call us the minute you can," Grant barked.

"Now, hurry." Audrey all but pushed him around the vehicle.

He backed around and barreled out of the driveway. Landyn was making strange noises that sounded frighteningly like what they'd called "transition" in the three childbirth classes they'd attended at the hospital in Cape.

At least he knew his way to the hospital, thanks to those classes. It was a twenty-minute drive—he'd clocked it last time they'd driven to class—but he pulled into the emergency room bay exactly sixteen minutes later.

He laid on the horn, then jumped out and ran around to open Landyn's door.

"I can't walk, baby. I can't do this."

"Yes you can!"

He tried to help her down from the high seat, but she slumped over and slid from the seat like a rag doll. Chase caught her before she hit the pavement.

"Here! Right behind you!"

Chase turned at the shout. Two uniformed men

336

were hurrying toward him with an empty wheel-chair. He half dragged Landyn and helped her into the chair.

She was weeping openly now, saying unintelligible words, but he knew she was talking about the babies and worried they were in danger.

"You Spencer?" the younger orderly—or EMT or whatever he was called—asked.

"Yes. How'd you know?"

He nodded toward Landyn. "Her dad called. Said you were on your way."

"She's in labor. Twins. But she's not due till April. April first."

"April second," Landyn grunted.

"Seriously? You're going to quibble about that now?" Chase almost laughed.

But he had to run to keep up with the men wheeling his wife toward the wide doors marked ER.

"You're going to need to move your car." The guy directed him to the parking lot around the side of the building.

"Just ask the reception desk when you get inside. They'll tell you where to find us."

"Okay." He dug in his pocket for Grant's keys, then realized he'd left them in the Highlander. And left it running. *Great move, Spencer. Get it together, man.*

"I'll be right there, baby," he hollered to the two uniformed backs shielding Landyn from view.

No reply. He watched them disappear into the building with his wife. With his family.

He ran around to the driver's side and climbed in. This was it. The real deal. At least they'd made it to the hospital.

He sucked in a breath of air and realized he was trembling almost as hard as Landyn had been. He hadn't had time for more than a desperate prayer, thrown up as they rushed to the hospital, but he prayed now. Prayed as earnestly as he'd prayed that wintery night after the ambulance had whisked Landyn away and he'd been left behind, staring at her mangled car.

"Please help her, God. Help *us*. Help me be what she needs me to be."

The room was deathly cold. And deathly silent.

Landyn stared at the table in the corner where they'd taken her baby. She raised up in the bed and strained to see past the knot of doctors and nurses working—frantically, it seemed to her— over the table. "Is the baby okay? Is it—"

Another contraction started, taking Landyn's breath away. She tried to breathe the way they'd shown her in the childbirth classes, but nothing was working the way they'd said it should. Her body had betrayed her and she felt at its mercy.

Chase stood at the head of the delivery bed, holding her hand, giving her ice chips, whispering encouragement. But all she could think about was the tiny, purple body they'd whisked away from her the minute it had slid from her body. She didn't even know if she'd delivered a boy or a girl.

The pressure built and she braced herself for the inevitable pain.

Dr. Gregory's voice came as if he were calling from a tunnel. "Push, Landyn. I need you to push."

She tried. But she was exhausted. Her body would not obey her brain's commands.

"Come on, baby. One more time. You can do it." Chase's voice sounded falsely bright. And that fear had never left his eyes.

"I can't."

"Yes, you can. You can do it, Landyn. I know you can."

She wanted to. She'd tried so hard. For more than ten hours she'd labored. Twice she'd heard them discuss the possibility of a cesarean section. She'd convinced them she could do this. But had it been for nothing?

She glanced over at the table again, praying to hear a baby's cry. And hearing only the hushed murmurs of the medical team working on her baby.

She and Chase had decided they wanted to be surprised about the babies' genders. But why hadn't they told her now? Something must be terribly wrong. She tried to ask Chase, but she was too exhausted even to turn her head and look at him.

His voice stirred her now. "Landyn? Stay with me, baby."

The contraction finally subsided, but another one began with barely a second's pause between. She just wanted this to be over. She was so tired. So very tired . . .

And then, a quiet cheer rose from the gathering in the corner. And the most beautiful sound she'd ever heard. A whimper at first, building to a squall, and then a furious, glorious scream.

At the foot of the delivery table, Dr. Gregory laughed. "That one is going to give you a run for your money."

"Is it . . . a baby?"

Chase laughed. "It's a girl, Landyn. A little girl. Didn't you hear us?"

Had they told her? How could she have missed that? Why did she feel so light-headed?

"The first baby was born at eleven-fifty-six," a nurse said. "If you want your twins to share a birthday, time's a wasting."

"Yes, it is." Dr. Gregory sounded concerned. "Landyn, we still have another baby to get out of there. Come on, Mommy. I need you to push."

She felt another contraction starting and took a deep breath, steeling herself for the agony that had come with every push. This time, the pain didn't seem quite as strong. She summoned every last ounce of strength and strained until she thought she might pass out. A second later, she felt the baby slide from her body.

Almost instantly, a cry identical to the noisy one still going on in the corner filled her ears.

"That's more like it," the doctor said, smiling. "Another healthy girl. But you missed March 1 by three minutes."

"Two birthday parties every year?" Chase groaned.

"It's a girl? Two girls?" Landyn struggled to stay awake.

"That's right. Another little girl," Dr. Gregory said.

"Two girls . . . Wow." Chase looked a little dazed.

Dr. Gregory shook his head. "Brace yourself, Dad. You're badly outnumbered."

"Not complaining," Chase said. He leaned down to kiss Landyn's forehead. "You did it, baby. I'm so proud of you."

"I thought we lost our—" The tears came then. Buckets of them.

Chase put his cheek next to hers and cradled the other side of her face in the palm of his warm hand. "No! No, babe. We didn't lose anything. Everything is fine now."

"They're okay then? Both of them? Two girls?" She couldn't seem to stop crying.

He nodded against her cheek. "Two perfect little girls. March 1 and March 2. You did great."

"We'll let you hold them for a few minutes," a nurse said. "But they're a little small, so we want to get them right into the warmers."

"How much do they weigh?" Chase asked.

Dr. Gregory looked to the nurses and aides, waiting for a reply.

"Baby A is five pounds, three ounces. And baby B is not quite five pounds. Looks like . . . four pounds, fourteen ounces. They're both doing well."

Chase beamed. "That's ten pounds of baby you've been hauling around."

She gave a wan smile, feeling light as a feather. But feeling herself fading fast. "I should write a diet book," she mumbled. "Make a million . . ."

That made Chase laugh.

It was a good sound to fall asleep to. A very good sound.

40

The damp breath of April blew across the creek, and Audrey breathed in the first scents of spring. Standing on the back deck, looking down the hill to the kids' climbing tree, she could just make out a mist of a million green buds beginning to unfold in its branches. And along the banks, the daffodils were popping open en masse.

"You want to go for a walk?"

She hadn't heard Grant come out. "Sure. Let me change into my tennis shoes."

A few minutes later, they padded across the spongy, greening grass, headed down to the creek. Unconcerned, a pair of rabbits munched early sweet clover at the foot of a stand of firs, and a fat robin pecked for worms nearby.

"Are the babies coming tomorrow night?"

"They'd better be. I haven't seen them for ten days."

"Well, you've seen them since I have," Grant said. "Maybe you should remind them?"

"If I talk to Landyn, I'll say something. But I'm really trying not to interfere." Chase and Landyn had bowed out of family night last Tuesday, pleading exhaustion.

"I don't see why that would be interfering." It came out a little like a whine.

She knew he had been disappointed, but she didn't blame the new little family for not wanting to subject themselves to the craziness that was Tuesday Family Night at the Whitmans'. "Grant. Surely you haven't forgotten how you felt when my mother would badger us about 'bringing the baby over' after Corinne was born?"

"Yeah, well now I get why she did that. We should have listened to her and obeyed."

Audrey laughed and took his hand. "I'm sure you'll get plenty of time with those babies. This time next year, when they're mobile, you'll probably be wanting me to call Chase and Landyn and tell them *not* to come."

"That will never happen."

Without missing a stride, she stood on tiptoe and planted a kiss on his cheek.

But Grant surprised her by stopping in the middle of the meadow and pulling her into a full embrace. After a long minute, he drew away, kissed her, then took her hand and continued on to the creek.

"What was that for?" She gave him a sidewise look.

"That was because I love you."

"Well, I knew that." She studied him. "Everything okay?"

He turned to look her square in the eye. "Everything is more than okay. For now anyway. Let's enjoy the lull between catastrophes while we can."

She giggled. "You got that right. If someone had told us a year ago that by spring we'd have Landyn back home, and five granddaughters . . . Five!" She shook her head.

"Only five? I hope that's just a drop in the bucket. But I wouldn't mind if one of our children would see fit to produce a *boy*. I'm starting to feel mighty outnumbered."

"I'm sure you can handle us."

His laughter joined the bright clear notes of an oriole in the top of the Osage Orange.

Audrey's heart lifted yet another notch. It had been a long winter, but finally spring was here.

Landyn tiptoed out of the nursery and pulled the door closed with a sigh of relief. She went to open the windows that looked out over the back of the storefront that was now their home. It had turned out to be a pretty great little space, too—especially Chase's studio in the loft over their apartment.

As the days had grown longer, they'd grown warmer too. The birds sang their hearts out and everywhere she looked, things were turning green or blooming. The sound of the creek rose up to meet her. Chase had discovered it was the same creek that flowed behind Mom and Dad's house. The clear water flowed deeper and faster here in town than it ever had on Chicory Lane. But still, it was a familiar sound, one she loved.

"Hey, baby?" Chase's voice floated down from his studio directly above her. "You got a minute?"

She ran to the bottom of the stairs. "Shh! I just got the girls to sleep." She heard stirring in the nursery and held her breath, then sighed when it grew quiet again.

She slipped off her shoes and padded up the open staircase. She didn't know how they'd keep the girls off the stairs once they were big enough to start crawling and climbing. But she loved this place. They'd figure something out.

It amazed her how God had brought her back

home in the truest sense of the word. Home to the godly man He'd given her. Home to the little girls they were raising. Even home to a view of the very same creek she'd loved for as long as she could remember.

Chase had even discovered an Osage Orange tree growing on the banks below their property. "We may not live long enough to see it become a climbing tree, but Grace and Emma just might."

Landyn loved that thought.

Chase met her at the top of the stairs. "Sorry. Hope I didn't wake anybody up."

"No, they're zonked. Hopefully for a few hours."

"Come here . . ." He took her hand and led her over to the worktable he and Dad had built from reclaimed lumber. "I wanted to surprise you."

Leaning against the galvanized metal wainscoting were two plaques made from old pallets. "Oh, Chase! I love them!"

"I thought maybe we could put them over the crib. And I made one for each so when they start sleeping in separate beds . . ." He shrugged, looking humble and sweet and handsome as all get out.

Chase had painted the girls' names—pink paint in a swirly font—on the pallet slats. *Emma Corinne* and *Grace Danae*. She loved that her babies, sisters, were named after her own sisters. She hoped their girls would be as close as she and her sisters had become.

"They're perfect, babe. Just perfect. When did you even have time to do this?" Her poor husband had been working twelve-hour days trying to keep two Brooklyn galleries supplied—and Miles happy.

He shrugged again. "It didn't take that long. I did most of it that day you and your sisters went to lunch. Gracie woke up before I finished, so I brought her swing up here and she watched me work."

"Aww! I wish I had a picture of that."

He grinned, looking embarrassed. "Don't worry, there'll be plenty of chances for pictures."

She reached for one of the plaques, then drew back. "Is the paint dry? Can I pick them up?"

"Sure." He picked up Emma's plaque and handed it to her.

She inspected it, overwhelmed with love for this man. "Chase, these are just beautiful. You could sell these in a heartbeat."

"No, thank you. I only do those for my own girls."

"Well, they are masterpieces. I can't wait to hang them up."

He got a funny look on his face.

"What?"

He cocked his head. "I was just thinking . . ." He reached out and traced Emma's name on the plaque. "My masterpiece—*our* masterpiece is those little girls sleeping downstairs. When I look at them . . . I feel like I'm getting a second chance at . . . everything that went wrong—" His voice broke.

She went to him and took the plaque from his hands, and leaned it back on the worktable. Then she wrapped her arms around his waist and lay her head on his broad chest. She loved the strong, steady beat of his heart against her ear. "I didn't think I could possibly love you more than I did the day our girls were born, Chase. But I was wrong."

"That goes both ways, babe."

She sighed and snuggled closer to him. "We're blessed, aren't we?"

"Yes, we are."

A wail from downstairs made them both jump.

"That's Grace." Landyn sighed and untangled herself from her husband.

He gave a wry laugh. "I'd say we're doubly blessed."

And at that, Emma joined her sister's chorus.

Group Discussion Guide

1. Landyn is the youngest and a bit of a "daddy's girl." Do you think that stereotype for the "baby of the family" is an accurate one or an unfair one? What role, if any, do you think birth order plays in your own life?

2. Chase and Landyn grew up in the same small town but came from different sides of the track, so to speak. How much do their differences in this regard play in to their marital problems? What role do Landyn's parents' attitudes play in how Chase and Landyn handle their issues?

3. Chase Spencer felt God was leading him to make a life-changing decision, but he did so without consulting his wife. Do you think there is ever a time when one spouse must follow God's leading, despite how the rest of the family feels about that decision? Cite examples.

4. If you were in Landyn's shoes and your spouse had forced a relocation, how do you think you would handle it? Landyn chose to separate from her husband, at least for a time. Do you agree with her decision? Why or why not?

5. Landyn discovers that she's pregnant at a very inconvenient time in her marriage. Because she knows her husband will be upset about the pregnancy, she hides the news from him for almost half of her term. Do you believe Landyn had a good reason to keep this news from Chase? What rights or responsibilities do you believe the father of an unborn child should have?

6. As newlyweds, Chase and Landyn have big dreams and small finances. They also can't seem to agree on what their life should look like. They see-saw from one apartment to another, one job to another, one decision to another. Were you like that in your youth (or maybe even now)? Or have you always known what you wanted and how to get it?

7. The Whitman family is very close-knit, and most of Grant and Audrey's children live nearby. While this allows them to be together often and know each other well, it also sometimes creates problems. What is your family situation? Share some of the pros and cons of having family close by or having family scattered far away.

8. Do you think Grant and Audrey became too involved in Chase and Landyn's lives? Were they as likely to get involved when the couple

lived far away? Do you think the Whitmans had more right than the average parent to intervene (or interfere, depending on your perspective) in the newlyweds' lives because of *Chase's* family situation?

9. Grant has made some fairly large sacrifices in order to allow Audrey to fulfill her dream of owning a bed-and-breakfast. Have you ever made a significant sacrifice so that someone you love could fulfill a dream? If so, were you ever tempted to feel resentment afterwards? Or a right to control that person you sacrificed for?

10. Audrey has realized her dream of owning and managing a bed-and-breakfast, but it comes with some unexpected facets. How do you imagine her grown children feel about their family home being turned into a place of business? About their mother becoming an entrepreneur? About their father spending most of his savings—and essentially their inheritance—to renovate and open the inn?

11. Landyn is resentful that her mother has turned the home Landyn grew up in into a business, including turning her childhood bedroom into a guest room. Do you think her feelings are justified? Why or why not? Do grown children have a right to expect their parents

to maintain their childhood home? To be available to babysit the grandkids? What obligations do parents have to grown children concerning grandparenting? finances? an inheritance?

Want to know more about
author Deborah Raney?

Be sure to visit Deborah online!
She loves hearing from her readers.

To e-mail her or to learn more about her books, please visit www.deborahraney.com.

Center Point Large Print
600 Brooks Road / PO Box 1
Thorndike, ME 04986-0001 USA

(207) 568-3717

US & Canada:
1 800 929-9108
www.centerpointlargeprint.com